TENDER EMBRACE

"Callie." Logan's heart leaped as she looked up.

"Good morning," she said, laying her cool hand against his brow. "Wonderful. No fever. Are you hungry?"

"A little." He started to push himself into a sitting position.

"Logan, you know you aren't supposed to exert yourself," Callie scolded him gently. "Let me help you. Put your arms around my neck."

With pleasure, Logan thought, tightening his hold.

Steadying him, Callie used her free hand to stuff extra pillows behind his back. When she eased him down, he held on to her, taking her with him. She nuzzled her face into the curve of his shoulder, and her nails rasped ever so lightly against his skin.

Logan's muscles tensed and Callie felt as well as heard his sharp gasp. She raised her head and started to pull away.

"No, don't," he pleaded.

"Logan—" Callie's protest was lost beneath his kiss.

His lips found hers, t tasting, claiming, con enough of her, couldn sweet, wild need, utte suming, drove him onw

Arizona Captive

LaREE BRYANT

ZEBRA BOOKS
KENSINGTON PUBLISHING CORP.

ZEBRA BOOKS

are published by

Kensington Publishing Corp.
475 Park Avenue South
New York, NY 10016

First printing: July, 1989

Printed in the United States of America

DEDICATION

For Michele and Robin. Sisters are forever friends.

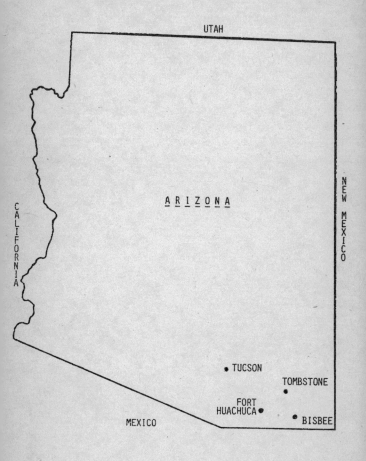

PROLOGUE

"All right, Hezekiah, what do you plan to do now?" Jasmine propped balled fists on her hips and stared at her husband. Fear-tinged anger sharpened the tone of her voice. "I don't care what the sheriff says, I don't believe the shooting was an accident! Doesn't he realize how close you came to being killed? No, Sheriff Culpepper's wrong! It wasn't some drunken cowboy; that shooting was intentional."

"Now, honey —"

"Don't you 'now, honey' me, Hezekiah Kane! I'm right and you know it. Why don't you admit it? We've both been scared ever since we heard about the prison break last month."

"Now, sugar, you've got to quit fretting like this." Hezekiah attempted to wrap his long arms around his wife, but she adroitly sidestepped his effort. Letting his hands drop to his side, Hezekiah gave a small shrug of resignation. "Culpepper's doing his job best as he can. It's not his fault there weren't any clues as to who fired the shot."

9

Jasmine's head jerked back. Her dark eyes bored into her husband's. "We don't need any clues! Jennings did it. I know it. You know it. Have you forgotten how he vowed to get even with you and Hawk and—"

"Now calm down, Jasmine. Don't you remember that letter we got from Hawk and Sabra last spring? They were going to Europe for a grand tour. Jennings would never be able to trace them. They're safe."

Jasmine gave an elegant snort. "Well, that may be, but *you're* certainly not safe. Yesterday proved that, didn't it?"

Hezekiah sighed. "All right, for the sake of argument, let's say that it was Jennings who shot at me yesterday. Don't you think he'd have hightailed it out of here by now, what with the sheriff and his men roaming all over the place? You can't be wantin' to pull up stakes just when we've got everything going for us. A few more months on the job and I can finally buy you that house you've been wanting. Be sensible, honey."

Hezekiah might believe Jennings was gone, but Jasmine wasn't buying it for a minute. She wanted her husband out of harm's way, and the sooner, the better. But how was she going to accomplish that feat? Despite his naturally quiet and amiable personality, Hezekiah could on occasion display a real streak of stubbornness. Afraid he'd sacrifice his personal safety in pursuit of something as insignificant as a mere dwelling, Jasmine played her trump card.

"Have you forgotten about Logan? Jennings threatened him, too. If it was Jennings who fired at you, if he really is out to keep his vow of revenge, then Logan is in just as much danger as you are. And *he's* not in Europe."

Hidden beneath the folds of her calico skirt, Jasmine's slim brown fingers crossed in the hope that her ploy would work, that her husband's loyalty to his old army friend would prevail over his contrary determination to stay in town to save his job.

Hezekiah's mouth dropped open. His jaw wagged a time or two and then snapped shut when he could think of no good answer.

"Logan's still in Bisbee, Hezekiah. What if Jennings is able to track him down? What if Logan hasn't heard about Jennings's escape? Do you want to take that chance?"

With a sigh, Hezekiah shook his head. "No, you're right, honey. We have to warn Logan of the danger. We'll leave in the morning."

CHAPTER ONE

Bisbee, Arizona Territory—Summer, 1891

Callie Nolan gathered her courage and stepped down from the train.

An early morning breeze caught a puff of silver gray smoke and sent it swirling across the deserted railway platform, momentarily concealing the town from Callie's curious gaze before drifting on across the rutted dirt expanse that served as the community's main street. Behind her, the crouching black locomotive chuffed harder, as if eager to be once again on its way. The rhythm of Callie's apprehensive heart matched the engine's accelerating beat, and she fought a sudden irrational desire to climb back aboard the passenger car and flee for the familiar security of home.

The thump-bump of her trunks being lowered from the baggage car jolted Callie back to reality, reminding her it was much too late to change her mind. She hadn't traveled halfway across the continent to turn tail and run even before the plan to help

13

her family could come to fruition.

"It's all unloaded now, lass," the elderly conductor called. The wood-planked deck grumbled under the iron-rimmed wheels of the loaded baggage cart as he pushed it toward her.

"Thank you so much, Mr. O'Malley." Callie tucked a strand of ebony hair behind her ear and adjusted her straw bonnet a quarter of an inch. She eyed the wrinkles in the skirt of her blue serge traveling suit with dismay, but there was little to be done about them at this point. Still, she gave them a few perfunctory brushes with one dainty hand.

The conductor pursed his thin lips as he scrutinized the station's empty expanse.

"Well, now," he said in a mournful Irish brogue. "I must say I'm a wee bit surprised. I was sure Mr. Claymore would have somebody right here waiting for you, him being such a high muckety-muck in town and all."

Callie abandoned the fruitless attention to her skirt. Her head lifted and dark lashes fluttered upward to reveal eyes the color of lapis lazuli.

"Oh, you're a dear to worry, Mr. O'Malley, but I'll be fine. Really." The words were spoken as much to reassure herself as the kindly conductor who'd taken her under his wing during the long train ride to Bisbee.

"Would you be wanting me to go in the office and get the station master for you, lass? He shoulda been out here long before now. Ol' fool's probably taking himself a wee bit of a nap."

"No sense you going to all that trouble, Mr. O'Malley. I'm sure someone will be here soon."

14

Callie flashed him the most confident smile she could manage as she tugged the sleeves of her jacket into precise alignment against the stiff white cuffs of her shirtwaist. She refused to give in to the hollow feeling that had been growing in the pit of her stomach ever since she'd realized there was no one at the station to greet her.

Mr. O'Malley shoved his cap to the back of his head and scratched the sparse red fuzz at his hairline. His eyes were full of concern as he continued to watch Callie's nervous gestures.

"You sure he knew you were arriving on the early train today?"

"I'm exactly on schedule according to Mr. Claymore's last telegram." Callie patted her purse. "I have it right here. And I'm positive he and Mrs. Claymore wouldn't have employed me as governess for their children and had me come all this way for nothing."

Callie's hopeful gaze once again swept the station platform and the bordering street. Even at this early hour there were several dozen people straggling up and down the boardwalks, but none seemed to pay the least attention to the town's latest arrival. The only sign of life at the station itself was the desultory tail swishing of a wagon-hitched horse standing at the far corner of the raised deck.

A mournful whistle filled the air. The conductor slipped a watch from his vest pocket and snapped it open. "Well, Miss Nolan," Mr. O'Malley said with a sigh as he repocketed his timepiece, " 'tis Charlie the engineer, remindin' me of the schedule."

Callie forced a reassuring smile to her lips. "I'm

15

positive someone will be along very soon, Mr. O'Malley. If not, I can always ask for assistance." She offered a small hand in farewell. "Thank you again for your kindness during my trip."

"My pleasure, Miss Nolan, my pleasure," the conductor said, patting her hand. " 'Tis not often I get to enjoy the company of a fine Irish lass like yourself. I wish you luck in your new position—"

The whistle blew again, sharper, longer.

"Sounds like Charlie's getting impatient, Mr. O'Malley," Callie said, her tone teasing. This time the corners of her eyes crinkled when she smiled. "You'd best be getting along now. I'll be fine."

The conductor frowned and shook his head, clearly unhappy about leaving the petite young woman all alone. The whistle wailed once again, and O'Malley reluctantly climbed the train's steps. When he reached the small platform at the top of the stairs, he turned to wag a cautionary finger in Callie's direction.

"Now, listen to me, lass, don't you be wandering off by yourself. This is a fine little community, from everything I've heard. A mite rough around the edges on occasion, but what else can you expect from a mining town on the bare edge of civilization? But you must be rememberin' this is still frontier territory. Hasn't been that many years since Geronimo and his bunch whooped it up 'round here."

The puffs of steam came faster, and the big iron wheels began to slowly turn. O'Malley talked louder.

"Stay put. Don't be wandering off. You don't want to wind up in Brewery Gulch. It ain't no place for a nice young lady like yourself." Mr. O'Malley

16

punctuated the admonishment with an emphatic waggle of his head. "You wait right there. Mr. Claymore will be here soon. You'll see."

"Don't worry. I won't budge an inch," Callie called above the whoosh of steam and the screech of metal against metal.

Her words were uttered with heartfelt sincerity, for Mr. O'Malley's remarks had reminded her of just how far she was from the cultured city of Boston, not to mention the ever present familial protection she'd always taken for granted.

Slowly but surely the ponderous train gathered momentum. The engine huffed longer and louder, the wheels turned faster, and the train slowly eased away from the depot.

Callie watched and waved until Mr. O'Malley was a mere speck in the distance. The finality of his departure provoked a deep, ragged breath as she fully realized that she was on her own, utterly alone for the first time in her life.

Swallowing hard, Callie turned to survey her new home.

The town sat at the bottom of several intersecting gulches in the Mule Mountains. The floor of the largest canyon appeared to hold the business section of the town, although Callie could see a few homes scattered about. The narrow areas of level ground which snaked around and between massive folds of mountain were covered with buildings of all shapes and sizes, from small, false-fronted stores constructed of raw wood to two-storied structures of dull red or ochre-colored brick, some brand new, others weatherworn and more than a little ram-

17

shackle.

Callie made a slow circle, her gaze climbing the earthen bastions that surrounded Bisbee on all sides. Her tummy did a little flip-flop at the sight of the houses clinging stubbornly to almost perpendicular hillsides, with nothing more to support them than a chunk of terraced land and a few slender pilings. When the community had run out of level ground, it had simply gone upward, building level after level of homes on the switchback trails that zigzagged up the mountainsides.

Callie murmured a fervent prayer that her new employer lived in a house on one of the bottom levels. High, open places were one of her least favorite things.

Hastily dragging her eyes from the disquieting elevations, Callie availed herself of the sliver of empty space at one end of the baggage cart and sat down. She carefully arranged the hem of her skirt so that nothing more than the toes of her polished kid slippers peeped from beneath the fabric. Then, her back ramrod straight, she demurely clasped her hands in her lap to wait.

The minutes crawled by. As the last echo of the train faded into the distance, Callie began to wriggle in impatience. Needlessly she once again smoothed her skirt over her knees and tried to concentrate on the new life that lay before her.

Would the Claymores be pleasant to work for? The headmistress of her school had assured Callie's parents that Mrs. Claymore came from a wealthy, distinguished Tucson family. What would the children be like? Callie smiled as she remembered how

18

many people had pointed out to her that taking care of three youngsters should be a lark for someone with six younger brothers and sisters.

The one subject Callie avoided addressing was the gnawing question of whether she would always be as homesick for her parents, grandmother, brothers and sisters, as she felt right now. Callie's slim shoulders threatened to slump in despair at the overwhelming thought.

Determined not to give in to such morose considerations, Callie turned her attention to the town's early morning strollers. She half hoped to see one of Mr. O'Malley's Indians — buckskin-clad and feather decorated — sauntering down the town's streets. At least it would take her mind off home.

Long minutes later, her elbow on her knee, her chin in her hand, Callie still watched the procession of pedestrians. One and all, they were male, mostly young, and dressed in a ragtag array of rough work clothes. Short or tall, wiry or muscular, they all moved with the distinctive carriage of those accustomed to hard physical labor. Miners, Callie surmised. Perhaps some were on their way to work; others, from their grimy looks, had evidently just finished their shift. They came and went in groups of twos and threes and fours, their boisterous laughter and discordant voices occasionally carrying across the street.

Slowly Callie became aware of the faint, rollicking melody of a rinky-tink piano in the distance. Suspicion of the men's destination began to seep into her mind. *Saloons.* The infamous Brewery Gulch Mr. O'Malley had spoken of must lie down the road which intersected the main street catty-corner to the depot.

Callie peered intently, but all she could see through the hodgepodge of buildings was an occasional glimpse of the far end of the narrow road as it serpentined its way up the sloping canyon.

The thought of what lay along that street intrigued a city-bred girl whose past experience dealt with nothing more adventuresome than an occasional excursion to a traveling vaudeville show. To the dismay of her mother, Callie had been captivated by the romance of the frontier since childhood. More than once she had snuck a western penny dreadful home and concealed it in the bottom of her lingerie drawer, poring over it during the few moments of solitude she could manage to snatch in a home that housed ten people. Their florid word pictures now provided instant visions of smoke-filled betting parlors and shootouts over crooked card games, fallen ladies, and mustached gamblers with pearl-handled derringers hidden up their sleeves.

With avid attention, the butterflies in her stomach forgotten for the moment, Callie perused the intersection, her toe unconsciously tapping to the music as she zealously reflected on what lay beyond.

Half an hour later, Callie's speculations had begun to lose their appeal. Aggravation replaced the apprehensions she had managed to forget for a few minutes. The flow of pedestrian traffic had slowed to a dribble and she was seriously debating whether to search out the missing stationmaster when two figures rounded the far corner and started walking in her direction.

Engrossed in each other, the couple ambled down the boardwalk, two tropical birds in what had heretofore been a procession of plain brown wrens.

The man was tall, head and shoulders over most of the men who effusively greeted the couple as they passed by. He walked with the easy, rhythmic stride of a big cat. A halo of wild curls, the rich tawny color of old gold, capped his majestic head and coiled against the collar of his shirt. Fawn-colored trousers molded muscular thighs and slim hips. The matching jacket, anchored in place with the help of a bent elbow and one crooked finger, was draped nonchalantly over one shoulder. The gesture stretched pale-blue linen tight across unbelievably broad shoulders and a deep chest.

He was quite the most magnificent specimen of manhood Callie had ever seen.

The man bent his head toward the woman, his deep rumbling voice eliciting a cascade of bright laughter. For the first time, Callie's full attention turned to the man's companion. Sunlight sprinkled ruby sparks through the woman's impossibly titian hair and Callie's eyes widened with interest. Her girlhood friend Judith Ryan's hair had been carroty orange, but Callie had never seen hair as vividly red as this woman's.

Dyed! Callie thought in awe. *And that dress!* Though cut to perfection, the emerald taffeta of the woman's gown was far too flashy for a morning dress. The skirt swished seductively against the man's long legs as the redhead tightened her possessive hold on his muscular arm and tilted her head to smile up at her escort.

21

"Oh, my," breathed Callie, her eyes wide with curiosity. That must be one of *those* women—the fallen angels described so vividly in her dog-eared pulp publications. And the man—was he gambler or gunslinger . . . or worse?

Raptly Callie watched the exotic pair as they neared a small wood-framed building marked "Restaurant." They paused at the entrance, turning to exchange a few low words. Callie's eyes widened further as the woman reached a familiar hand upward. Bold as brass and without even the most cursory glance around to see if anyone might be watching, the redhead cupped the back of the man's neck and dragged his head down for a skillful kiss.

The man's appreciative chuckle rolled like summer thunder through the clear morning air when the woman finally released her hold and pivoted toward the restaurant's entrance. Callie's mouth formed a small shocked 'O' when he reached out and gave the redhead's retreating emerald-clad fanny an affectionate pat just before she disappeared through the door.

The banging of the restaurant door caught Callie by surprise. She had expected the man to follow his companion inside. Instead, he hurriedly raked one hand through his tousled curls, turned on the heel of his boot, and walked to the edge of the boardwalk. Then, as if suddenly aware of being watched, the man stopped.

Frowning, he hastily glanced across at the seemingly deserted railway station, and then perused the street, up one side and down the other. The frown deepened as his gaze returned to the depot, his scrutiny more thorough this time. His slow gaze swept the area, coming to rest square on the loaded baggage cart and Callie.

Heat flowed up Callie's throat and into her cheeks as the man's dark eyes raked her appraisingly. Her stomach slid all the way to her toes when his mouth suddenly turned up at the corners, tilting in a wide, slow grin that revealed a row of strong teeth, startling white against the rich golden tan of his skin.

He paused only long enough to drag the coat from his shoulder and fold it over his forearm before stepping down onto the street. A ray of early morning sunlight speared through the crystalline mountain air, momentarily setting his tumbled curls aflame with golden highlights. Pale clouds of dust puffed in response to each long-legged step as he sauntered across the street in that lazy, hip-rolling gait, his devilish eyes still fixed steadfastly on Callie.

Callie's mouth snapped shut in alarm. *Oh, my!* she thought, tiny frissons of excitement skipping through her veins as she realized the man was well aware that she'd been staring at him in the most brash manner.

"Dear me," Callie whispered aloud as the man's gaze never wavered and his grin grew even wider.

She jerked her eyes from his. Surely he hadn't construed her avid interest as something more than simple curiosity.

Callie's runaway imagination conjured up one embarrassing finale after another, and she suddenly wished she'd paid more attention to her mother's admonitions about proper ladylike behavior.

A surreptitious glance through sheltering lashes did nothing to relieve Callie's anxiety. The man was still headed straight toward her. What would she say if he actually approached her?

Callie began a worried search of the street. Her trepidation doubled when she realized there wasn't a soul in sight. Where could they have all disappeared to so fast?

The only thing louder than the beat of her heart was the thud of the man's boots, coming nearer and nearer and nearer.

Callie's fingers tightened on her purse strings. It wouldn't make a very formidable weapon if the man became persistent, but it was all she had. Surely he wasn't in search of a further assignation. Only the worst kind of rogue would come directly from the embrace of one woman to accost another. Locking her gaze on the knotted fingers in her lap, Callie prayed that the man was simply headed toward the rig at the end of the platform.

Her prayers went unanswered.

CHAPTER TWO

Callie wished she hadn't wedged herself into the minuscule space at the end of the baggage cart. She was as good as trapped. If she were on her feet, she could at least run if the man became too tenacious in his endeavors.

Suddenly another disturbing thought blossomed to life. Good Lord! What if he had a gun? Didn't all desperados wear six-shooters? For the life of her, she couldn't remember if there'd been a pistol strapped to the man's hip or not. What if he pulled it on her and forced her to go with him? What could she do if he did? If she screamed, would the stationmaster hear?

And why on earth did she keep thinking of how handsome the man was rather than how dangerous he might be?

Her heart felt as if it might hammer itself right out of her chest, but Callie struggled to keep her anxieties hidden as the footsteps came nearer. She kept her head down and prayed that the man would keep on walking.

No such luck.

Through a fringe of dark lashes she saw two booted feet come into view, the pointed leather toes aimed straight toward her. Callie swallowed hard and stiffened her spine, prepared to give the man a scathing reply at his first improper suggestion.

"Miss Nolan?"

The unexpected use of her name surprised Callie so much that her mouth dropped open and her head jerked up. Her round blue eyes encountered broadcloth-covered thighs, solid as tree trunks beneath the tight-fitting pants. She forced her eyes higher. Lean hips, a shiny belt buckle riding low on a flat stomach. *No gun.* She blinked and drew a sigh of relief.

Callie's gaze continued upward, slipping quickly past the wedge of crisp spun-gold hair curling in the open vee of the man's shirt, until it collided with a pair of sparkling brown eyes. It was finally beginning to dawn on Callie that she'd let her imagination get totally out of hand, that her fears had been unfounded.

Slowly her body began to respond to what her head was comprehending. There was no danger. The man had simply come to meet her train.

Callie had never felt more absurd. All she could do was hope that the man hadn't noticed her peculiar behavior. He'd think her an utter fool if he realized the crazy thoughts that had been running through her mind. She smothered a grimace. What a wonderful first impression she was making on her new employer cowering among the baggage like a silly schoolgirl while visions of renegade cowboys and Indians ran amuck in her altogether too inven-

26

tive head!

"How do you do, Mr. Claymore," Callie managed to say, hoping for all she was worth that she sounded professional and intelligent and competent and not in the least given to wild fantasies.

Much to Callie's chagrin, the man threw back his head and laughed, a deep rumbling sound that made Callie want to sink right through the ground. *Oh, heavens!* she thought in despair. He did know what she'd been thinking! She was desperately trying to formulate an explanation that wouldn't make her look like an even bigger fool, when the man spoke again.

"No, ma'am, I'm not Mr. Claymore." He shook his head and the thick taffy curls shimmered against his ears. His grin broadened. "But you are Miss Callie Nolan, aren't you?"

"Y-yes, I am," Callie managed to answer, her befuddled head trying hard to ignore the odd little thrill which had pulsed through her at the pronouncement that he wasn't the married father of three who had contracted for her services. Callie shook the feeling off and tried to concentrate on the situation at hand. If he wasn't Claymore, who was he?

"Logan Powers," the man said, as if he could read her mind.

Before Callie knew what was happening, the man reached out and clasped her hands. Her purse swung like a pendulum from the braided cords linked over her wrist as he effortlessly pulled her to her feet.

"Mr. Claymore asked me to meet your train."

Callie's eyes were fixed on the sight of their still

27

joined hands. His were huge; hers had nearly disappeared inside his folded fingers, and the flesh of his palms felt warm against her fingertips. The work-roughened pads of his fingers brushed against the sensitive skin of her inner wrists as he loosened his hold.

Shocked at the unexpected rush of pleasure his touch elicited, Callie snatched her hands away, clasping them tightly in front of her.

Tilting her head, she stared upward. He was so tall and so close. The air suddenly seemed sparse, devoid of all movement. *It must be the altitude,* Callie quickly rationalized. She wished Logan Powers would back up, even a few paces, and give her a little breathing room. But he didn't budge an inch; he just stood over her and kept watching her with those big brown eyes.

Callie took a hasty backward step, only to be brought up short as the calves of her legs pressed hard against the edge of the baggage cart. The few inches she'd gained didn't seem to help in the least; she still felt as if she couldn't quite breathe a good deep breath.

"Are . . . are you a friend of the family?" Callie asked, her oxygen-starved brain seizing the first thought that came to her mind.

Logan Powers chuckled again. The first tendrils of irritation began to feather through Callie's body, blessedly banishing the initial mortification she'd felt. Was he deliberately making fun of her?

"No, ma'am. Just the hired help."

"I see," said Callie, not at all sure that she did. She'd never seen "hired help" who looked — or acted—like Logan Powers.

"Actually Mr. Claymore hired me as his body-guard, but I don't know why—that kind of service hasn't been called for. I do a little of everything—run errands, deliver supplies out to the mines . . ." Logan Powers leaned a little closer. A roguish grin tilted one corner of his mouth. ". . . pick up pretty ladies at the train station."

Callie's mouth thinned in irritation at the man's presumptuous attitude. "Well," she retorted before thinking, "let's hope you can perform *some* of your duties in a more satisfactory manner."

The pale-blue fabric of Powers's shirt pulled tighter across his chest as he lifted his broad shoulders in a nonchalant shrug. "You were early."

That did it. A jab of swift Irish anger surged through Callie, chasing away the last vestige of embarrassment.

Oh, marvelous! Now it was somehow her fault that he was tardy. And he was wrong, besides. The train had been exactly on time! If the man had been doing his job instead of lollygagging around with one of those . . . those fancy women, Callie fumed inwardly, she wouldn't have had to sit and wait; she wouldn't have had the time to formulate all those foolish fantasies.

Unconsciously, her chin lifted another inch. "I beg your pardon, the conductor said the train was exactly on time."

Callie longed to give Logan Powers a dressing down on the virtues and good manners of promptness, but then, remembering how much she needed this position and how far she'd come to secure it, she bit her tongue and kept quiet. After all, she had no way of knowing how entrenched Logan Powers was in the Claymore household, and in her circumstances she couldn't take the chance of offending someone important.

Logan simply grinned. "Sorry. I had a little business to tend to, and I guess I lost track of time. It's been a bit of a problem since I forfeited my watch in a poker game last week. I really did plan to be here before the train got in."

"Of course," Callie said, the words clipped.

Sorry, hummph! The man might not be an out-and-out desperado as she had at first feared, but his morals were certainly suspect. Lost his watch in a poker game, indeed! Back in Boston, no upstanding gentleman would indulge in such peccadillos, much less admit them to a perfect stranger.

And did he think all he had to do was flash that big, charming smile and say "I'm sorry" and she'd forget what he'd been doing when he was supposed to be seeing to her welfare? *Business, my aunt Fanny!* Callie thought in irritation. It was evident to her that the only kind of business Mr. Logan Powers was interested in was "monkey business."

Taking a slow, deliberate breath, Callie slammed a mental door against the rankling thoughts. What did she care? Logan Powers was nothing more than a fellow employee of the Claymore family. His choice of acquaintances—business or otherwise—didn't matter a hill of beans to her. All she wanted him to do was take her to the Claymore house, then he could go right straight back to his redheaded hussy—or the devil—for all Callie cared.

Logan Powers watched Callie's lips momentarily thin in irritation and wondered if she was always so testy. Granted, he'd been a few minutes late meeting her train, but that hardly justified the flash of blue fire he'd seen in her eyes.

For just a moment, she reminded him of the wild black kitten Betsy Claymore had dragged home several months before. Half a pound of yowling, fighting determination and independent spirit. All soft warm fur and cuddly sleek curves on the outside, the tiny ball of fluff possessed the heart of a mountain lion and was given to displays of sheer bravado when anyone or anything came too close. When confronted, particularly by Betsy's father or her two brothers, the kitten could react with surprising ferocity, its delicate back arched stiffly, tiny milk-white fangs bared, spitting and hissing for all it was worth.

Betsy loved the kitten she had named Shadow desperately. While Logan had no particular affinity for cats, he was terribly fond of Betsy. He'd helped her tame the little creature, at least enough to preclude Owen Claymore's threat to ban it from the house, which would have broken Betsy's heart.

Still a runt despite Betsy's overindulgent care and feeding, the ebony-furred creature now stalked the house like a dowager queen. Betsy had been the first to receive any real sign of affection from Shadow. Logan had been forced to work harder to be admitted into the inner circle—an accomplishment he wondered if he should have pursued when the cat began to creep into his room at night. More than once he had awakened from a sound sleep to find the feisty feline sprawled atop his chest, purring like a runaway railroad engine.

Callie Nolan had the same kind of spunkiness. She was small, almost delicate. All glossy dark hair and big blue eyes. A porcelain complexion with just a smattering of pale golden freckles across the bridge of her pert, tip-tilted nose. But underneath, Logan sensed a strength every bit as indomitable as Shadow's. It would be a bigger challenge to tame this little wildcat, but that was all right. Logan Powers loved a challenge.

"I assume these trunks are yours?" Logan said, his eyes crinkling at the corners as his lips turned up again in that wide, lazy smile.

Callie started, caught off guard once more. "Wh-what?" She squashed a quick surge of guilt and dragged her eyes from the intriguing dimple that winked in Logan Powers's bronzed cheek every time he smiled. "Oh, yes. Yes, they are."

"I'll get you settled in the wagon, and then I'll load your trunks."

"Thank you." This time Callie kept her eyes carefully averted.

Logan slipped his hand under her elbow and led her to the wagon tied at the end of the platform. He tossed his jacket over the backrest, and then turned to help Callie. She had no choice but to place her hand in his. As she hoisted her skirts with her free hand and stepped upward, she felt the disconcerting warmth of his palm against the small of her back.

"Comfortable?" Logan asked as Callie settled herself in the far corner of the seat. She simply nodded, not trusting her voice at the moment. "Good. Be right back," he said, throwing another of those disconcerting grins over his shoulder as he strode back toward the baggage cart.

Callie quickly busied herself with smoothing her skirts and arranging them decorously about her feet, and tried not to notice the way the muscles across Logan Powers's back and shoulders flexed as, one at a time, he effortlessly lifted her two trunks and transported them to the bed of the wagon.

Logan wasn't even breathing hard when he climbed up beside her and took up the reins. Irritated at herself for noticing, Callie swiftly turned the thought aside and hugged her corner of the wagon seat even harder as the plank sagged under his weight. He clicked his tongue and the bay pricked up its ears and leaned its weight against the harness. The wagon began to move.

Pulling her thoughts from the man at her side, Callie tried to concentrate on the potpourri of people and establishments they were passing. There were more important things to consider than her disconcerting welcome. This would be her home for the next year; the sooner she learned her way around the town, the better.

Although still deeply rooted in the days of the raw frontier, Bisbee was clawing its way toward the twentieth century. The town appeared to be bulging at the seams with a large and considerably diversified population.

According to Logan's rambling discourse, people from all points of the compass had heard about the glittering promise of riches to be wrested from the earth and had come in search of silver and copper and gold. Others had quickly followed, eager to reap

33

their own fortunes through trade, be it the necessities of life or the pleasures so near and dear to a boom town's heart. Many a saloon owner was making easy dollars, thanks to the hard-drinking, free-living, card-loving miners.

The wagon rolled past half a dozen buildings in various states of construction, and Logan explained that new businesses were springing up all over the community, a plethora of markets, breweries, saloons, hotels, and boardinghouses. Occasionally there were patches of gardens, whose produce would end up in the kitchen, but Callie saw no sign of the colorful flowerbeds or carefully manicured lawns so familiar to many Boston neighborhoods. The town was oddly lacking in trees of substantial size and, for the most part, scatterings of olive-drab bushes and strange desert plants provided the only greenery to be seen along the packed-earth thoroughfare.

Traffic on the boardwalks and dusty paths between seemed to double by the minute as the town shook itself awake and came out to greet the new day. Housewives, baskets over their arms, hurried to do their daily shopping. Children scampered up and down the shadowed side lanes, their laughter ringing gaily. The doors of markets and dry goods emporiums were propped open by men in starched shirts with gartered sleeves. And the ever-present clusters of miners still strode the weathered pathways.

The big bay was more than happy to amble along at a reduced rate of speed while Logan provided Callie with a continuous monologue of people, places, and history, which was interrupted with great frequency by the folks they passed—especially the women.

"Mornin' there, Logan." A short, thick-waisted woman paused in sweeping the boardwalk in front of her restaurant to lift a hand in greeting.

"And a good morning to you, Miss Lucy," Logan called in return, that big white smile flashing again.

"Gonna have fresh berry pie today."

"Umm hmmm! I do love your berry pie," Logan responded. Callie rolled her eyes heavenward when the woman simpered like a schoolgirl. "You be sure and save me a piece, you hear? A nice big one. I'll be by later," he promised.

"I surely will," the hefty little woman replied, her answering smile revealing front teeth as widely spaced as a picket fence. She eyed the woman beside Logan with frank curiosity. Then, as if remembering her manners, Miss Lucy politely bobbed her head in Callie's direction and went back to her sweeping.

Evidence of Logan's popularity grew as the wagon bumped its way over the deeply rutted road. Miners, store owners, two kimono-clad women in a second-story window, a gaggle of boys and girls playing hide-and-seek, all took the time to wave or call out greetings as they passed. Callie wondered how long Logan Powers had been in Bisbee, for he seemed to know everything about the town and the people in it.

"What's all that smoke?" she asked, shielding her eyes to gaze at the pall of greenish gray hanging over several shedlike buildings on the side of a far hill.

"The new smelter. The first one was built back in '80, and they've been improving or building new ones ever since. Always eager to up the production ratio. The town really boomed after they put in that first smelter. Made copper production a viable business for the area, especially after Phelps Dodge built the railroad."

"Phelps Dodge?" Callie repeated, her nose wrinkling delicately as a wisp of acrid-tinged breeze wafted their way. "Who is he?"

"It's not a he." Oblivious to the exasperated glance the grin accompanying his answer elicited, Logan continued his explanation. "Phelps Dodge is the biggest mining company hereabouts. There're also a couple of medium-sized companies. Actually Mr. Claymore's organization is the largest of that lot. And the town's still got a fair amount of independent miners, although the number's been going down the last year or so."

"Why is that?" Callie asked, curiosity overpowering her irritation.

Logan's broad shoulders lifted in that now familiar gesture. "It's always been tough for the independents to survive. It's not just the long hours and hard work. You've got to have a grubstake, enough money for supplies and equipment until you strike a vein rich enough to pay off. Lately some of the big companies have been trying real hard to convince the independents to sell out."

"Why would they do that?" Callie queried, consternation knitting two little lines between her brows. "Surely the independents aren't much competition for the big companies."

"No, they're not competition, but mining is based on volume. And the more claims the big boys own, the more profit they make. They'd swallow up all the independents if they could."

Callie pursed her lips and considered Logan's statement. "Well, if it's so tough to be an independent, perhaps the larger companies are doing them a favor in offering to buy them out."

Logan didn't say a word. He just turned and gazed at the woman by his side, one dark-gold brow lifted in contemplation. *Beauty and brains,* he thought in surprise, even if her reasoning was skewed the wrong way.

Callie Nolan was more than a little disconcerting. He was used to women who rarely thought of much more than new gowns or the town's next social event. Della Maxwell had certainly never taken an interest in such issues, one way or the other. Nor had Edith Claymore, whose husband owned the second largest mining concern in the area.

Callie squirmed under Logan's scrutiny. "I mean, wouldn't it be more profitable for the independents to sell? At least then they'd have guaranteed wages."

Caught up in the unfamiliar enjoyment of sparring with an intelligent *and* beautiful woman, Logan responded with another teasing remark. "If I didn't know better, I'd think you were a Phelps Dodge representative rather than a governess. You certainly spout some of the same rhetoric as the local big boys."

Callie bit back a retort. He was doing it again! Making her feel foolish when, for the life of her, she didn't know what she'd said or done wrong. "Mr. Powers, it was not my intention to get into some controversial discussion with you. I was merely commenting on the financial significance of the situa-

37

tion."

Logan knew he should let well enough alone, but something drove him onward. He threw Callie another slow grin, thinking how fetching she looked with that flush of high color on her cheeks. "That's your privilege, of course. But a lot of folks hereabouts like the idea of being their own bosses. That's why they came West. If they'd wanted to be company men, they'd have stayed back East and worked in the factories and refineries."

"You sound like you agree with the independents, Mr. Powers. Isn't that in conflict with your position with Mr. Claymore?"

My, my! She gets her back up as fast as Shadow! Logan thought, suppressing a chuckle.

Just then an ominous reflection flickered through Logan's mind and he was suddenly sorry he'd let the discussion go so far. Good Lord! What could he have been thinking of? He'd taken the job with Claymore for the express purpose of obtaining information that might help George Anderson and his people, and now he might very well have jeopardized that vital position for the sake of a little flirting.

What if Callie happened to repeat his words to Owen Claymore? The disturbing thought curbed Logan's tongue quicker than anything Callie could have said.

Irritated at his own stupid behavior, Logan flicked the reins over the bay's back and fervently hoped that Callie would forget all about their conversation. A definite wariness had replaced the teasing sparkle in his eyes when he next glanced Callie's way.

"No, ma'am," Logan said, "I don't aim to be in

conflict with anybody, and certainly not the boss. Now, let me show you the local churches . . ."

Although surprised at Logan's abrupt change of tone, Callie took one look at the pugnacious tilt of his jaw and decided the subject was best left alone. With a dismissing sniff, she turned her attention back to the sights being pointed out as they progressed beyond the business section and into the fringes of the residential area.

"Whoa, Flapjack." The wagon was just rounding a sharp curve at the bottom of a hill when Logan pulled the reins taut. They came to a halt in front of a two-story house of weathered silver wood.

Wrapping the reins around the whip holder, Logan turned to Callie. "Hope you don't mind if we make one stop on the way. I promised to drop something off. It'll just take a minute."

Before Callie could say a word, Logan swung down from the wagon, almost grateful for this small reprieve. He swore silently that when he returned he'd be more careful about what he said.

Leaning over the sideboard, Logan grabbed a large sack of flour from behind the seat and hoisted it on his shoulder. "Be right back," he called as he strode across the broad front porch and disappeared through the door.

The small yard, bare of grass, was spotlessly clean. Three rockers, calico cushions in place, graced the far end of the porch. Callie had just noted a "vacancy" sign in the front window when Logan returned.

Wouldn't you know it? she thought in exasperation, noting the blond-haired woman trailing close behind him. Couldn't the man go anywhere without a female in tow?

"Don't know what I'd do without you, Logan. Thanks so much," the woman said, laying a slim hand on Logan Powers's arm.

While not the breathtaking beauty the redhead had been, the blond was attractive. From her looks and actions, it was quite clear to Callie that the woman was exceptionally fond of Logan Powers.

"I don't want to hear another word about it, Henrietta." Logan Powers looped his arm about the woman's shoulders for a quick hug. Then he took her hand and tugged her toward the wagon. "Come on over here and let me introduce you to Miss Nolan."

The last thing Callie wanted to do was meet one of Logan Powers's women, but she pasted a smile on her face and tried her best to look delighted at the prospect. At least this one looked more respectable than the redhead.

"Henrietta, this is Miss Callie Nolan, the new governess I told you about. Miss Nolan, may I present Henrietta Winslow, proprietress of the best boardinghouse in town."

"Pleased to meet you," Henrietta Winslow said, her welcoming smile more genuine than Callie would have expected under the circumstances. "Hope you'll enjoy your stay in Bisbee."

The woman was older than Callie had at first thought. Gray strands flecked the pale golden hair at her temples, and tiny, fine lines bracketed her hazel eyes. But Henrietta Winslow's figure was still slim and youthful, and she held herself with quiet dignity. Callie could see what might attract Logan to the woman despite the obvious age difference. Besides, if his response to every female they'd passed during their ride was any indication, Logan Powers apparently gave little attention to such matters. He seemed to be attracted to almost anything in skirts.

"Thank you. I'm sure I will," Callie answered graciously, although she was beginning to have her doubts. She only hoped her first two hours in town weren't an indication of what lay ahead.

"What do you think of our little community so far? I don't suppose you've met the family yet?" Henrietta questioned.

"It seems very nice. Quite different from Boston," Callie said. "And no, I haven't met the family yet, although I'm looking forward to it."

"I just picked Miss Nolan up at the depot," Logan interjected. "We're on our way up Quality Hill now."

"Ah." Henrietta lifted a hand to smooth a stray curl. "Well, I wish you the very best. Betsy is an angel, but I'm afraid you'll have to be on your toes when it comes to those boys. Richard and Thomas can be more than a handful, if you don't watch out. They come down every once in a while to play with my two, and I'll have to admit they keep me hopping. Last time they actually tried to set the outhouse on fire!"

"Fire?" Callie repeated in alarm, the comment quite wiping out her speculations about the father of Henrietta's children.

Henrietta's pale blond brows drew together, and sudden distress filled her eyes. "Oh, drat! I shouldn't have said anything. I'm so sorry. I sure didn't mean to upset you. They're good children at heart; they're just . . . uh . . . high-spirited. I really believe it must be the lack of discipline, that's all."

Callie stifled a groan. Was it going to go from bad to worse the whole day long? "Lack of discipline?" she echoed. "But I thought they'd had governesses all along."

The look of dismay on Callie's face brought a surge of unexpected contriteness to Logan. Oh, he knew that Henrietta hadn't purposely upset the Claymores' new governess, and he'd certainly never considered that the conversation would turn in this direction. Still, he couldn't help thinking how hard it must be for a young lady to leave home and take a position far away, even under the best of circumstances. And Logan suddenly felt exceedingly guilty because he knew that life at the Claymore house was not going to be anywhere near the best of circumstances.

For reasons totally unfathomable to Logan Powers, he suddenly wished he could go back and start the day over. If given the opportunity to do so, he not only would bypass the early morning romp with Della Maxwell, but he would be on time at the train station, and he wouldn't foolishly jeopardize the Association's safety by teasing Callie about the mining issues.

Right now, Logan very badly wanted to put things to right, but most of all he wanted to wipe that worried look from Callie Nolan's pretty face.

"Look, Miss Nolan, I'm sure you won't have any problems. I've heard Mrs. Claymore comment on how difficult it's been to get dependable help way out here. From what I know, the family has had more than a dozen governesses in the last couple of years."

"A dozen?" Callie squeaked, her eyes growing even larger.

"Yeah . . . but, you have to understand how it was," Logan hastened to explain. "They weren't *real* governesses, like you are. Some were from Tucson, others were young local Mexican girls. I'm positive none of them had your credentials. You can't expect everyone to know how to handle three rambunctious children. Why, the girl who's been taking care of them until you could get here is little more than a child herself. I'm sure it'll be a lot easier for you, you having had experience and all."

Callie's worried gaze traveled from one hopeful face to the other. *Experience,* she thought with dismay. She had no real experience. She'd obtained the position because the headmistress of her school had recommended her. Her merits included high grades in all her studies and many years of helping care for six younger siblings. The Claymores knew that they weren't getting a seasoned governess . . . didn't they?

But right at the moment, Callie wasn't so sure. Miss Thorndike had known of her family's precarious financial situation, but surely she wouldn't have misled the Claymores just because she knew Callie needed the position. Would she?

Oh, my! Callie thought in despair. What if they really did think she was experienced? And what if she couldn't handle the children? Was her position — and the opportunity to help her family — in jeopardy before it even began?

"I'm sorry, Logan. I should have thought before speaking up." Henrietta Winslow looked truly remorseful.

"No harm done, Henrietta," Logan quickly soothed. "I'm positive Miss Nolan's going to do just fine with the children."

"Well, I've taken up too much of your time already," Henrietta said, giving him a gentle shove toward the wagon. "You best get Miss Nolan on up to the house."

"Reckon you're right." Logan clambered aboard. "I'll see you later."

"Drop by anytime, Miss Nolan," Henrietta called as the wagon began to roll again.

"Wh—? Oh, yes. Of course. That's most kind of you." Callie's response was automatic. At the moment, she was too busy dissecting her new worries and wondering what awaited her at the Claymore house.

CHAPTER THREE

Callie drew a deep breath as the wagon angled up yet another steep switchback on the narrow, rutted lane. With deliberate effort, she willed her white-knuckled hold on the wagon seat to loosen. Logan hadn't even given a second glance to the disconcerting void just inches from the wagon's wheels, and she'd be damned if she'd let him know how uneasy heights made her.

"Is that it?" Callie asked, praying the answer would be yes. She wasn't sure how much higher she could go and still keep the quiver in her stomach out of her voice. She kept her gaze locked on the large gingerbread-trimmed house straight ahead in an effort to avoid another heart-stopping perusal of the sheer dropoff at her side and the steep rock-tumbled hillside that swept downward to the floor of the canyon. The two-story structure she was eyeing with such intense hope was nestled on a large plot of flat land that cut back into the side of the mountain.

"Yep, that's it."

"Oh, good," Callie said fervently. At least the house sat on the mountain side of the narrow road and didn't hang out over the canyon as did some of the homes they'd passed on their way up. She could stand the awesome sight of the narrow valley as long as it was from a safe distance.

Flapjack abandoned his usual lazy gait as he neared home, his feet plopping against the road in hasty rhythm. Logan had just begun to guide the wagon through the final jouncing turn toward the house when two small forms barreled out of nowhere and into the road.

"I didn't!" a towheaded urchin threw back over his shoulder, his high-pitched words aimed at the larger boy charging after him. The small boy's scrawny legs poked out from ragged-edged shorts, and his knobby, scab-dotted knees pumped up and down like small pistons. He jerked to the side, momentarily avoiding his pursuer's grasp.

"You did!"

"I didn't!"

The biggest boy launched himself in a flat dive, catching the smaller one about the knees, and down they went in a tangle of flailing legs and arms. Callie cried out in fear as they disappeared from sight right under the horse's nose.

"Son-of-a—!" Logan sawed on the reins, pulling Flapjack to a stop with only inches to spare. Dust from the youngsters' tumblings mingled with that raised by the bay's prancing hooves.

The horse's bulk obstructed her view and Callie surged upward. Just as she craned her neck to see what had happened to the boys, she caught another

46

movement out of the corner of her eye. "Oh, no!" she wailed at the sight of the tiny girl toddling from the shadows.

Oblivious to their narrow escape and the still present danger from Flapjack's dancing feet, the boys continued to roll upon the ground, first this way and then that. Grunts and squeals sounded as fists more often than not buffeted little more than thin air. Some found their mark, though, and the towheaded urchin yowled in surprise when one of the bigger boy's blows connected with his nose.

Their wallowings took them near the edge of the cliff and Callie screamed again, her gaze swiveling back and forth between the boys on the precarious edge and the little girl who was trudging steadily onward, heedless of the frightened horse's hooves. Logan vaulted from the wagon, covering the space separating him from the pint-sized pugilists in three long strides. Almost simultaneously, Callie scrambled down her side of the wagon, ran forward, and scooped the cotton-topped girl from harm's way.

Clutching the child to her breast, Callie whirled in time to see the struggling duo just as Logan reached them. A swift sigh of relief rushed past her lips as Logan's long fingers closed over bedraggled shirt collars and he hauled the boys to their feet.

"Richard! Thomas! Stop it this instant!" The youngsters dangled from Logan's big hands like two disheveled puppets. He gave them each a vigorous shake. "What's got into you boys? You were told to be on your best behavior this morning!"

For a long moment, all that could be heard was the harsh rasp of the youngsters' breaths, Flapjack's agitated snorts, and the jingle of harness as the bay tossed its head.

"I'm waiting," Logan prompted, punctuating his statement with another shake.

Finally Thomas gulped a big draught of air and drew his forearm beneath his nose, smearing the drop of scarlet his brother's blow had drawn across one dirt-laden cheek. Hair as fine and pale as corn silk dangled over his forehead. The thrust of his bottom lip became even more pugnacious as he glared at his older brother.

"Richard said I did it on purpose!"

"You did!"

"I didn't!"

Logan's fingers hauled the collars higher; the boys came up on tiptoe. Their angry glares gave way to wary glances in Logan's direction, and their small chins retreated an inch or two from their former belligerent angles as they concentrated on keeping their balance.

"One at a time," Logan warned sternly, careful to maintain his holds. "Thomas, what did Richard say you did on purpose?"

Thomas's eyes dropped. "Let his stupid ol' rabbit go . . . but I didn't—"

"You did!" Richard intervened.

"Yeah, but it wasn't on purpose," Thomas defended, his bottom lip taking on a decided quiver. "All I wanted to do was pet it. Richard never lets me pet it."

"And the rabbit got loose?" Logan asked.

His corn-silk hair bobbed in response to Thomas's forlorn nod. "But I still didn't do it on purpose," he

48

muttered again.

Logan's eyes met Callie's across the expanse of road. His broad shoulders moved in characteristic gesture. His annoyance with the boys dimmed as he shot her a look of apology.

"Richard," Logan said, squatting down so that he was on eye-level with the two boys. "I thought we talked just last week about sharing. Didn't we?"

Curls the color of dark honey shimmered as Richard ducked his head in shame. "Yes, sir," he mumbled.

"Then what's this all about? You know you were supposed to behave yourselves this morning. What's your new governess going to think, seeing you two acting no better than heathens?"

Richard's chin shot upward again. "Don't need no governess," he said belligerently. "I ain't no baby. I don't need no babysitter."

"Maybe not," Logan said with a weary shake of his head. "But it certainly sounds to me like you could use a few lessons in proper English."

He stood, releasing his hold on the boys' collars and letting his hands slide down until they each cupped a small, bony shoulder. Gentle pressure angled the boys until they were face to face.

"All right, fellas, I want to hear some apologies. Thomas, you apologize to Richard for not being more careful. Richard, you apologize to Thomas for saying he let the rabbit go on purpose."

Twin blue gazes flickered upward, exchanging hesitant glances.

Callie watched the scene in mild amazement. She would never have expected Logan to be so good with children. Just how many more surprises did this man hold?

"I'm sorry," Thomas mumbled.

"Me, too," Richard replied.

"Now, shake hands," Logan instructed. They did, and Logan gave their shoulders an affectionate squeeze. "Good. That's over and done with. I don't want to hear any more about it. Understand?" They nodded. "Fair enough. Now come on over here, boys, and meet Miss Nolan."

"Yes, sir."

They turned toward Callie. For the first time, Logan noticed the small bundle in her arms. A smile tugged the corners of his mouth upward. "I see you've already met Betsy."

Callie's gaze dropped to the child in her arms. A riot of almost white curls framed Betsy's cherub face. One grubby thumb was tucked in her rosebud mouth, but she removed it long enough to flash Callie a smile that would melt the hardest heart before turning her attention to the others.

"Hi, Mr. Logan," Betsy chirped. "Richard and Thomas have been bad again." The words were delivered in a babyish lisp, coming out "mithter" and "Wichard" and "Thomath." As soon as Betsy's pronouncement had been delivered, she once again leaned contentedly against Callie's shoulder.

Logan watched in fascination as Betsy's curls brushed against the pale ivory of Callie's throat and one small hand splayed innocently against the gentle swell of the new governess's bosom.

A slow warmth curled deep in Logan's chest.

Her gaze steadfastly on the child in her arms,

Callie failed to notice Logan's hungry eyes. Betsy's utter serenity in the face of such chaos created dire speculations about the frequency of the boys' fisticuffs. Was this an everyday occurrence?

"Yes, I know," Logan finally responded to Betsy's comment, the tiniest hint of amusement in his voice. "But they're going to behave themselves now. I'm sure of it."

"If you say so," Betsy said, nodding her head in solemn agreement, as if all Logan had to do was "thay tho" and everything would be all right.

Callie, her arms still tight around the comforting warmth of Betsy's small body, watched the little girl's brothers edge forward in a reluctant shuffle and once again wondered what she'd let herself in for.

"Well, what do you say?" Logan prompted when Richard and Thomas came to a halt in front of Callie.

"Pleased to meet you," the boys muttered in unison.

"I'm very pleased to meet you, too," Callie responded, hoping the smile she forced to her lips looked sincere. "I'm sure we're going to have a grand time. I've brought some new picture books, and I know games . . . lots of games—"

"I'll bet it's all sissy stuff," Richard muttered.

"Yeah, sissy stuff," Thomas echoed.

Betsy tried the phrase, repeating it several times in order to enjoy the intriguing sibilant sounds the words made.

Callie tried another tack. "Oh, you might be surprised. Do you boys know how to play baseball?"

They frowned and shook their heads.

"Well, I do." Callie's dark curls bobbed enthusiastically. "And I know blindman's buff and king of the hill, and . . ." She searched for a clincher. "And I can turn cartwheels with the best of them—"

"Cartwheels," Richard said in awe. He exchanged a speculative glance with Thomas, their past differences completely forgotten at the thought of a grown-up doing such a thing.

A low whistle sounded. "Now, *that* I'd like to see," Logan said, his head suddenly filled with thoughts of swirling petticoats and tempting glimpses of well-turned ankles.

Callie's head jerked upward and her gaze collided with sparkling brown eyes. She shot Logan a reproachful look before turning her attention back to the children. She hadn't won them over yet, not by a long shot. And maintaining her precarious toehold on their attention was more important at the moment than putting Logan Powers in his place.

"Daddy's gonna be mad when he finds out you were fightin' again," Betsy informed her brothers.

Sudden dismay flooded the boys' faces. Callie frowned and then shot Logan a quick glance. The look in his eyes was sufficient to convince Callie that there might be reason for the youngsters' fears.

Inspiration blossomed. "I'll tell you what," Callie said quickly. "Why don't you two boys run on ahead? This horse moves pretty slow. I think there might even be time enough for you to clean up before we get to the house. What do you say?"

Richard and Thomas exchanged a quick glance. Was Miss Nolan suggesting what they thought she was?

"I'm sure it'll take a while to unload the wagon, and I have to meet your parents. That'll take ever so long." Callie's eyes grew wide, as if she'd just realized something utterly surprising. "Why, when I see you again, it'll almost be like we're meeting for the very first time."

The boys were bright enough to recognize reprieve when it was offered. "Yes, ma'am! they echoed. "We're going."

"Me go, too," Betsy declared loudly. Determined not to let her brothers out of her sight, she wriggled in protest.

Callie eased the child to the ground. She barely had time to straighten Betsy's badly smudged pinafore before the boys each grabbed one of her small hands and led her off at a trot that kept her little legs pumping. In a flash, they were gone.

Once again the rumble of Logan's laughter sounded. Her chin high, Callie stared him down, daring him to reproach her tactics.

Sunlight danced in Logan's taffy curls as he shook his head slowly from side to side. "You're a real softy, Miss Nolan." His teasing tone effectively concealed the admiration he was feeling.

One dark brow winged upward in response, but Callie held her tongue, more interested in information than retaliation. "The boys seemed genuinely disturbed when Betsy mentioned their father's wrath. Tell me, is Mr. Claymore really that formidable?"

Logan's lips parted, closed, and parted again as he mentally framed answers and discarded them. "Let's

53

just say he's not the easiest person in the world to get along with," he finally said.

"I see," Callie said.

The idea of children being frightened of their father didn't set well with her at all. She came from a home where along with the discipline, love had always been dispensed in heaping handfuls. Her contemplations of the Claymore family were interrupted when Flapjack, tired of waiting for his oats, put his velvety muzzle in the small of Callie's back and nudged—none too gently.

Caught off balance, Callie stumbled forward and landed squarely in Logan Powers's embrace. His arms closed around her, pinning her against the hard strength of his chest. She gasped as he lowered his head just a smidgen, suddenly afraid he was going to kiss her, inexplicably afraid he wasn't.

But all he did was smile down into her mesmerized eyes. "Is this a sample of the kind of games you like to play, Miss Nolan."

"Oh!" Callie fumed, furious at herself for falling under his spell for even one moment. The man was insufferable! She was not—repeat *was not!*—going to be one of Logan Powers's harem!

Her small hands flat against his chest, she shoved hard. So hard that she staggered backward a step when he released her without protest.

Her tip-tilted nose thrust skyward, Callie stalked back to the wagon and climbed aboard, Logan Powers's husky chuckle rumbling in her ears. She kept her gaze fastened steadfastly on a hawk soaring high above in the periwinkle blue sky while Logan gave Flapjack a tender pat on his nose and promised him an extra ration of oats. She ignored him when he climbed up beside her, and even congratulated herself on her continued display of intestinal fortitude as the wagon rolled slowly up the drive and stopped in front of the house.

By then Callie felt almost giddy with success until Logan reached up and bracketed her waist with his big hands. That's when her disloyal heart stopped dead still and then began to beat in double time. Dismay banished the last vestiges of her smugness. How could she maintain her determination to ignore him when his most innocent touch sent her senses reeling?

"I'll see you into the parlor, and then I'll come back and unharness Flapjack," Logan said. He lifted her down as if she weighed no more than Betsy.

Callie barely managed to suppress the temptation to jerk her arm from his grasp when Logan mounted the steps behind her and captured her elbow. Swallowing hard, she strove to compose her features. "Fine." The word barely squeaked out as she allowed him to lead her up the stairs and across the porch.

The trip across the painted boards seemed to take forever. The time spent standing side by side with Logan Powers while they waited for an answer to his knock seemed even longer.

Finally, the ornately carved front door swung open and they were greeted by a young Mexican girl.

"Ah, *Señor* Logan," the girl said, her round brown face brightening at his sight. "I was getting very worried about you."

Good grief, here we go again, Callie thought with irritation.

Almost as an afterthought the girl addressed Callie. "Welcome, *senorita*. Mrs. Claymore is in the parlor. Please follow me."

Callie took a deep breath and did as she was bid. Logan trailed behind.

Once inside the parlor it took a minute for Callie's eyes to adjust to the gloom created by the tightly shut drapes, and another few seconds to reconcile the picture she'd had in her mind with the woman ensconced on a dark velvet chaise in the far corner of the room.

Average. That was the first word that came to mind when Callie viewed her new employer. Average height. Average build. Average mousy brown hair that held little hint that it had once been as blond as her children's. Average pale-blue eyes. Eyes that held none of the sparkle and spunk of her three offspring. Average features that seemed to fade from memory almost immediately. It was like the spark of life inside Edith Claymore had gone out, leaving nothing but an empty shell.

But to Callie's surprise, Mrs. Claymore's voice wasn't average. Despite its softness and the hesitant deliverance of her welcoming speech, Edith Claymore's soprano held a surprising richness. The sparrow had the voice of a canary.

"I . . . I hope you'll excuse me. I suffer from . . . from rather exhausting headaches at times, and the only things that seem to help are my medicine and rest in a quiet, dark room." Edith hoisted the crystal glass clutched tightly in her grip and took a sip. "Come closer so I can see you. The light . . . it's so dim it makes it rather hard to see."

Callie obeyed. Her eyes widened in surprise as she caught a strong whiff of alcohol when she drew near the couch.

Something glinted in Edith Claymore's eyes. Anger? Fear? Resignation? "Another pretty one," the mistress of the manor mumbled, her voice very low. Mrs. Claymore's eyes went unfocused and she clasped the glass with both hands and lifted it again.

"Beg your pardon?" Callie said, not at all sure what to make of her mistress's remark.

Edith's head jerked up. "What? Oh. Nothing. Nothing." Her eyes slid to the Mexican girl still hovering in the doorway. "Paloma," Mrs. Claymore called, "will you ask Consuela to send the children down?"

Paloma's dark gaze darted toward Logan. Her brows lifted a fraction of an inch and she shook her head. The last time she'd seen the children's current keeper, Consuela, she had been asleep in a corner of the back porch. There was no telling where the children were.

Logan was quick to the rescue. "Why don't you check upstairs, Paloma? Maybe they're getting all spruced up for their meeting with Miss Nolan." He ended the exchange with tiny reassuring nod.

Relief flooded Paloma's brown face. *"Sí, senor."* She gave a quick bob and scurried from the room.

Logan turned to Callie. "I'll get your things unloaded and up to your room."

"Thank you." Swift conflicting emotions flooded through Callie. She'd be relieved to finally have some distance between herself and Logan Powers, a chance to take control of the peculiar feelings he

57

elicited in her. But there was also a strong desire that he stay right by her side, that he not leave her alone in this uncomfortable encounter. Callie bit back the plea, but she couldn't stop her wistful gaze from following his departure from the room.

Silence fell. Edith Claymore leaned wearily against the back of her chaise, both hands still hugging the glass. Callie shuffled uncomfortably, not knowing what to make of the whole strange situation. She'd expected instructions, and a discussion of the children's lessons, time tables, and schedules. All the information she needed in order to do her job well. But Edith Claymore seemed totally unaware of such necessity.

Callie waited. And waited. And finally could wait no more. She cleared her throat nervously. "Is this a convenient time to discuss the children's schedule? And I'd like to know what subjects they have been studying and how far each has progressed in their lessons—"

"Lessons?" Edith repeated, her brows drawing together in muzzy contemplation.

"Yes, ma'am. The children's lessons," Callie prompted gently. "I'm sure you have certain expectations as to the children's schooling. And their agendas . . . I want to make sure that I conform to your wishes."

"My wishes?" Edith repeated as though the thought were utterly foreign. Apprehension joined the confusion in her eyes. "Oh, no. You don't understand. Mr. Claymore takes care of those things. He wouldn't . . . I mean, I couldn't. You'll have to talk with Mr. Claymore. He handles everything."

"Oh." Callie could think of nothing more to say. Something was wrong. Very wrong. Miss Thorndike's description of Edith Claymore — Edith Weatherspoon when they'd known each other — buzzed in her head. The picture Callie's headmistress had painted of her old school friend had nothing in common with the woman she was viewing. What had happened to the laughing, inquisitive girl Miss Thorndike had described?

Callie was saved from further speculation by the arrival of the children. The boys had managed to remove the majority of dirt from their faces. Their hair was slicked into a semblance of neatness, and someone had tied a red ribbon atop Betsy's pale curls.

The sham of introductions was over within seconds. Edith seemed relieved when Paloma, with instructions to show Callie to her room, led them all from the parlor.

The children's shoes clattered against the polished steps as they scrambled up the staircase to the second floor, the boys racing to see who would be first. "Rotten egg, rotten egg," Betsy repeated, her little legs straining to take the broad steps.

As they climbed, Paloma described the layout of the house in her heavily accented English.

The downstairs was divided by the broad entryway and the grand staircase. Down the left side lay the parlor they'd just been in, Mrs. Claymore's bedroom, a living area, and the kitchen. On the right was a study/office combination for Mr. Claymore. Paloma intoned grave warnings about never disturbing Mr. Claymore in his study unless expressly summoned. Next in line was the master's bedroom.

Callie remembered the big feather bed her parents shared, the huge carved headboard, the bright patchwork quilt. It had offered safe haven during storms, a gathering place for early Sunday morning stories and tickling sessions before they all dressed for church. Had the Claymore children ever enjoyed such small pleasures? Paloma's final words about the dining room and kitchen and the small quarters she shared with Consuela barely penetrated the disturbing thought.

The upstairs was likewise divided by the stairway, which opened onto a small landing. The boys shared connecting bedrooms on the left. Paloma stopped long enough to open the door to the next small room, a cubicle barely large enough for the porcelain bathtub and washstand it held. At least bathing facilities would be convenient. From the present appearance of the children, Callie feared they'd be needed on a very frequent basis.

The front right corner held the nursery, the large room Callie would use for lessons. Then came Betsy's room and next to it was Callie's.

"This opens onto the gallery," Paloma said, opening the glass-paned door off the hall landing.

Callie stepped through to look around. The children eagerly followed, surging ahead to lean precariously over the railing.

"Oh, Betsy, be careful!" Callie cried, suddenly afraid the little girl would tumble headfirst over the banister.

Richard eyed the new governess with mild annoyance. "She's all right. We play up here all the time.

We even know how to climb down the trellis."

Wonderful. Callie tried to still the rapid beat of her heart at the mere thought of such a feat. She managed a weak grin before turning her attention back to her surroundings.

The upper veranda ran the length of the rear of the house, with a staircase angling off to the left. The view offered little more than the barn and some sheds below, and straight ahead was the vast mountainside that climbed upward behind the dwelling. That suited Callie fine. It would be a good place to do lessons on pleasant days, as long as she ignored what lay beyond the railing.

"Mr. Claymore prefers that the children use this staircase. That way they do not disturb him at work in the study," Paloma explained.

Callie raised one brow but said nothing.

They stepped back inside to the hallway. There was still one closed door on the rear left side, directly across from the one Callie would use.

"And what's in there?" she asked.

"Oh, that's Senor Logan's room."

CHAPTER FOUR

"Where shall I put this?"

Callie whirled to find Logan's big frame blocking the doorway to her quarters, balancing one of her trunks on his shoulder. The room she'd thought so large and airy a moment ago now seemed to shrink in size as Logan stepped through the portal.

Her gaze darted about the room. "There," she finally answered, pointing to the empty corner near the massive pine wardrobe.

Logan's heels thudded against the floor as he crossed to the designated spot. Callie's heart thudded in unison, and she watched in silence as the trunk was effortlessly lifted from his shoulder. Despite her best efforts otherwise, her eyes fastened on the sleek flex and slide of muscle under the thin blue fabric of his shirt as he slowly lowered the cumbersome chest.

The trunk thunked against the floor, and Callie jumped when, in one fluid movement, Logan straightened and began to turn. She whisked her gaze away, determined he wouldn't catch her staring again. But the slow smile that tipped his generous mouth as he faced her left her less than sure she'd succeeded.

Callie, despite the strong impulse to back away as he crossed toward her in that slow, hip-rolling gait, stood her ground at the side of the bed. Was she mistaken, or did Logan's gaze linger overly long on the bed's colorful expanse of patchwork quilt as he came nearer? She tried to concentrate on the distant sound of the children chattering in the nursery, but the happy noises faded as he came closer.

Finally he stopped, so close to the edge of the bed that his pants leg brushed up against the corner of the quilt. "I'll go get your other trunk now."

"Th-thank you."

Callie waited until he'd traversed the room and disappeared through the doorway before approaching the chest he'd carried in. She told herself that it was just a matter of minutes before Logan would be out of the room for good—and out of her mind. Why, in the course of a normal day, she assured herself, she probably wouldn't even see him. Surely Mr. Claymore's business kept Logan too busy elsewhere for him to hang around the house. More than likely she'd see him only on rare occasions.

Like every day as he goes in and out of that room across the hall, a wee small voice in the back of her mind taunted.

Quickly brushing the troublesome thought aside, she knelt in front of the trunk and turned her attention to the lock. The key turned easily enough but the hasp refused to release. Muttering a word her mother wouldn't have approved of, Callie yanked harder. The lock finally gave way and the trunk lid flew upward, banging against the wall.

Blindly she grabbed a handful of folded garments and stalked to the chest of drawers, jerking the top drawer open with such force that one edge slipped from its runner and the drawer stuck halfway open. Lifting the clothes high, Callie prepared to shove them inside anyway, but her hand froze in midmovement.

Callie's startled shriek echoed through the upstairs just as Logan's foot touched the bottom step of the grand staircase. Without hesitation he dumped the trunk from his shoulder and took the stairs two at a time. The babble from the nursery ceased abruptly as he reached the landing and sprinted for Callie's room. There was a clatter of little feet as the children raced out of their room and after Logan.

"What is it? What's the matter?" Logan's voice was raspy as he rounded the entryway. His desperate gaze raked the room, but he saw nothing out of place save for the small pile of tumbled clothing at Callie's feet.

Callie didn't even look in his direction. Like a statue she stayed poised before the open drawer, her head bent forward at an odd angle. "I think perhaps you'd better have a look at this," she said, her lips barely moving.

Logan heard a strangled "uh-oh" behind him as he moved swiftly to Callie's side. Stepping between Callie and the tall chest, he peered down into the drawer's depths.

In the dark recesses of a back corner lay a coiled snake, its bands of red, yellow, and black muted by the shadows. Its cold reptile eyes glittered menacingly, and the tiny forked tongue darted in and out, in and out in hypnotic rhythm.

"Damn," Logan breathed. "Back up, Miss Nolan. I need to get our little visitor here into a bit more light before I can tell for sure—"

"Tell what?" Callie asked, bumping Logan's arm as she totally disregarded his directions, raising on tiptoe in an effort to see around his broad shoulder.

Logan pushed aside the distracting thought of how very soft and warm Callie's flesh felt against his arm. This wasn't the time or the place to indulge such fantasies. Reaching out, he rapped his knuckles against the side of the drawer. The snake gave a soft sibilant hiss and slithered catty-corner toward the other side.

Logan's breath whooshed out. "Just what I thought," he said, relief tinging his voice.

"What?" Callie questioned, pressing even harder against Logan. "Thought what?"

There was a severe scowl on Logan's features as he stepped away from Callie's disconcerting nearness and turned toward the doorway. Only Betsy still stood inside the room, but Logan's sharp eyesight caught a flickering glimpse of retreating shadows against the far wall of the entryway.

"Thomas! Richard! Come here this instant." No one would have dared disobey the tone of Logan's voice.

The two little boys crept through the doorway, heads tucked tight into their drawn-up shoulders.

At that moment Paloma reached the doorway, her large bosom heaving with the exertion of her race from the kitchen and up the stairs. *"Madre dios! What has happened? You have alarmed Mrs. Claymore."*

"It's all right, Paloma," Logan assured. "Nothing to worry about. I'll take care of it. Go down and tell Mrs. Claymore that everything is all right."

Paloma eyed the shame-faced boys for a long moment before she acknowledged Logan's directions with a quiet *"Sí, señor,"* and withdrew from the room. They could hear her muttering in rapid-fire Spanish as she descended the stairs.

"Now, what is the meaning of this?" Logan demanded. The boys flinched under the sternness of his voice and ducked their heads even lower.

Callie's mouth dropped open, and her gaze swung to the two sheepish figures hugging the rectangular framework of the doorway. "You mean the boys put that snake in my drawer?"

Logan's gaze stayed pinned on the culprits. "I'm afraid so."

"Well," Callie said with relieved sigh. "Then it must not be poisonous."

"No, of course not. I presume they just wanted to frighten you."

The tangle of abandoned clothing on the floor snagged the toe of Logan's boot as he turned and took a step toward the boys. He looked down at the obstacle and then up at Callie.

"Oh, my!" she said, her eyes following his gaze. "I'm sorry. I'll get them."

But it was too late. Logan had already bent to retrieve the scattered clothing. Heat began to climb in her face as Logan's big hand closed over the

66

tumble of lace-edged undergarments. His fingers were long and golden brown against the gossamer fabric. Callie found it suddenly hard to swallow when a delicate length of blue ribbon shifted and settled against the tawny-dusted back of his hand. She watched him slowly rub the pad of his thumb against the topmost camisole and her mouth went drier still. Spots of color stained Callie's cheeks. She snatched the offering from his grasp and whirled toward the chest, jerking the second drawer open with enough force to make the wood squeal against the runners.

With difficulty, Logan forced his thoughts back to the business at hand. Barely inside the door, the boys still shuffled nervously. Richard dared a quick upward peek at Logan, but Thomas kept his head so low that the cowlick at the crown of his unruly blond hair poked straight toward the ceiling.

Logan glowered, his face as dark as the thunder-clouds that often roiled over the Mule Mountains. "I can't believe you two would pull such a low-down, dirty trick on Miss Nolan after what she did for you this morning. What have you got to say for your-selves?"

"We forgot," Richard muttered so low under his breath that they could barely hear his words. "We put it in there early this morning—"

"Yeah, real early," Thomas echoed, though he still refused to meet Logan's gaze.

Richard ignored his brother's interruption. "We didn't know Miss Nolan was going to be nice. 'Cep-tin' for Miss Walker last year, we ain't liked anybody who's come. We figured she'd be like all the others.

We just forgot about the snake, that's all."

Finally Thomas snuck a repentant glance upward, his eyes aswim with remorseful tears. "Honest. If we'd a remembered, we'd a taken it out. Miss Nolan was nice to us. We wouldn't a scared her if we'd knowed she wasn't like the others."

Richard's chin rose belligerently. "What difference does it make anyway? The nice ones never stay."

Compassion filled Logan's eyes. He was searching for an answer to the little boy's plaintive remark when Callie returned to his side.

"Would you kindly explain how to tell this one isn't poisonous?" She thrust the length of wriggling snake under his nose.

The unexpected gesture caught the big man by surprise. His balled hands dropped from his hips and he stumbled back a step. The beginnings of giggles escaped from the boy's mouths. Logan's head jerked their way and the sounds died.

"Well?" Callie prompted.

Shaking his shaggy head from side to side, Logan scrutinized the small figure before him. Callie seemed not in the least perturbed to be holding the writhing reptile.

Logan drew a deep breath. "Damn, lady, don't you ever react in normal female fashion?"

"Sorry to disappoint you, Mr. Powers, but I grew up with three younger brothers who at times could put Richard and Thomas to shame. There's not anything slimy, hairy, or crawly that I haven't found in my belongings or on my person at one time or another. Now, I ask again, how do you know this one isn't poisonous even though its colors match the descriptions I've read of a coral snake? I don't want to make the same mistake again."

Logan fought back a grin. Callie Nolan was a constant source of amazement. He knew it wouldn't do to let the boys see his amusement; they still had to atone for their behavior. "That's a Sonoran shovel-nosed snake. The colored bands are arranged in the same sequence as the coral snake's, but there's one important difference. Look at the red bands. On the shovel-nose they don't encircle the body. Don't worry, it would rather dine on insects and spiders than humans."

Lifting the snake, Callie turned it this way and that as she peered at the red semicircular bands that left its underside bare. The boys watched Callie's movements gape-mouthed; only by sheer willpower did Logan keep his own mouth tightly shut.

Betsy's small voice finally broke the spell. "Are you going to keep him for a pet?"

Callie smiled in the little girl's direction. "No, Betsy, I'm not. God's wild creatures belong outside." She crossed the room and held the snake out to the boys. "Put him back where he belongs."

"Yes, ma'am!" Richard eagerly took the snake.

Logan could do no more than shake his head while he watched the two boys disappear as if by magic.

"I have a pet, Miss Nolan," Betsy solemnly said.

"You do, darling?" Callie replied, placing her hands on her knees and bending toward the little girl.

"Yes. Her name is Shadow. I'll share my pet with you, if you'd like." Betsy's blond curls bobbed in response to the nod of her cherubic head.

A shining smile wreathed Callie's face and she stooped to give Betsy a swift hug. "That's quite the nicest offer I've had all day."

"I wouldn't be too sure of that," Logan muttered under his breath, well aware of Shadow's spit-fire personality where most of the human race was concerned.

Caught up in Betsy's glowing description of her pet, Callie appeared not to have heard Logan. With another shake of his head he eased past the enthralled duo and went to retrieve the abandoned trunk.

When Logan returned, he found Callie alone. "Where's Betsy?" he asked.

"Here I am," the little girl answered, darting past him to join Callie on the edge of the bed. "I had to get Shadow." Sure enough, there was a black bundle of fur clutched tight in her small arms.

"Oh, no," Logan groaned, rolling his brown eyes heavenward.

He quickened his pace, eager to rid himself of the trunk and save the new governess from injury. But by the time he deposited his burden beside the first trunk, Callie had the half-grown kitten in her arms and was raising it toward her face. Logan could almost see the four slashing lines that would soon mar the soft ivory velvet of her cheek.

"Don't do that!" he admonished, knowing he couldn't reach Callie in time.

"Do what?" Callie asked, her eyes wide and innocent as she cuddled the cat against her bosom. Just then Shadow arched her head against the delicate

70

underside of Callie's chin, a loud purr echoing through the room as she stretched and preened and rubbed her ears sensuously against the soft, satin skin.

"Oh, never mind," Logan muttered wearily.

A decidedly uncomfortable feeling flowed through Logan as he watched Callie stroke the kitten. What strange magic did this petite miss possess? She'd tamed the boys. She'd tamed Shadow. Who did she plan turning that peculiar sorcery on next?

Well, Logan vowed, his mouth thinning into a stubborn line, it damn well wouldn't be him. Much as he admired the female race, he had no intention of curling up and becoming some woman's domesticated pussycat!

CHAPTER FIVE

Callie approached the door to Mr. Claymore's study with a mixture of apprehension and relief. She'd made it through her first day as governess on intuition and frequent prayers; she fervently hoped that the children's father would shed some light on the subject of schedules, goals, and discipline. Thank goodness there hadn't been much time for that today. But tomorrow still loomed ahead, and all the tomorrows of her one-year contract.

By the time Callie had unpacked her belongings, it had been time for the midday meal, a meal she and the children had shared alone at the small table in the nursery. Edith Claymore had not appeared for the meal, or at any point thereafter. When questioned, Paloma had answered that Mrs. Claymore usually took a tray in her parlor—if she ate at all.

Callie couldn't help but wonder if Logan ate in the kitchen with Paloma or if perhaps one of his lady friends provided his repast. Heaven knew, Callie thought with a grimace, there were probably a dozen of them falling all over themselves to feed him.

She'd made a game out of letting the children help her put away the books and teaching materials she'd purchased with the draft Mr. Claymore had sent before her departure. The afternoon had flown swiftly by, the children overjoyed that no lessons were to be forthcoming on the day of Callie's arrival.

Supper had been taken at the same table in the nursery. Shortly afterward, she'd supervised Betsy's bath and inspected the results of the boys' obviously hasty contact with water. She made a silent vow to hold a lesson on the benefits of cleanliness as soon as possible. Then she read the children two stories, and they were now tucked snug in their beds.

Callie had looked forward to a leisurely bath for herself and a full night's sleep after the long days of travel, but Mr. Claymore's unexpected summons had caused a postponement of her plans.

The rap of Callie's knuckles against the polished wooden door sounded alarmingly loud in the dim hallway. Hearing a muffled "Come in," Callie drew herself up stiff and straight. She gave a hasty pat to her ebony curls and smoothed her fingers across her skirt one last time. Then she placed her hand on the ornate brass knob and gave it a twist. The door swung open on well-oiled hinges.

Except for two bright pools of light cast by kerosene lamps atop a massive desk on the far side of the room, the area was engulfed in gunmetal-gray shadows. Callie's new employer was nowhere in sight. Her brows drew together in a perplexed frown and she hesitated in the doorway.

"Come in, my dear." Owen Claymore's rumbling bass filled the room. "Come in and close the door."

Callie did as instructed. As the door clicked shut, the oversized leather chair behind the desk swiveled around, bringing Owen Claymore into view. Placing his hands flat on the top of the walnut desk, he stood to greet his new employee.

The man's stature was a perfect match for the huge desk and the high-backed chair. Claymore stood several inches taller than six feet, his weight well over two hundred pounds, although there was no hint of fat to his massive girth, just an overpowering bulk and presence. An impeccably tailored red silk smoking jacket encased his broad shoulders, thick arms, and barrel chest. Velvet lapels bracketed an artfully draped white silk cravat. Owen Claymore obviously enjoyed fine things.

Silver frosted his thick, light-brown hair. Lips that were full, almost pouty, peeked through a gray-sprinkled close-cut beard. His face was big, almost round, his nose fleshy and rather flat. But his most striking features were his eyes. Eyes the color of pale topaz. The predator eyes of a rogue lion.

"Well, Miss Nolan. I'm delighted to finally meet you." His lips turned up at the corners, and one huge hand gestured toward the chair near the corner of the desk. "Come in, come in. Please have a seat and make yourself comfortable."

The hem of Callie's gown whispered softly against the nap of the rug as she crossed the room to perch nervously on the edge of the indicated chair. Owen Claymore emerged from behind the desk, moving

74

with exceptional grace and silence for a man of his size.

"Would you care for a glass of sherry? I was just about to have a little refreshment myself, and I'd be pleased if you'd join me."

"No thank you, sir," Callie answered in a voice barely above a whisper. "I'm afraid I'm not accustomed to spirits."

"Ah," Claymore said, with an approving nod of his leonine head. "Young and innocent, obviously gently reared. Excellent. I've chosen well. You'll be a fine influence on the children." With those words he sauntered to a sideboard and poured a splash of amber liquid into a heavy glass tumbler.

When he returned, he surprised Callie by electing to prop one haunch on the edge of the desk nearest her chair rather than once again taking his place behind it. Callie shrank from his unexpected nearness, unconsciously shifting until her spine was pressed firmly against the corner of the wing-back chair in which she sat. Frissons of unexplained discomfort butterflied through her stomach.

Nerves, she thought. Just nerves at finally meeting her employer, propelled by her fervent desire to please, to do a good job. She still didn't understand how she'd been lucky enough to be selected for the position, right at a time when her family was in such difficult financial straits. The salary she'd been offered was excellent, and her head was filled with thoughts of how much three-quarters of her wages would help her family each month. She wanted so badly to make a good impression on her new employer, to ensure her position for the promised term of one year. By then her father would be well and able once again to provide for the family.

"I hope you had a pleasant trip." Claymore slowly raised his glass and took a sip of the whiskey, those pale hunter's eyes watching her unblinkingly over the crystal rim.

Callie forced a trembly smile. "Oh, yes, sir. The arrangements were excellent. It . . . it was quite interesting. I mean, seeing the country . . . and all the different sights."

You're babbling, Callie admonished herself. But she couldn't seem to help it. She very much wanted to like the man who would be her employer for the next twelve months, but something about Owen Claymore made her decidedly uncomfortable. The questions she'd prepared concerning schedules and lessons had completely vanished from her mind.

"I apologize for not being here to greet you at the time of your arrival. I had an early appointment with a prospective employee."

"Oh, please, sir, think nothing of it. I know you must be a very busy man."

Owen Claymore smiled benignly. "Yes. Yes, I am. But I just want to assure you I had planned to be here. It was just that this man has some . . . uh . . . rather unique qualifications and I felt it necessary to conduct the interview myself." Claymore's thoughts seemed to turn inward and he fell silent for a long moment.

Callie felt compelled to say something to break the ensuing silence. "I hope it went well, sir" was all she could think of.

"What? Oh, yes. Yes, it did. I do believe I've

finally found the right man for the job." Owen's smile was almost smug. "Well, enough of business. How about you? I trust Logan took care of everything in a satisfactory manner?"

Logan. Callie suddenly wished he was there to act as a buffer during this first interview. His presence would be greatly appreciated right at the moment although she hardly considered her welcome to Bisbee as having been "handled satisfactorily." But she certainly wasn't about to say so to Mr. Claymore. She had the very distinct feeling that it wouldn't be smart to earn his displeasure. Annoying though Logan had been at times during their ride to the house, Callie had no intention of putting him in an awkward position with their boss.

"Yes, sir. Everything was perfect."

"Paloma tells me that you met Mrs. Claymore."

"Yes, sir, I did."

Claymore's words brought a vivid picture of Edith Claymore to Callie's mind. Sparrow and lion. How had these two ever managed to become man and wife? Callie had never seen a more mismatched pair.

Something flashed in Owen Claymore's eyes. It was quickly banished by the look of deep sadness which settled on his face.

"My poor, poor darling," he said with a shake of his shaggy head. "You see . . ." He gave a great sigh. "My wife suffers from a peculiar illness. Quite debilitating at times. I've had untold specialists look at her, but the doctors don't seem to know what to make of it."

Callie's gaze dropped to the whiskey-filled glass in Claymore's hand, then her eyes cut swiftly away.

Although she suspected at least one reason for Mrs. Claymore's impairment, she held her silence. Who was she to say anything? After all, she could have been wrong this afternoon. Maybe the medicine had an aroma similar to that of whiskey. She had no proof regarding what Mrs. Claymore had been drinking.

Callie knew she had no business poking her nose into such issues; the children were her responsibility. Nothing else. She'd do well to remember that if she wanted to keep this job. Rich, socialite families didn't take kindly to their employees offering unwanted opinions or advice.

The children. Oh, yes. Their schedules and lessons. Callie swiftly turned her mind to matters more appropriate for a newly hired governess.

Owen Claymore's answers to her questions were less than satisfying. Virtually all decisions would be left up to Callie. The main thing that the children's father seemed concerned with was that they be well supervised and kept out of the way unless summoned.

"Oh, yes," Claymore finished. "Logan will be available to take you and the children about as needed. Last week I prevailed upon him to take over the empty room upstairs on a permanent basis. It's much more convenient that way . . . no more messages to the boardinghouse, all that nonsense. All you have to do is give him a little advance notice. Just tell him when to have the wagon ready and where you want to go and he'll take care of everything else. I occasionally have chores for him to take care of, but for the most part he'll be at your disposal every day." Claymore was inordinately pleased with this current decision. He'd have Logan close at hand just in case things did get out of hand in the future, and, in the meantime, he could earn his pay by keeping a watch on the children.

Callie gulped. *Every day? See Logan Powers every day? Not if she could help it!* "Oh, surely that won't be necessary, Mr. Claymore. Bisbee isn't that large. I'm sure we can walk just about any place we'd like to go."

"I'm afraid not, my dear. You're on the frontier now. You must remember that. There's still an occasional Apache about. And we've been having a little trouble with some of the miners lately—all the wealth from the mines has drawn some rather unsavory characters to the area. It's best to be cautious. That's the one thing I will insist upon. Logan must accompany you and the children if you leave the immediate area around the house."

Wonderful! Just wonderful. "Yes, sir," Callie said, trying not to let her vexation creep into her voice.

Claymore apparently didn't notice Callie's reluctance. "I believe the children enjoy nature study; at least that's what one of the past governesses said. Rather a good idea, I think. It does keep them out of the house and allows their poor mother to get a little rest. Just ask Logan. He'll see to everything."

Callie simply nodded.

"Anything else I can do for you, my dear?" Claymore asked, leaning toward her.

"N-no, sir. I can't think of a thing." He'd done quite enough all ready.

Claymore stood and held out his hand toward her,

a pleased smile wreathing his broad face. "Well then, Miss Nolan, let me escort you to the door. I'm sure you've had a busy day, and I've already kept you up much too late."

"Thank you," Callie said, bewildered that Owen Claymore seemed inordinately pleased with their first visit while she was filled with a lingering uneasiness. *It's only the thing with Logan,* she assured herself. *That's all.* Mr. Claymore had been exceptionally nice even if he hadn't shown much interest in the children. There was no reason to feel so . . . so discomforted in his presence.

Callie placed her hand in his and allowed him to pull her to her feet. His palm was soft and slightly damp. Her uneasiness intensified. Sliding her fingers from his grip, she quickly sidled around the chair and began edging her way toward the door.

But Owen Claymore wasn't that easy to escape.

Just as she turned she felt his big hand close gently over her upper arm, a mannerly, solicitous gesture that shouldn't have bothered her at all. But it did. His steps were slow, almost languid, as he guided her toward the door. He reached with his other hand to turn the knob, maintaining his hold on her arm until they were in the hallway just outside the study.

"Pleasant dreams, Miss Nolan."

"Thank you. Good night."

Relief flooded through Callie as she slipped from his grasp. She forced herself to walk decorously toward the stairs. Once there, she hiked her skirts and began a hasty ascent, anxious to escape to the comfort and security of her room.

As she reached the top landing, Callie threw one last look over the banister. Owen Claymore stood in the precise same position, one long finger softly stroking the silvered hair beneath his meaty bottom lip. His yellow cat eyes watched her until the railing finally obscured him from view.

The warm water closed over her shoulders as Callie sank deep in the porcelain bathtub. She leaned her head wearily against the rim of the tub and let the liquid heat work its magic on her taut muscles. It would be midnight before she climbed into bed, but the luxury of a long, soothing soak was worth the loss of sleep.

The children were deep in slumber. The house was quiet. She lay in the hot water Paloma had so thoughtfully prepared for her and contemplated the peculiarities of the day, not knowing quite what to make of those in the Claymore household.

The children. The thought brought a smile to her lips. Betsy was a delight. Callie could see no problems there. The boys were going to be a handful, but she felt she'd made a fair amount of progress with them. At least they looked at her now with a little respect. The snake had done the trick.

Callie chuckled softly as she remembered her initial reaction at the sight of the reptile coiled in her drawer. Her brothers would have loved it. Travis, Gerald, and Andy were in constant competition to outdo each other when it came to playing tricks on Callie, Jenny, Marcy, and Tina. Not that the four sisters hadn't been able to get in a few licks of their own once in a while.

Lord, but she missed her family! Mother and Father. Grandmother Nana. And the whole rowdy bunch of brothers and sisters that filled the Nolan house with such love and laughter.

What a difference it was to compare the home she grew up in with the Claymore home. No wonder the boys were little hooligans. And it was just this side of a miracle that Betsy was as sweet and pliant as she was. She obviously adored Richard and Thomas. And, according to Logan, she served as their faithful shadow unless they somehow managed to elude her—something that happened rarely, he had assured her with a grin. Callie was more than a bit surprised that Betsy hadn't yet begun to copy her brothers' wild antics.

Edith Claymore was an enigma. Was she really ill, or was the pain in her eyes the result of other problems? What could make a woman withdraw from life in such a way? Turn her back on her children and leave their rearing to strangers? Something haunted Edith Claymore, something Callie didn't understand. But somehow she knew it was there.

And Owen Claymore. What about the master of the house? Never in Callie's life had she felt such an instinctive discomfort at the first meeting with a person. Perhaps it was because the Claymores were head and shoulders above the Nolan family's social strata, with mannerisms so different from what Callie was used to. Maybe she'd read more into Mr. Claymore's demeanor than was warranted. Still, she'd felt a real surge of relief when he'd made it evident that his business hours often ran late and she wouldn't be expected to spend much time around him.

That was all right with Callie. She would manage quite well with no help from either of the Claymores. It would be just her and the children.

And then there was Logan Powers.

Callie scowled at the memory of Owen Claymore's pronouncement concerning Logan and his duties. Her employer's words had certainly banished her earlier conviction about seeing Logan only rarely.

Now the ghost of the devilish rogue returned to haunt her. She hadn't seen him since the incident with the snake. Perhaps he'd gone to see the redhead. The thought deepened Callie's scowl.

"What do I care?" she muttered, jerking upright so swiftly that water sloshed over the edge of the tub and two pins fell from her hair, allowing delicate ebony ringlets to curl provocatively against the back of her neck. Grabbing the cake of soap from its dish on the small side table, Callie began scrubbing her skin with unnecessary intensity.

But the memories of Logan weren't as easy to wash away as the dust of the day. Her vigorous efforts created little wavelets that spread outward, lapping against the rim of the tub with soft, liquid gurgles.

Like it or not, she was stuck with the situation. She could either stay at the house and see if she could keep three exuberant children pacified with whatever diversions she could find close by, or she could learn to overcome the decidedly peculiar and disconcerting feelings Logan evoked in her.

"I won't take the coward's way out," Callie vowed with soft vehemence. "It wouldn't be fair to the children. They need fresh air and sunshine and a place to run and play and shout." So be it. She'd handle Logan Powers. One way or another.

The water's warmth had seeped away. Callie glanced at the wrinkly pads of her fingers and knew it was time to relinquish the tub. With a heartfelt sigh she rose and reached for a towel just as the hallway door swung open.

Too surprised to scream, Callie whipped the length of toweling in front of her, clutching it for dear life as she gaped open-mouthed at the man in the doorway.

Logan looked as shocked and astounded as she was. He swallowed hard, his Adam's apple bobbing visibly. His voice cracked the first time he tried to speak. He swallowed again.

"I . . . I'm sorry. Really. I'm sorry. I never dreamed anyone would still be up this late."

The towel was large enough to swathe Callie from neck to knees with the bottom edge of it trailing in the water, but a red-hot blush climbed her cheeks just the same. Had she managed to get the towel in place soon enough? She didn't know. And the peculiar look on Logan's face did little to reassure her.

Callie's chin snapped upward. "Would you mind?" she demanded, a slight tremble in her frosty voice.

"Mind?" Logan repeated. Hell no, he didn't mind. She was quite the loveliest sight he'd seen in a long time, all flushed and damp from her bath, her eyes large and luminous, a froth of dark curls grazing her temple and trailing down the delicate length of her neck. Sweet heaven, he didn't mind at all.

Callie gave a little hiss of anger when Logan failed to move. Her eyes narrowed dangerously.

Sudden awareness blossomed in Logan's eyes. "Oh," he said, realizing that he was still standing in the open doorway and Callie wore only a towel that was becoming increasingly more transparent and clingy as the material soaked up the bathwater.

"Oh," he said again, at a loss for words. "Sorry." The door slammed shut behind him.

CHAPTER SIX

*Get hold of yourself, fella. She's not your type!
Not your type at all.*

The stern self-lecture Logan had been delivering to
himself every day since Callie Nolan's arrival did no
good. Not one tiny bit of good.

He knew all the reasons why he should put her
out of his mind. He'd listed them so many times the
last few weeks that he knew the litany by heart.

His motto had always been "love 'em and leave
'em." Enjoy a woman as long as it was fun and free
and unrestricting. But with one hint that the woman
was looking for a more permanent relationship, Logan had always been off and running like a bear
with a hive of wild bees at his back. That's why his
friendship with Della Maxwell had lasted so many
years. She put no pressures on him, asked for no
commitments.

But Callie . . . ah, that would be a different story.
She would settle for nothing less than commitment.
Marriage, a vine-covered cottage with a picket fence,

children. Everything.

Everything or nothing.

So why was he wasting his time mooning around like some lovesick schoolboy? Why did he look for excuses to hang around the Claymore house when he could have been enjoying a lusty romp with Della?

Why, he'd barely seen the redhead since Callie's arrival five weeks ago. Della knew better than to push, but she had casually mentioned his uncharacteristic absence the last time he'd seen her on the street. He didn't even remember the excuse he'd stammered. She'd cocked her head to one side and scrutinized him in a way that had made him feel like he had a good case of poison ivy all over. But, to Logan's profound relief, she hadn't questioned him any further.

Other things about his life had changed during the past five weeks. He hadn't been spending near enough time looking for information that George Anderson and his mining association could use to fight whoever was sabotaging the independent miners in the area. Hell, that was why he'd taken the job with Claymore in the first place, not to mention moving into the Claymore house, so he could find out the truth.

Was wealthy, pillar-of-the-community Owen Claymore the ruthless person behind all the dirty, underhanded tricks that had been going on the last few months? The stolen supplies. The undermining of the shoring timbers in Dave Guthrie's mine. The tampered fuses that had caused a premature explosion and the death of Gene Bradshaw and his boy Curtis. George was positive Claymore was the guilty party. It was Logan's task to verify those suspicions. So why wasn't he putting forth more effort in doing his job?

Why did he spend every morning loitering in the barn, hoping against hope that Callie would send word to hitch up the wagon for an afternoon excursion? Since when was driving a wisp of a woman and three children around for "nature studies" or picnics the most exciting thing he had to look forward to each day?

What in hell was wrong with him anyway? He was no better than a kid with his nose pressed against the display case in a candy store, knowing he didn't have the coins it took to make a purchase, knowing that the luscious treats behind the glass barrier would never be his. Looking only made him hungrier.

Never taking his eyes off Callie, Logan sighed and shifted on his hard rock seat. God, she was beautiful. Just watching her made his breath come faster and evoked a crazy little swirling tickle deep in his stomach.

Surrounded by the children, Callie sat on a faded old patchwork quilt spread under a towering tree. All four of them had abandoned their shoes and stockings at the edge of the blanket. The gnarled trunk of the tree served as her backrest, and though she'd carefully tucked her gingham skirt around her legs when she'd sat down, a persistent breeze had finally plucked one fold loose, occasionally lifting the hem past bare toes to give Logan a tempting glance of shapely ankles.

The boys were sprawled on their stomachs, their

chins on folded hands, their bent legs slowly kicking back and forth. Betsy had burrowed under Callie's arm, curling up at her side like a little kitten. Wriggling and scrunching around until she was comfortable, she'd finally wound up with her flaxen curls pressed against the soft swell of Callie's breast and one small hand propped negligently on Callie's gingham-covered knee. Lord, but he coveted what Betsy was taking for granted.

Logan had refused their invitation to join them on the quilt, afraid that he'd give himself away, afraid that Callie would be able to read the desire in his eyes. So here he sat on a nearby rock, a safe three feet away, listening to the melody of Callie's voice as she once again read from the children's favorite story, *Alice in Wonderland*.

Sunbeams speared through the softly swaying branches and dappled the quartet with golden coins of bright yellow light. Cedar-scented wind stirred the ebony curls at her temple and she automatically lifted one slender hand to smooth them back in place before once again anchoring the pages of the storybook against the zephyr's playful fingers. Her voice carried on the breeze, tones, inflections, accents changing in the most delightful manner as she portrayed each character in the tale, the flow of her words stopping only long enough to show the children the colorful illustrations before she turned each page and took up the story again.

The boys loved the Red Queen. "Off with their heads!" they shouted with glee. Betsy preferred the White Rabbit, and often urged Alice in little breathy whispers to hurry and catch "wabbit" before it was too late for the tea party.

Logan was beginning to think he knew just how Alice had felt when she'd stepped into the dark and fallen down the rabbit hole, her stomach sinking to her toes, her heart in her throat as she tumbled end over end in a plunge over which she had no control.

He'd fallen down the hole the night he opened the door to the bathing room and found Callie naked as a wood nymph.

They'd never spoken of the incident again, but Logan had lain awake many a night remembering every tiny detail. One short moment in time, a bare flicker in the light beam of eternity. But that flicker had rocked him clear to the tips of his toes.

Why? Why such a reaction? He could name a dozen women more voluptuous than Callie. More available. More willing. But, when reviewing all of those accessible delights, none seemed so enticing, so heartbreakingly alluring as the slender young Callie Nolan.

All Logan had to do was close his eyes and he could play the whole scene again in his mind. The proud swell of her breast above a tiny hand-span waist. The pert uptilt of her nipple, the same rosy pink as the camelias that used to grow in his grandmother's front flowerbed. The gentle woman-curve of her hip and long, lush line of her alabaster thigh. The memory was so sweet, so tantalizing that he had only to conjure it up and his rebellious body reacted instantaneously.

He tormented himself with the question of what she would have done if he'd stepped inside and closed the door behind him, secluding the two of them within the dark shadows of the room. Alone. All alone.

Logan sighed. He knew what she would have done. What she'd do any time in the future. Draw herself up as proud and tall as her tiny stature would allow and then pierce him with those huge, innocent eyes that bespoke without a doubt exactly the kind of woman she was. The kind who would give herself only to the man she loved. And then, only then, would the bud blossom. She would turn her face up to the sunshine created by such a relationship, and unfold petal by magnificent petal as she willingly, joyously gave herself to the man who'd won her heart.

A muscle ticked relentlessly at the corner of Logan's clenched jaw. He forced his mind back to reality, berating himself for acting like some foolish fourteen-year-old, wet-behind-the-ears kid. He'd made up his mind a long time ago to steer clear of commitments. And a relationship with a woman like Callie called for a commitment, which all boiled down to love and trust and responsibility.

And that was the problem. When love was concerned, people began to depend on you, and sometimes you let them down no matter how hard you tried. Sometimes terrible things happened because people believed you worthy of that love and trust. The mere thought of being responsible for another person's well-being made Logan nervous as a cat in a cactus patch.

No. Never again. It was far easier for him to avoid such a situation than to take a chance at failing again.

Callie turned another page and tried to ignore the tiny frissons of excitement she felt up and down her spine whenever Logan watched her. A deep breath, then another, did little to still her quaking stomach. She'd been so sure it would get easier as time went on. But the more hours she spent with Logan, the more he intrigued her.

The last five weeks had been a study in confusion. Logan was nothing like she'd first supposed. She'd come to realize that his teasing was just that; there was nothing caustic or hurting about his bantering. It was just one more facet of his intriguing personality. It gave Callie great satisfaction when she could best him in some of those lively exchanges, and even greater pleasure when she realized that Logan himself took delight in her small verbal victories. Their relationship had changed from that of wary adversaries to a tentative friendship—a friendship that Callie was beginning to fear might all too easily lead to something else.

And that possibility Callie was determined to avoid. She couldn't deny that she liked Logan, perhaps considerably more than she should. But every honest examination of those feelings led to the same conclusion. Logan was nothing like the man of her dreams, the kind of man she planned to spend her life with eventually. She'd always assumed the man she would marry would have her father's traits. Gentleness. Dependability. A soothing sense of stability. He would be a source of serene, unending love and devotion. A placid sea of contentment in a world too often filled with turmoil.

Ah, but Callie knew, knew without a doubt, love

with Logan wouldn't be tranquil. Logan would be fire and ice, mountaintops and ocean depths. He would command emotions so overpoweringly strong that they would consume her, body and soul. She knew better than to let herself fall in love with Logan. When her contract was up, she was going back to Boston and live the same sort of life her parents had always lived, with a man as kind and gentle and dependable as her father.

Logan Powers wasn't the man for her. He wasn't.

So why did her heart jump every time he came close? Why did she look for excuses to take the children out so she could be near him? She knew she could just as well have stayed at the house today and read storybooks.

Callie told herself it was because the children loved getting away, loved being able to run and play and shout without worrying about disturbing their mother or drawing their father's ire down upon their heads as had happened several times in the past weeks. She told herself it was because the fresh mountain air and golden sunshine were good for the children.

She told herself a lot of things, but more often than not lately she wondered if she was about to follow the tempting White Rabbit of her own emotions on a chase as foolish and confusing as the one Alice had embarked upon.

Callie closed her mind to the disturbing thoughts and finished the last few lines of the book. "The end," she concluded. There was a soft little plop as Callie closed the book.

"Again, Miss Callie. Again. Please!"

"Yes, please."

The children's voices rang out in routine protest to the end of the story.

Callie shook her head.

"Please, please, Miss Callie. Just one more time. Just the first part till Alice finds the key."

"I think not." Laying the book aside, Callie bent forward and rumpled the hair of the boys' heads until it stood on end like two small haystacks. "I think that's quite enough for one day. You should know the whole thing by heart by now. Let's go exploring. All right?"

"Ya hoo!" Thomas and Richard were on their feet and chasing each other in circles around the small square of blanket before Callie even had time to scoot Betsy aside so she could stand up.

"Boys. Boys! You're going to make me dizzy!" Callie's sweet laughter rang out and she aimed a playful swat at the nearest little-boy fanny. "Hurry and get your shoes and stockings on so we can go."

The boys collided in midcircle and fell to the ground in a giggling tangle of arms and scabby-kneed legs. Betsy eyed them with such a pure, feminine look of disapproval that it was all Logan could do to keep from laughing aloud.

The little girl gave one slow shake of her head in dismissal of such silly antics before turning her attention to the footgear that Callie handed her. She promptly applied herself to getting her shoes back on the proper feet, a task she was just now mastering.

"This one, Miss Callie?" Betsy asked, holding one small slipper next to her right foot. "Is this the right one?"

"Yes, darling, it certainly is. You haven't made a mistake all week. Isn't that marvelous?" Callie beamed with pride.

Betsy tucked the tip of her little pink tongue in the corner of her mouth and diligently applied herself to working an upside-down stocking on to her foot. Occasional giggles still broke from the boys as they struggled with their own stockings and boots.

Logan was fine until Callie began to follow suit. He tried concentrating on Betsy's engrossed manipulations, but time and again his gaze slid back to Callie as she drew first one stocking upward and then the other.

Agony.

Sheer, sweet, blissful agony.

What would it feel like to cup one of those slender feet in the palm of his hand? Would the bones across her arch and forming the slim ankle be as delicate, as birdlike as they looked? Her flesh had the same mellow coloring and texture as a magnolia blossom. Would it feel as soft, as silky as that flower's creamy petals?

"Sweet Lord!" Logan muttered under his breath, lurching up from the rock and stomping over to where Flapjack was munching on a particularly lush patch of grass. Had he gone right around the bend? Here he was fantasizing about toes and ankles when he could be down in town enjoying a double handful of Della's abundant attributes.

Something was wrong. Mighty wrong. And if he didn't get hold of himself soon, someone was surely going to come and take him away in a straitjacket.

Flapjack's hobble was all right, but Logan checked it anyway. It gave him something to do besides salivate over the exceedingly unattainable delights of Callie Nolan.

"You coming with us?"

Logan jerked upright so quickly that he bumped his head against Flapjack's prominent belly, causing him to stagger backward a step before he could regain his balance.

Her hands clasped demurely in front of her, a saucy smile on her lips, Callie waited for his answer.

Logan took a deep breath. Did she have any idea what she did to him? Probably not, he thought morosely. "Uh . . . sure, I'm coming. I guess I have to, don't I? Mr. Claymore told me to keep a close watch on the kids." At least he could still save face by blaming Claymore for his presence. Callie need never know he was beginning to believe he would have found a way to be with her regardless. Automatically Logan's hand went to the holstered gun on his hip, making sure it was in place. Then, in a deliberately casual manner, he ambled toward Callie.

"What are we looking for today?" he asked. He kept his tone a bit on the gruff side, hoping she wouldn't realize just how much these afternoons had come to mean to him.

Each time they took the children out, Callie made it a game, a treasure hunt. Armed with her illustrated pamphlets on local flora and fauna, she would designate a certain flower or a shrub or a type of rock or an animal as the "treasure," and the children would vie for the privilege of being the first to spy it. Richard and Thomas did fairly well. Betsy often received prompting from Logan, a breach of the unspoken rules which everyone graciously ignored.

It was all good-natured fun, and the children looked forward to the game with more eagerness than Logan would ever have expected. The respect he felt for Callie was growing. The children were having a marvelous time and they were also learning.

Hell, *he* was learning. He could name bushes and birds that he'd never paid attention to before.

"Shall we see if we can find a rock squirrel?"

"Yes!" chorused the children.

One quick perusal of the illustration in the book and the hunt was on.

Up slopes, through gullies, winding in and out of clumps of dusty green vegetation they searched. Richard and Thomas whooped and ran and chased, making enough noise at times that even if there had been a squirrel nearby, it would have fled for dear life. Betsy ambled along in her usual determined manner, her little legs pumping as steadily as pistons as she pursued her brothers. Callie and Logan brought up the rear.

"Uh . . . you . . ." Logan cleared his throat nervously, fighting but losing to the growing need he felt to know more about the small miss by his side. These excursions offered him the perfect opportunity to feed that unexplainable compulsion. "You didn't get to finish telling me about your family last time we were out." He grinned in memory. "Actually, if I remember correctly, you only got as far as your parents before Richard discovered the skunk."

Laughter sweet as the tinkle of silver bells made

Logan's heart contract when Callie reacted to a mental recall of the incident. "Ah, yes. What an interesting afternoon that was." Richard's discovery had almost resulted in a good dose of the startled skunk's protective essence for all of them.

"How many brothers and sisters did you say you had?" Logan persisted.

The amused smile on Callie's face turned absolutely radiant as she thought of her family. "Six. Three brothers. Three sisters."

"And you're the oldest?"

"Yes. I am." She cocked her head sideways and peered up at him. "Are you really game for a run-down of the Nolan family tree?"

Logan nodded his head solemnly. "Sure." Sure he was. Anything to keep her talking so he could continue to enjoy the sweet lilt of her voice. Besides, whether he wanted to admit it or not, he liked hearing about her family.

"All right," Callie agreed with a grin. "I'm the oldest. Then there's Jenny and Marcy. They're seventeen and fifteen. And then the three boys: Travis is fourteen, Gerald is eleven, and Andy is eight. Tina is the baby. She's only six."

Logan shook his head in wonder. He'd grown up with only one sister. He couldn't imagine a household so filled with people. "No wonder these three don't get under your skin."

"Not hardly." A small chuckle accompanied Callie's answer. She stumbled a bit on a rocky hillock and Logan's hand automatically shot out and grasped her elbow. The ground soon leveled again, but Logan seemed not to notice; his strong grip

98

stayed securely in place. Was he merely being polite or did he want to touch her as much as she sometimes wanted him to? Callie struggled with the relentless question she'd been dealing with for the past five weeks. Should she pull away—put some safe distance between herself and Logan—or simply let herself enjoy these few moments of closeness. Her head said one thing; her heart another.

With him so near, Callie found it hard to concentrate on what she'd been saying. "Then, well, let's see . . . then to round out the rest of the family, there's my mother and father."

"Elaine. Right? Elaine and Robert Nolan." Putting names to the unseen faces seemed to breathe life into the family. *Family.* The word conjured up poignant memories. Lord, what he would have given for a real family like the one Callie had grown up with.

"That's right. And Grandma Nana, my father's mother." *That's it. Nice and calm. Just answer his questions like a rational person,* Callie instructed herself as Logan's fingers continued to sear the soft flesh of her upper arm. *He's only being polite. He doesn't even realize how his touch affects me. Why should he when he has practically every woman in town at his beck and call? He certainly doesn't need me.* The thought brought a frown to Callie's face. Her lips thinned stubbornly. *Besides, I wouldn't have him if he did.*

"She's always lived with you?"

"Who?" Callie asked, startled back to reality.

"Your grandmother."

"Oh. Oh, yes. As long as I can remember. My

99

grandfather was killed in the war, and my father insisted that Nana stay with him. She's wonderful. I can't imagine what families without grandmothers do." The words tumbled out in a rush. *You're babbling again!* Why, *why* did her brain always seem to turn to mush whenever Logan Powers was around?

Two deep furrows formed across the bridge of Logan's nose as he considered Callie's statement. "Yes. I . . . I suppose some of them are very special."

Logan didn't have many fond memories of his own childhood. He remembered his grandmother, and the long years he and his sister Sabra had lived with his grandparents after their mother's death. But none of his memories reminded him of the things Callie spoke of. Not that his grandparents had been unkind to Logan and Sabra, but somehow he remembered his childhood years as his always having felt more like an intruder than part of a family unit. Perhaps that was simply because of the terrible way his mother and baby sister had died. Perhaps it had something to do with his ensuing estrangement from his father, and his own unconscious feelings of guilt.

Years later, Logan had tried to decipher the essence of his childhood, wondering if two small children had simply been too much work for people his grandparents' age. He could envision just how much change had take place in the elderly couple's lives with the unexpected addition of two lively youngsters. Maybe the answer was that simple. It wasn't too difficult to accept that having two small children thrust upon you when you were already up in years might be more than most folks could cope with. He could hardly blame them for the lack of love he'd felt during those years.

Logan's fingers unconsciously tightened on Callie's arm as he asked another question. The strange tone in his voice drew her attention. She cocked her head and eyed him surreptitiously through a fringe of dark lashes, wondering what had prompted the sudden melancholy quality to his words.

Logan had never mentioned his family. The only thing she knew about his past was that he'd been an officer in the Army for several years, that he'd been stationed at the fort located about thirty miles from Bisbee. It had a funny name, an Indian name that sounded almost like a sneeze. Huachuca. That was it. Fort Huachuca. Logan had told her it meant Thunder Mountain. That's all she knew about Logan Powers.

No. Wait. There was something else. Hadn't mention been made of the fact that his father had also been an officer at the fort? She was sure it had. Was his father still there? As far as she knew, Logan had never been to the fort to visit him. Maybe the elder Powers had been transferred. But some inner sense told Callie it wasn't that simple. There was something else in Logan's background, something hidden, something sad.

Her thoughts were interrupted by Logan's next question. "So how did you wind up in Arizona?"

A small sigh escaped Callie's lips. "My father was injured in an accident last year. He's been unable to work since then. There were a lot of medical bills at first. Our savings were dwindling fast. Miss Thorndike—that's the headmistress at the school I was

101

attending—knew our circumstances. It seems that she and Mrs. Claymore knew each other a long time ago. Somehow she found out that the Claymores were looking for a governess and she recommended me. The offered pay was very generous. Well, with things the way they were, I could hardly turn down the opportunity. It meant one less mouth to feed at home—" She ended the statement with a little shrug of her shoulders.

"I see," Logan said, knowing instinctively that there was more to the story than that. He would bet everything he owned that Callie sent a large portion of her wages home to the family she so obviously loved.

Once again, being with Callie set Logan's head awhirl with some unknown restlessness. For a while, seeing her during these little excursions with the children had been enough but not anymore. His frustrations were increasing daily. No matter how hard he tried, he couldn't stop himself from wanting something other than casual conversation, simple friendship. He wanted something . . . something more. But what?

"Come look, Miss Callie, come look! Richard found something!" Betsy's call terminated Logan's befuddled thoughts.

"I guess we'd better see what it is," Logan said, thankful for the distraction.

"I guess so," Callie agreed, a small smile playing on her lips. "With Richard's luck, it could be another skunk."

Logan's old familiar grin surfaced, the discomforting thoughts of the prior moment gratefully pushed aside. "You're right. We might be wise to hurry." So they did.

The children had formed a semicircle around a small clearing at the base of a tumble of rocks. The object of their scrutiny hovered just under one thick pad of prickly-pear cactus.

"Do you see him, Mr. Logan?" Betsy whispered as they drew near. "Bend down here, like this," she instructed, giving the sleeve of his shirt a tug. "You can see his eyes—they're all glittery—and his whiskers go wiggle-waggle, real funny like." Betsy capped the rush of information with a giggle.

Obediently, Logan squatted to get a better look at Richard's find, instantly recognizing the cornered pack rat. "Watch," he said, rising enough to slip a shiny copper penny from his pocket. Ever so gently he leaned forward and dropped the penny a few inches from the rodent's shadowed hiding place. "Be very still."

Sunlight speared off the coin. Nothing happened for a long moment, then a tiny twitchy nose poked from under the cactus pad. Long whiskers quivered as the pack rat daintily sniffed the air. Another long wait and he thrust his head out far enough to reveal two shiny black shoe-button eyes.

"Don't move," Logan cautioned in a soft whisper.

The children barely breathed.

Tiny step by tiny step, the rodent departed his refuge. Then in a flurry he rushed forward and grabbed up the coin, turning tail to once again disappear under the spiny shelter of dusty green pads.

"Oh!" Betsy exclaimed.

"Shh!" Logan admonished softly. "Stay very still. The show's not over yet."

"What's going to happen?" Thomas whispered.

"You'll see."

Callie's heart gave a little lurch as Logan's gaze met hers over Betsy's fair head. The sunlight painted his hair as bright as the coin he'd thrown. For just a moment she felt as if she might drown in the sparkling depths of his deep brown eyes. The roguish smile appeared again, and Callie's lips turned up in response. She wondered if he even realized how effectively his caring and kindness to the Claymore children put the lie to the scoundrel facade he tried so hard to maintain.

"He's coming back."

Callie experienced a sharp surge of regret when Betsy's awed murmuring broke the spell. Reluctantly, she dragged her eyes from Logan's enticing face and turned her attention back to the arena.

Sure enough, the little rodent scampered forward, a shiny pebble in his mouth. He cocked his head and eyed the statuelike humans with apprehension; then, quick as a wink, he dropped the pebble where the coin had been and vanished back into his hole.

"Gee willikers!" Richard said in surprise. "He traded!"

Logan reached out and rumpled the boy's hair. "That's right. Our little friend's a pack rat . . . some people call them trade rats. When they take something, they always leave something in return —"

Logan's head snapped upward at the sudden clatter of small rocks rolling down the mountainside. His hand went reflexively to the butt of his gun and

104

his sharp gaze swept the area, snapping back to the far right at the glint of sunlight on something shiny. Shielding his eyes against the sun, he peered intently at the spot. Nothing moved. The metallic glitter was gone—if it ever had been.

"What is it, Logan?" Callie asked.

"What? Oh, nothing, I guess," Logan answered, dropping his hand from his gun. "Must have been a deer."

Callie nodded in acceptance.

Betsy gave his sleeve a tug. "Will the trade rat come back, Mr. Logan?"

"Probably not, Betsy," Logan replied, scooping the little girl up in his arms. "He's made his bargain for the day. I imagine he'll take his prize home. And, speaking of home . . ." Logan shaded his eyes with one hand and squinted at the sun. "I guess we'd better think about getting packed up ourselves. Isn't this the night for the big dinner?"

"Oh, dear. You're right." Callie's shoulders slumped at the thought of the weekly dinner with Owen and Edith Claymore. Mr. Claymore had instigated the dinners during her second week of employment, ostensibly as a means of discussing the children's progress.

When Paloma had passed on Mr. Claymore's request for that first meeting, Callie had felt immediate remorse at the thoughts which had been lurking in her mind, thoughts concerning how very little attention the Claymores paid to their children. She'd had great visions of how the evening would go, how she would discuss the children's progress and plan their future activities with their concerned parents.

She couldn't have been more wrong.

Except for a few perfunctory remarks about the children's lessons, Owen Claymore had spent that first dinner expounding on his own exploits and triumphs while Edith sat quiet as a mouse at her end of the table, sipping at her glass of "medicine" and hardly uttering a word. The second week had been a repeat of the first. The only evening that had been halfway pleasant had been the third one, when Logan was included. He at least seemed to be able to draw more than monosyllables from Mrs. Claymore. And Edith seemed less inclined to pin Callie with those long, watchful glances when Logan was present.

Tonight would be the fourth dinner, and Callie dreaded the evening.

"Is there any chance Mr. Claymore will ask you to join us for dinner?" she asked hopefully.

" 'Fraid not," Logan said. "I've been instructed to deliver some supplies to one of the outlying mines. I probably won't be back till late." His eyes took on a distinctive twinkle. "Why? Will you miss me?"

Callie blushed and ducked her head. Yes, she'd miss him. For more reasons than she cared to admit.

CHAPTER SEVEN

Reflections of candlelight danced on the highly polished surface of the dining table. For a moment nothing but the clink of silver against china sounded in the room. Callie toyed with the food on her plate, cutting the blood-red slice of beef into small pieces and then pushing the pieces first to one side of the fragile gold-rimmed plate and then the other.

"Is the meat not to your liking, Miss Nolan?"

Callie jumped at the sound of Owen Claymore's deep voice, her startled gaze flying upward at the question. "It's fine," she assured quickly. "Just fine." The last thing she wanted to do was complain about the food. The weekly dinners with the Claymores were uncomfortable enough already. To give credence to her statement, Callie speared another bite with her fork and carried the repulsive morsel to her mouth. It proved as difficult to swallow as the last portion.

Claymore smiled ingratiatingly. "I could have Paloma bring you something else, if you'd prefer."

"No, it's fine . . . really." Callie could feel Edith's

quiet gaze upon her in response to Owen's solicitous tone.

Mrs. Claymore emptied her glass with a slow lift of her wrist. She placed the drained goblet on the tabletop with precise and careful attention before speaking. "Please don't be afraid to speak up if you'd care for something else, Miss Nolan. Owen quite forgets that not everyone likes their meat so rare. I'm sure he'd be glad to take *your* preferences into consideration."

"No, really—" Callie's hasty assurance was interrupted by Owen.

"Edith, darling, I wish you wouldn't worry yourself about such matters. Paloma and I will see that Miss Nolan's needs are not ignored."

Owen's eyes narrowed momentarily as he stared down the expanse of the table at his wife. Their eyes held for a long, uncomfortable moment before Edith lowered her gaze and began to fiddle with her napkin.

"Yes, Owen. Of course you will, " she replied in a subdued tone. "I didn't mean to imply . . . I just thought . . . I mean, you know that I would like—"

"Now, Edith, you know I don't want you to worry about such matters. Just put all these little details right out of your head. We don't want you to bring on one of those dreadful headaches again, do we?"

Callie eyed the untouched slice of meat on Mrs. Claymore's plate as she listened in utter confusion to the curious exchange between her host and hostess. Had Mrs. Claymore meant to imply that her husband would give consideration to the family's governess but not to herself? Oh, surely not.

Callie's worried gaze moved from husband to wife and back again as she wished desperately that the evening would be over. The whole situation was beyond her comprehension. As uncomfortable as Owen made Callie feel, she could find no fault with his behavior toward his wife. He appeared devoted to Edith, making frequent excuses for her often peculiar behavior. Callie had never heard him say an unkind word to the woman — or about her, but a tiny little voice in the back of Callie's head nagged that, while Owen's words were always correct, on occasion his tone of voice had seemed tinged with anger. Well, Callie rebutted silently, only a saint could deal with a sick wife and all the attendant problems without occasionally showing some sign of annoyance.

But, still, there was something . . . something not quite right about the Claymores' relationship. While everything seemed proper and correct, it bothered Callie that she had observed none of the signs of love she was used to seeing between her own parents. Where were the soft, sentimental gestures her parents used so naturally? The tender words? The loving glances? The small, routine touches and pats that, to Callie, conveyed love and reassurance?

Well, she again argued to herself, perhaps the Claymores were just more reserved in their displays of affection. She knew from experience at her friends' homes that not every family was as open and loving as her own.

Still, the persistent inner voice insisted, *you'd think there'd be some obvious signs of affection at least for the children. Logan shows them more atten-*

tion and love than their parents.

Logan. Pictures of the tall, tawny-haired man instantly filled Callie's mind. Memories of how his dark brown eyes had watched her that afternoon as she read to the children — long, slow perusals she was sure he thought she was unaware of. Looks that brought a quickening to her heartbeat and a peculiar shortness to her breath, making it even more difficult to pretend unawareness of the constant scrutiny he tried so hard to conceal. Memories of the sudden warmth that pervaded her body these past weeks each time he reached to help her from the wagon or took her arm as they walked, a languid, flowing warmth that lapped at the bulwark of long-instilled sensibilities and threatened to wash away all the arguments and resolutions with which she tried to fortify herself.

Once again she wished Logan had been invited to share dinner with them. At least he seemed to know what to do, how to soothe Mr. Claymore's bad temper, how to ease Edith's tension without making it appear that he considered her an invalid — or worse.

With grim determination Callie pushed the wishful thoughts and disturbing recollections from her mind. The Claymores were enough trouble to contend with at one time. She certainly didn't need her head muddled by memories of Logan Powers.

Callie's chin inched upward. She had no business letting herself feel dependent on him. There was no denying that Logan was utterly charming, and far too appealing. Oh, he might give her looks that would melt a glacier, he might turn her bones to

110

butter with his touch, but Logan wasn't the man for Callie, and she knew it. She'd already made the decision to keep her relationship with him strictly one of friendship. Friendship and nothing more. It was foolish to dwell upon the matter any further.

With a sigh, Callie turned her attention back to the Claymores just as Owen carefully placed his cutlery on the edge of his plate. His elbows on the table, he steepled his thick fingers together.

"Edith, my dear, you're looking quite pale tonight. Would you prefer to finish your meal in your room?"

Callie wriggled uneasily in her seat. There was that tone again. On the surface, Owen's words sounded sincere and concerned, but Callie suddenly felt quite sure they held an underlying threat. Edith could "behave" or be banished. Fastening her gaze on her plate, Callie prayed that Edith would cease her behavior. The atmosphere in the room was decidedly tense, but it was certainly preferable to being alone with the master of the house.

The awkward silence stretched endlessly while Callie waited and hoped. She snuck a quick glance at Edith. Compassion flowed through her as she watched Edith's knuckles grow as white as the linen napkin her fingers clutched.

What had fueled Edith's uncharacteristic show of emotion this evening? Usually she was as silent as a statue.

At last Edith placed the napkin back in her lap, taking a long, long time to smooth it into place. "No, Owen."

Edith's voice was properly subdued, but Callie

thought she could still detect a hint of steel in the softly spoken response.

"Your medicine is gone, my dear. Perhaps you'd better have another draught to ease your nerves." Owen lifted the small silver bell at his elbow and gave it a shake. Paloma appeared almost instantaneously. "Paloma, would you replenish Mrs. Claymore's tonic?"

"*Sí, señor.* Right away, *señor.*" The Mexican maid quickly retrieved a tall smoked glass bottle from the sideboard and refilled Mrs. Claymore's goblet. "Anything else, *señor,* before I go upstairs to check on the children?"

Owen frowned. "I thought Consuela was seeing to the children."

"*Sí, señor.* Consuela readied them for bed but I want to make sure they're asleep."

"Very well. Miss Nolan, can Paloma get you anything else?"

"No," Callie said with a quick shake of her head. "Thank you anyway." She watched Paloma scurry away, envious of the Mexican maid's freedom to escape the thick tension of the room. Past experience told her that it would be at least another hour before she could follow suit. Lord, how would she stand it?

An uneasy silence ensued. Callie searched her mind for a topic of conversation that might relieve the tension. Not the children, and certainly not anything to do with Mrs. Claymore. Callie had the uneasy feeling that, despite Mr. Claymore's outward calm, Edith had said or done something to anger her husband. Although she didn't understand what had transpired, Callie certainly didn't want to reopen any touchy subject.

All right, what then? Books? Poetry? The theater? Callie dismissed each and every subject. Owen seemed to have no interests other than mining and money. Well, mining it would be, then. Anything to pass the time.

Callie cleared her throat nervously. "I-I'd love to hear how you got started in the mining business, Mr. Claymore."

Surprise bloomed on Owen's face, quickly replaced by delight at Callie's unexpected request. "Why, of course. I'd be very pleased to tell you." His dinner forgotten, he leaned back in his chair and began his tale. "Actually I was little more than a lad when I left North Carolina, a young man intent on making his fortune in the West. Ten, fifteen years ago this was a real wilderness. Raw frontier. But I'd heard about the riches just waiting for the plucking — if you were smart, if you were determined. And I was. Oh, yes, I was." Owen nodded in recollection.

Callie prayed that she looked appropriately interested as Claymore continued. "Why, I had only a few dollars in my pocket when I hit Tucson. But I was ambitious. I applied myself and worked hard. Before long, I'd earned enough to invest in a mine here in Bisbee."

Edith's mouth thinned at her husband's statement. Engrossed in the tale of how be became a wealthy entrepreneur, Owen paid not the slightest bit of attention to the pain-tinged anger that blossomed in his wife's eyes.

"With a great deal of hard work and diligence, I've managed to build my mining company into one

113

of the finest in the territory." Claymore leaned back in his chair, thumbs linked in the edges of his vest, a smug look on his face. "I would hazard a guess that if they fashioned a list of the wealthiest men in Arizona, I'd be on it. And all from that first little grubstake."

Edith's fork slipped from her stiff fingers and clattered loudly against the edge of her plate. She snatched at the utensil as it skittered along the polished surface of the table, but her effort did more harm than good. The back of her hand hit the crystal goblet, sending it crashing into a hundred pieces. Amber-hued liquid splashed across the table and spilled onto Edith's lap while another rivulet seeped toward Callie. Only a few drops landed on Callie's dress before she dammed the flow with her napkin.

The legs of Claymore's chair scraped protestingly against the floor as he lunged to his feet. "Good Lord, Edith, what is wrong with you tonight?"

Edith shrank in her seat at her husband's angry tone. Her fingers pressed tight to her ashen lips, she snatched one stricken look at Callie and then dropped her eyes in embarrassment as Owen continued his tirade.

"Just look what you've done to Miss Nolan's gown. It's ruined!"

Callie gasped at the unwarranted harshness of the man's accusation. "Oh, please, Mr. Claymore," she protested. "My gown is fine. Really."

Despite Callie's reassuring words, Edith pressed herself even deeper into the corner of her chair as she watched her husband advance toward her. The

114

fingers at her lips began to tremble.

"It was just a few drops. It'll wash right out, I'm sure," Callie insisted.

Claymore froze in place as Callie's words finally penetrated. He drew several deep breaths before the mottled red of anger began to fade from his face. When he spoke again the volume of his voice had dropped by half and his words rang with tender concern.

"Edith, darling, you're soaked to the skin. We'll have to get you out of those wet things immediately."

Callie stopped sopping at the tabletop with her napkin long enough to ask, "Can I help?"

Owen shook his head. "That's very kind of you, Miss Nolan, but Edith much prefers that I attend to her needs myself. Poor dear, it can be so difficult when one of these spells comes upon her. Would you be so kind as to excuse us?"

"Yes, of course," Callie said quickly, eager to put an end to the whole confusing episode. "Take care of Mrs. Claymore. That's all that's important. The progress report on the children can wait."

Owen took a few steps toward his wife and then halted again. His amber eyes drifted slowly over Callie's face. "Oh, yes. The progress report. I'd quite forgotten in all the . . . uh . . . confusion." He cocked his shaggy head to one side. "Perhaps we'll still have time to discuss the children after I get Edith settled."

Fire flashed in Edith's eyes at her husband's suggestion.

"Oh, please," Callie protested, sure Edith's agitated state would require prolonged attention. Besides, she was grateful for an excuse to end the unpleasant evening. "Don't even think about that now. You just take care of Mrs. Claymore. We can postpone our discussion until next week."

Claymore sighed. "I so look forward to these little chats about the children, but you're right, of course. Edith needs my attention right now." He pulled a pocket watch from his vest and snapped it open. "And I do have a late appointment with a business associate. Even if I can get Edith settled quickly our meeting would be rushed. I suppose we must postpone."

Attributing the strange look in her host's eyes to the embarrassment of the moment, she hastened to expedite his leavetaking. "Absolutely. I think we'd accomplish much more at a later date."

The timepiece was repocketed with a small shrug. "Quite right." Claymore's leonine head bobbed once in affirmation. "There'll be other opportunities. But, please, finish your meal, Miss Nolan. Don't let Edith's little mishap spoil your supper."

Callie's eyed the unappealing sight of her barely touched plate. Her stomach flipped in protest at the thought of taking another bite. Her first impulse was to shove the plate aside, but good manners prevented the gesture. She managed a weak smile.

Claymore stooped over his wife and gently grasped her arms. "Come along, Edith, darling."

Edith tried to jerk her arm away. "No."

"Now, you mustn't argue, dear. We want to do what's best for you. I'm afraid I miscalculated badly. I thought these little evenings with the children's

116

governess would be good for you, but they're obviously too taxing for your delicate health."

Owen hauled Edith to her feet as if she were no more than a small child herself. "Don't worry, dearest," he said. "I won't subject you to such stress again. I'll handle them myself from now on. Your presence won't be required."

Anger flashed in Edith's eyes and she renewed her struggle to free her arm. "I know what you're up to, Owen. I know! And I won't stand for it again."

"Edith," Owen admonished in a stern, condescending voice. "I must insist that you get hold of yourself. Now, do come along like a good girl . . ."

Owen cast Callie an apologetic look. She could only stare in bewilderment as the man led his still protesting wife from the table.

"Please excuse us, Miss Nolan," Claymore called back over his shoulder as he opened the carved door leading to the hallway.

The door swung shut and Callie slumped against the back of her chair.

"Oh, my!" she gasped, her head awhirl. She listened intently to the fading sounds of arguing, willing herself to wait until the Claymores had time to clear the hallway before she left the room. All she wanted to do now was escape without further unpleasantness.

Assuming that enough time had elapsed, Callie pushed back her chair and tiptoed to the door. Easing it open she cocked her ear to the crack and listened for a long moment. Reassured that the hall was empty, she slipped through the portal. She traversed the corridor with careful footsteps, making

117

sure the heels of her slippers didn't click against the polished floor.

Callie was almost past the door to Edith's room when the sound of breaking glass brought her up short. She froze in place, afraid the partially ajar door to Edith's room might swing open at any second. Heaven knew she didn't want to see either of the Claymores again tonight. Should she run for the stairs or scurry back to the dining room? She stood rooted to the spot, unable to decide which way to go, while Edith's voice rose shrilly on the other side of the door.

"You can drop the act now, Owen. You no longer have an audience."

"Edith, dear, I wish you wouldn't say such things."

"I'm sure you do. You like it much better when I sit quietly and let you do exactly what you want, don't you? You think it's just going to go on and on like that. Well, it's not. You've had your way all these years, but that's over. Do you hear? Over! No more pretending. No more turning a blind eye to your peccadilloes."

"I don't know what you're talking about, Edith. You're letting your imagination run away with you."

"Do you think I'm blind, Owen? Do you honestly think you've fooled me all those times?"

Owen's placating tone was one which might have been used on a naughty child. "You're overwrought, Edith. You must sit down and try to calm yourself. What would your parents think if they could see your behavior? Civilized women don't throw fits and break things. I want you to stop acting like this."

"My parents?" Bitter laughter tinged Edith's re-

118

tort. "Oh, I wish they *were* here to see this. I wish they knew what is really going on. Wouldn't they be surprised?"

"I think they'd be ashamed to see their daughter acting in such a manner," Owen replied.

Edith's voice grew more strident. "No! They'd be appalled at how you've treated me."

"Good Lord, woman, what are you babbling about? How could you possibly consider yourself mistreated? You don't have to lift a finger. What do I ask of you? To hostess a few dinner parties? To entertain business acquaintances now and then? Nothing more than any wife should do."

"Business! The company! That's all you ever cared about, Owen. And the mines. Those damn mines! I have to hand it to you, Owen. You should have been an actor. So clever, so persuasive. You had me fooled for a long time. And you've managed to keep Mama and Papa fooled all these years. But it's got to stop. You can't get away with your wicked deceits forever. It's time the truth came out."

"The truth? And what is that, Edith dear?"

"That you've used me. And my family. That you care for no one but yourself. Not me, not the children."

"Really, Edith, how you do go on. Haven't I always seen to the children's needs? Don't they live in a fine house? Haven't I provided them with all the necessities of life, not to mention a good many luxuries? Clothes, toys, the best governesses money can buy."

"Ah, yes, the governesses. How thoughtful of you to hire such fine ladies. So talented, so young, so

119

. . . beautiful. How lucky that you're so concerned with the children's needs."

"I don't think I like the tone of this conversation, Edith. I don't know what you're insinuating, but I refuse to discuss such rubbish with you. It's your illness that makes you think such things. Now, drink your tonic like a good girl, and put those foolish thoughts right out of your head."

"Tell me, Owen, is our lovely Miss Nolan to be the next one?"

Callie had just gathered a double handful of voluminous skirt in preparation for a scurry toward the staircase when Edith's taunting words halted her in midstep. She frowned and let her skirt fall back to the floor. Whatever did Edith mean? The next *what?* Curiosity compelled Callie to edge closer to the cracked door to see what else Edith might have to say.

"Our dear Miss Nolan was quite impressed by your story, wasn't she? Wouldn't she be surprised to know how you really got your start."

"I think you've said quite enough, Edith."

"Oh, no. I don't think so. Perhaps I should tell her that the only ambitions you had when you reached Tucson were to snare a wealthy wife. And, I, fool that I was, fell for your sweet lies, your effusive promises."

"Edith —"

"And what if I told her that it was *my* money — my dowry — you used to finance that first venture? If you hadn't had my family's good name to trade on, you'd never have been able to build your little empire. Without their help, you wouldn't be such a

120

high and mighty businessman. Don't you think I know that you've borrowed from them over the years? Don't you think I know that's the only reason you want me around—just to keep the channels to Papa's money open? If they only knew the truth!"

"I'm warning you, Edith, you're going too far."

"Too far?" Hysteria edged Edith's voice. "Too far, you say? What about you? What about your recent activities? Wouldn't our dear little Miss Nolan say *you'd* gone too far, if she knew?"

"I've heard all of this drivel that I intend to. Lord knows, I've tried to be patient with you, Edith. I know you're sick—"

"I am not sick, dammit! It simply serves your purpose to have people believe that. Well, I won't sit idly by this time while you start up another af—"

"Enough!" Owen roared.

There was a sudden silence and then the soft sound of weeping began.

"You'd best give it a great deal of consideration before you say anything else."

Owen's softly spoken sentence sent shivers up Callie's spine. Shocked at the ugliness she'd just overheard, she hoisted her skirts and bolted for the stairs.

CHAPTER EIGHT

Not as much as I'd hoped for, but at least the evening wasn't a total waste. Logan closed the weathered door to the barn and ambled toward the back staircase of the Claymore home, his mind filled with what he'd seen and heard that night.

He'd arrived at the mine just after dark. Evidently Claymore wasn't aware of Jack Wilson's fondness for whiskey. But, thanks to a random comment by Della several weeks prior, Logan was. At the last minute, he'd decided to make a quick stop at the Silver Lily Saloon on his way out of town to pick up a bottle of Jack's favorite libation.

The slight delay in reaching the mine had proved extremely worthwhile. One glimpse of the bottle and Jack had greeted Logan with far more enthusiasm than at any time in the past. Half a bottle later, Jack's tongue had begun to loosen. He'd spouted enough innuendos about "setting those independent scalawags right" and "teaching the bastards a lesson" to convince Logan that Claymore was indeed behind the attacks on the independent miners.

But Logan knew that liquor-fueled bragging and groundless threats wouldn't hold up in a court of law. George Anderson and the Independent Miners Association needed more than that.

If they jumped the gun, Claymore could always claim he was innocent. Even if the root of the trouble could be traced back to Claymore's organization, he could claim that the deeds had been committed without his knowledge. Claymore was too smart to be involved directly. No, he'd want to be sure his hands stayed lily-white in case someone slipped up. Claymore would delegate all those nasty little duties such as tampering with fuses and stealing supplies and weakening mine supports . . . but to whom?

Logan frowned when he remembered Jack's casual remark about the "new man who was finally going to take care of things." Damn but he wished Zeb Taylor and Andy Bircham hadn't wandered into the mine cabin just then. There'd been no way for Logan to pursue the subject without alerting the other two men. He certainly didn't want them getting the idea that he'd been pumping Jack for information.

If he kept his eyes and ears open, he might eventually find out who the "new man" was. Meanwhile, he'd just have to keep on as he had been. To put a stop to Claymore's shenanigans, he needed some *real* evidence, evidence that would prove beyond a shadow of a doubt that Claymore himself was ramrodding the takeover scheme.

Evidence. Something concrete. Something undeniable.

Yes, but what?

A shift in the night breeze brought the pungent scent of pine. Before continuing his journey across the yard, Logan paused long enough to sniff appreciatively and to peruse the clear star-sprinkled sky.

His mind quickly returned to the problem at hand. Evidence. Perhaps paperwork of some sort. Files or maybe letters. But where would he find them? A mental picture of the fat leather briefcase Claymore carried back and forth between his home and his downtown office popped into Logan's head.

Of course! Why hadn't he thought of it sooner? There might be something of use in that briefcase.

And, what if there is? he thought in sudden irritation. *Fat lot of good it'll do any of us. There's not much chance of getting a look at the contents of that case. Claymore does everything but sleep with the damn thing!*

Sleep! Sweet heaven, that just might be the answer. What did Claymore do with the briefcase at night? When he retired for the evening, did he take it to his bedroom or did he leave it in the office? Lord above, if it were only true that he left it in the office!

All right, Logan thought, ideas beginning to buzz like bees in his head. Say he got lucky and Claymore did leave the briefcase in the office, would it be worth jeopardizing his cover story to attempt to get a look at the contents of the case? Did he dare take that chance?

"Hell, yes," Logan muttered. He was ready to put an end to his masquerade and get on with his life. This fiasco had gone on long enough.

He'd agreed to George's request for assistance for several reasons. George was a friend and Logan Powers wasn't the kind of man who refused his friends when they needed help. Plus, it galled Logan to know that some big fellow was trying to stomp down a bunch of little guys who'd done nothing but mind their own business and work their claims.

Hell, the independents were no threat to Claymore's organization; they simply stood in the way of his dream to be as big as Phelps Dodge in the mining industry. Greed motivated Owen Claymore, pure and simple greed and the hunger for power.

Logan had a more personal incentive for helping the independent miners. Just before coming to Bisbee, he'd traveled to Tucson and filed a claim on a mine of his own. He hadn't had much chance to work it yet, but if the vein was as rich as it looked, it would be well worth the effort. So, in one way, he'd been protecting his own interests when he took the job.

Very few people in Bisbee knew about Logan's mine: George, Henrietta, Della, maybe one or two others. Logan's old army buddy, Hezekiah Kane, and his wife Jasmine knew, but they were far away. Matter of fact, he hadn't heard from them since Hezekiah took that foreman job up by Tucson a few months back.

Actually, Logan's mine was a legacy from his sister Sabra and her husband, Hawk. Hawk hadn't cared anything about working the mine himself. He already had his family's lumber business to run, and, besides, neither Hawk nor Sabra had wanted to stay in Arizona. There were too many memories concerning Sabra and Logan's father. Major Powers's death had almost cost Hawk his life.

Thank heaven they'd discovered the real culprits in time to save Hawk from the hangman's noose. Mortimer Henderson had escaped justice by conveniently dying of a heart attack during the trial, but Logan and Hezekiah's testimony had helped make sure Leroy Jennings would spend the rest of his life in prison in payment for his part in the major's murder.

During his run from a military posse, Hawk had stumbled across a promising vein of silver in an old Indian cave up in the Mule Mountains. Before he and Sabra left the territory, he'd taken Logan aside and told him about it. Logan hadn't given the cave or the silver much thought for the next year, but when his army enlistment was up, he'd decided that Bisbee was as good a place to go as any.

Logan had run into his old friend George Anderson just a few days after arriving in the booming mining town. It hadn't taken much urging on George's part for Logan to delay his plans for working his own mine. He'd been so sure he could get the goods on Claymore quickly. But the days had stretched into weeks, and the weeks were now becoming months, and they still didn't have anything on Claymore.

Logan had hoped the move to the house would help him accomplish his goal, but so far it hadn't helped a bit. In fact, rather than solve the initial problem, the move to the Claymores' house had presented Logan with a brand-new dilemma, a dilemma in the form of a small Irish lass.

Callie. What in the world was he going to do

about Callie?

Lord but there were times Logan wished he was back in his old room at Henrietta's boardinghouse. Just knowing Callie was across the hall in the Claymore house was playing havoc with his mind. How could he be expected to concentrate on the problem at hand when he spent half the night lying awake thinking about Callie and the other half dreaming of her?

She was making a pure mess of his life. Take tonight for instance. He'd bumped into Della during his quick stop at the saloon. She'd been so pleased to see him, and her invitation to return later that night had left no doubt in Logan's mind as to what would be in store if he did.

So why wasn't he on his way back to the saloon? Once again, he was passing up a night with Della to lie in his lonely bed and torment himself with impossible dreams about Callie. If he didn't know better, he'd think he was falling in love.

Logan's foot froze in place on the bottom stair. *Whoa!* his shocked mind retaliated. *Just a damn minute there! I'm not falling in love with anybody! Not me. No, siree. That's pure-dee foolishness.*

He'd admit to lust maybe, but not love. He'd made up his mind about that a long time ago.

With an irritated shake of his head, Logan continued his ascent and his arguments. The only reason Callie was getting under his skin was because she was off limits—definitely off limits. He'd always known it would be poor planning to get messed up with a "nice" girl. Nice girls meant commitment, responsibility, marriage.

Well, here was proof positive of how much havoc nice girls could wreak on a man's life. He'd forgotten his number one rule and he was damn sure paying for it now.

Yes, it was definitely time to put an end to the situation. He had to get into Claymore's study as soon as possible. Maybe even tonight.

If he could get the goods on Claymore he'd be free to move out of the house. He definitely needed to put some distance between himself and Callie before things got out of hand. And the sooner, the better.

His face grim with determination, Logan strode across the second-story porch and reached for the door. His long fingers wrapped around the knob and he gave it an irritated twist. The door flew open and Callie fell right into his arms.

Much to his astonishment, she gave a small, startled shriek and then burst into tears.

Logan's mouth dropped open in utter astonishment. Instinctively he folded Callie inside his embrace, steadying her wobbly balance with his firm body. Wrapping her arms around his waist, Callie sagged against Logan as his hands began to slide up and down her back, stroking, patting, trying to reassure.

"There, there, honey," he crooned in an automatic litany as old as mankind itself. "It's going to be all right. I'm here. Now, you just take it easy. Whatever it is, it's going to be all right."

Logan experienced a swift jab of panic as Callie tightened her hold and only sobbed harder. Lord, what did he do now? He'd been confronted with

128

weeping women before but he'd always known what the problem was. Female vapors were certainly harder to deal with when a man was totally in the dark as to what had precipitated the crisis.

"Now, now. It's all right, honey. You just have a good cry. You'll feel better in a minute."

With Callie clutched tight against him, Logan began a slow shuffle across the porch in the direction of the rocking chair. Once there, he folded his long length into it and drew Callie onto his lap, cradling her against him much as he had done with Betsy on more than one occasion.

One slender arm looped around Logan's neck as she burrowed closer to him, pressing her face into the curve of his shoulder. For a long moment they simply rocked, Logan patting and stroking and murmuring soft, reassuring words to Callie while her tears soaked through his shirt and dampened his skin.

Gradually Callie's emotions calmed, and her sobs subsided until they were no more than little hiccuping sighs. Logan's senses began to stir to life.

Each arc of the rocking chair caused an errant lock of Callie's hair to whisk lightly against the hollow of his throat. The butterfly-soft brushes of silken curls elicited tiny sparks of primal response deep within him. Each sob caused the firm mounds of her breasts to press even harder against the muscular wall of his chest. Each fluttery expulsion of breath against the side of his neck sent tiny shivers up and down his spine.

The heat of her body began to warm his flesh, the sweet woman-weight of her whispered that he held no child in his arms but just the opposite. Callie was all woman, sweet-scented flesh and soft female curves that fit together with his body like the pieces of a puzzle.

The strong physical response was not unexpected by Logan. What threw him for a loop were the emotions that accompanied and overshadowed the familiar male urgings: an overpowering tenderness, an unfamiliar urge to safeguard, to protect at all costs the woman in his arms, even if it meant denying himself what his body demanded.

Logan was valiantly trying to decipher those peculiar, foreign feelings when Callie gave one last shuddering sigh and turned her face up to his.

Moonlight bathed her features, silvering the wet tear streaks left on her cheeks and glittering in the droplets left clinging to her eyelashes. Suddenly Logan felt as though a big fist had closed around his heart and squeezed hard.

"I'm sorry," Callie said with a little hitch in her voice. "I—I don't know what came over me. I haven't cried like that since I was little girl."

"Shh, it's all right," Logan soothed, giving her shoulder a little pat. He watched one last tear lose its hold on the thick fan of black lashes and glide over her sculptured cheek bone and down her velvet flesh. With gentle fingertips, he brushed the moisture from first one cheek and then the other.

"Want to tell me what happened?" he asked in a gentle, urging voice.

Callie shifted against him, pushing herself upright. "I don't really know. It's all so confusing."

"Did something happen at dinner? Say, did Claymore do something to you? Is that why you were headed out here?" Swift anger flowed through Logan at the sudden thought.

A vigorous shake of her head answered the question. "Oh, no! Mr. Claymore didn't do anything to me. I just wanted someplace where I could think and breathe some fresh air. It was just that dinner was . . . well, dreadful, but then they've never been what you could call comfortable, so I don't know why I was surprised."

"Then what has you so upset?"

"The Claymores. I—I really don't understand what happened. They got in this . . . this argument." Callie's brow furrowed as she remembered the scene.

"About what?"

"I really don't know. Mr. Claymore was talking about when he first came to Arizona and then Mrs. Claymore knocked over her glass. It was just an accident, but he got so angry with her." Callie's hands fluttered in accompaniment. "And he took her out of the room. And then, when I went down the hall to come upstairs, they were arguing. She was saying awful things to him, such awful things . . ."

The words faded away and Callie lifted her shoulders in a small, confused shrug.

Logan frowned. "I don't understand. Edith is usually so quiet. She hardly says a word to a soul, and certainly not to her husband."

"You know, I thought the same thing. She didn't seem like herself at all. I've even wondered if she wasn't a bit afraid of him. But now I don't know, not after hearing what she said tonight."

"What *did* she say?"

"It's hard to explain, Logan. Something about her money, that he only wanted her around for her money. And . . . Oh, I don't know. Parts of it didn't make any sense at all to me. She kept saying, 'You're not fooling me' and 'I know what you have planned' . . . and something about telling people and ruining his business. Oh, I don't know! It was awful. I never heard two people talk to each other like that in my whole life. My parents never—"

Afraid the tears were going to start again, Logan responded with another litany or reassurance. "Of course not, honey. No wonder you're upset. But you listen to me, the Claymores are kinda . . . uh, peculiar, different from most people. I don't rightly know what's going on, either, but it has nothing to do with you."

Callie sniffed and shook her head. "I'm not so sure. Mrs. Claymore did say something about me."

"She did? What?

"She asked Mr. Claymore if I was going to be the next one."

"The *next one?*" Logan repeated.

"Yes," Once again Callie's brow furrowed, her face a study in confusion. "Whatever do you suppose she meant by that?"

A red mist clouded Logan's eyes. Now he had reason number four to put a stop to Claymore's shenanigans. He'd heard rumors, and he was all too afraid he knew exactly what Edith Claymore had meant. But, heaven knew, he couldn't let Callie know what he was thinking. If he told her what he'd heard about why the last governess left, she'd be even more upset than she was now.

"I . . . I'm sure she didn't mean anything by it, honey. If they were arguing, she probably just said anything that came to mind. Now, you put all this right out of your little head, you hear?"

Callie nodded obediently. "I—I'll try."

"Good." Logan set Callie on her feet and then rose himself. Now, more than ever, he needed to get on with his work. For Callie's sake, if nothing else, he had to stop Claymore. And for his own sake, he had to finish up the job and get out of the house before she got so deep under his skin that he did something foolish. "It's been along day. You must be exhausted. Come on, I'll walk you to the door of your room."

Docile as a lamb, Callie let him lead her across the porch and through the door. Their heels clicked in unison against the polished floor as they traveled the few feet to her doorway. Logan turned the knob and the door swung open with a faint squeak of the hinges.

Callie started to enter, then turned back. She paused, raising her eyes to Logan's. A small smile lifted the corners of her mouth.

"Thanks for listening. I promise I won't go all weepy on you ever again. It's just that I miss my family. I guess I get a little homesick at times."

"Sure you do," he said softly.

Her smile went a bit trembly around the edges. "Thanks again. I . . . I don't know what I'd have done without you."

Before Logan knew what was happening, she'd raised on tiptoe and pressed a kiss on his cheek. And then she was gone.

133

As Callie's door clicked shut, Logan fingered the place her lips had touched. His stomach seemed to sink right down to his toes, his heart thumped so loud he was afraid she could hear it.

"Ah, hell," he muttered. "I think it's already too late."

CHAPTER NINE

His hands behind his head, Logan lay fully clothed on his bed. All was quiet. Only the occasional groans and creaks of the house settling marred the stillness of the night. The children had already been tucked in bed by Consuela and were sound asleep when he'd escorted Callie to her room.

Before retiring to his quarters, Logan had taken a quick look over the banister. The downstairs had also been dark and quiet, but he nevertheless had deemed it prudent to wait a while before tackling Claymore's study. He didn't want anyone — not even the servants — up and roaming around when he made his foray.

The ensuing interlude had given him time to think about Callie and his feelings. He'd been side-stepping the issue for the last week or so, scoffing at the idea of Callie's becoming an important part of his life — a much too important part. With constant effort, he'd managed to convince himself again and again he was simply enjoying the company of a spunky, witty, intelligent, altogether delightful young lady and nothing more.

But the situation had changed tonight when he'd held her in his arms and gloried in the way she fit so perfectly against him, when he'd breathed in the delicate rose-tinged scent of her soft flesh and felt his heart swell until he feared it might burst from his chest, when he'd realized that her happiness and well-being were far more important than his own physical self-gratification.

Yes, tonight he'd finally admitted he couldn't lie to himself any longer. He was in love with Callie. And he didn't know what to do about it.

He'd vowed long ago not to fall in love, not to become entangled with someone else's life, not to take on the responsibility for another person's happiness and well-being. It was simple: if you didn't love, you couldn't lose.

He knew how badly it hurt to fail those you loved, how devastating it was to lose someone dear to you. If you let yourself love, you became vulnerable to new losses, new hurts.

Logan had figured that out long ago, and he knew the solution. Don't tempt fate.

It hadn't seemed to be much of a problem before. He hadn't wanted to fall in love; ergo, he hadn't.

Simple enough.

Till now.

His chest rose and fell with the effort of his sigh. It appeared he'd become a bit too smug about his ability to remain uninvolved. It had seemed so easy for so many years that he'd become careless. Somehow, some time, when he wasn't paying attention, his foolish heart had overruled his head.

So, what did he do now? Did he try to put all those old fears out of his head? Did he build a relationship with Callie? Or did he stick to the rule he'd lived by all his adult life and walk away from his feelings?

Getting the cart before the horse, aren't you? the logical side of his mind questioned. *Who says Callie cares anything for you anyway? Who says she thinks of you as anything more than a friend?*

A friend.

Just a friend.

The thought brought a knife jab of sorrow. But that would be best, wouldn't it? Wouldn't that solve all his problems?

Callie need never know how he really felt. It didn't have to go any further. Her contract was only for one year. And then she'd be gone. Back to Boston, back to the family she missed so much. Back to the kind of life she was used to. Back to the kind of man who would fit in that life. A man who wasn't afraid of love.

Logan knew there was just one thing left to do: get George the evidence he needed and get out of the Claymore house. His earlier decision had been absolutely right. He'd be able to deal with his feelings if he didn't have to see Callie every day.

The desire to touch her would fade away. Unfueled by her presence, the need to be with her would eventually wither and die.

So what if she'd be in Bisbee another ten months. He could avoid her. Easy. He'd take his old room back at Henrietta's. Rekindle his friendship with Della. He sure wouldn't have to worry about running into Callie down in Brewery Gulch.

Besides, he had a claim to work. If temptation got too bad, he'd just make a permanent move up to the mine. There was water and ample grazing for his horse, and the cave would provide all the shelter he needed. Hawk had lived up there, so could he.

Logan lurched upright as another barrage of thoughts bloomed in his mind. Several things might happen, depending on what kind of evidence he was able to find against Claymore.

One, he might find only enough proof to scare Claymore into stopping the vendetta against the independents. It would change the way Claymore ran his business, but his personal life would probably go on as usual. His family might never know what had been going on. And Callie would finish up her term of employment.

But if he found some really damning evidence, Claymore could go to trial. What would happen to Edith and the children? Surely they'd go back to Tucson, back to Edith's family. Logan couldn't believe that shy, quiet, muzzy-minded Edith would try to make it on her own. Maybe she'd take Callie with her or maybe she'd release Callie from her contract and send her home to Boston. Either way, she'd be out of Bisbee.

And he would once again be able throw the walls up around his heart and return to his chosen way of life — a little wine, lots of women and good times. No ties, no promises, no possibility of pain.

If there'd been any doubt in his mind that he was going to search Claymore's study that very night, the doubt was gone now. All that was left was to do it.

With the resilience of coiled steel, he rose from his bed. Cat-quiet he slipped through the doorway, across the hallway, and down the grand staircase. On the bottom step, he waited for a long moment, his eyes searching the black-on-black expanse of the hallway, his senses primed for any sound or movement.

But all was silent, the inhabitants of the house obviously sound asleep. Satisfied, Logan eased down the hallway, more by feel than by sight.

At last his hand found the ornate brass knob of Claymore's study door. A quick twist and he stepped inside. The heavy wooden panel closed securely behind him. The breath he hadn't realized he was holding whooshed out in a gust of pure relief.

The moon's luminescence, pale silver diffused by the heavy lace panels covering the room's two tall windows, allowed him to make his way across the study to Claymore's massive oak desk.

Did he dare a light? Did he dare not? He *needed* that evidence in more ways than one.

The scratch of a match, the sharp tang of sulphur, a burst of flame. Logan winced as the glass chimney gave a muted screech against the base's brackets. He held the dancing flame to the wick. A golden glow blossomed in the ebony gloom. Logan quickly turned the wick as low as possible.

Raising the lamp, he moved the muted circle of light over the top of the desk. Once. Twice. His shoulders slumped in disappointment. Nothing. No sign of the briefcase.

Just take it easy, he berated himself. *What did you expect? That ol' Claymore would leave it sitting there, smack dab in the middle of this desk for your convenience?*

A tense grin tipped one corner of his mouth. All right. So what next? Where else might Claymore have put the damn thing?

Logan surveyed the room. The breakfront? Why not? He hurried to it. Squatting down, he pulled open one drawer after another. This time his disappointment was saber-sharp.

Rising swiftly, he held the lamp high, turning to scrutinize every corner of the room. The bookshelves . . . perhaps on the lowest level.

But no, the bric-a-brac-crowded bookshelves contained nothing more than porcelain figures and gilt-edged, leather-bound books by the old masters. He fingered one volume. It didn't look as though it had ever been opened. He shook his head. Simply

140

another embellishment for Claymore's aristocratic facade.

With renewed determination he continued his search, his senses tuned and alert for any unusual sound from the other parts of the house. He checked corners, stooped to look in the cavernous knee-hole of Claymore's desk, and felt behind cabinets. Totally engrossed in his search, Logan never considered the possibility of discovery by someone other than the people inside the house.

Outside, on the path to the barn, Owen Claymore reined his horse in and stared in confusion at the muted glow of light that bobbed and danced within his study. Who could possibly be in there at this late hour? And what in hell could they be doing?

It's time the truth came out. Wasn't that what Edith had said during their stormy conversation after dinner? Was she in his office? Was she looking for something to use against him, some way to carry out her vaguely veiled threat? The thought enraged Claymore. He silently swore expedient revenge if his suspicions proved correct.

With amazing grace for one of his size, he slid from his mount. He led the dark stallion to the far side of the yard, where he looped the reins over a low bush. After a final quieting pat of the horse's neck, he edged toward the house.

From a carefully selected vantage point in the inky darkness just outside the study window, Claymore watched with avid interest as a shadowy figure rose from behind the desk.

"I'll be damned!" he muttered in shock when he recognized the culprit.

What in hell was Logan Powers doing in there? Had Edith somehow convinced him to help her? Claymore's mouth thinned into an angry slash.

How very disappointed his loving little wife was going to be when her chohort's mission failed. Was she really stupid enough to think he'd leave anything incriminating at home? And, as for Logan Powers, he was going to be very sorry that he'd poked his nose where it didn't belong.

With careful, creeping footsteps, Owen returned to his waiting horse and mounted up. A small creak of leather, a light jingle of harness were all that proclaimed his leavetaking. With an angry jerk of the bridle, he rode off into the night, following the trail he'd just traveled.

Half an hour later, Claymore climbed the rickety step to the porch of a little used cabin on one of his mining claims. The cabin was dark and quiet, but at Owen's first footfall the planked door eased open a few inches. Moonlight gleamed dully on the barrel of a gun.

"You can put that up," Claymore said. "It's only me."

"I didn't expect you back tonight, Boss." Rusty hinges whined as the door swung wide.

The dim figure of a man moved aside, and Claymore brushed through the doorway. He stopped inside long enough to allow the other man

142

time to light the lantern resting in the middle of the battered table at the side of the room.

When the feeble light filled the small dwelling. Owen crossed the narrow room and took a place at the table. The dark-haired man pulled back the opposing chair, rough-cut wood scraping against the uneven floor. His slender fingers reached to adjust the position of the gun he'd laid within reach, and then he casually folded his arms on the scarred surface. A jerk of his head toward the half-empty bottle of whiskey brought a nod of assent from the big man across from him.

"Something wrong?" the man asked Claymore as he spilled amber liquor into two glasses.

Owen accepted the proffered refreshment and downed his portion in one gulp before answering. " 'Pears I have a little problem for you to take care of."

"Oh?"

"Seems one of the men who works for me has gotten a little big for his britches. Snooping around where he has no business being."

"That so?"

The dark man took a small sip from his glass, enjoying the tang of the liquid as it flowed across his tongue. It had been a long time since he'd enjoyed good liquor. A long, long time.

Reaching to refill his glass, Owen nodded. "Yes, I'm afraid it is. I must admit, I'm a bit surprised. I thought Powers was all right." His dark chuckle ribboned through the room. "Just goes to show

143

you, even I can make a mistake."

The dark man's mouth turned up in the semblance of a smile.

"That's all right," Owen said, wiping a drop of liquid from his mouth with the back of his hand. "I don't intend to make another one. From the looks of things, I don't think he found whatever the hell he was looking for."

"Got any idea what he was after?"

"Not the slightest. But, whatever it is, I think we'd better make sure he doesn't get a second chance. Think you might be able to handle that?"

"It would be my pleasure."

CHAPTER TEN

"Oh, you didn't have to bring the children's breakfast tray back, *Señorita* Nolan. I would have come after it," Paloma admonished.

Callie smiled and brushed aside the protest. "I didn't mind, Paloma, really. I was coming downstairs anyway."

Callie set the tray of dirty dishes on the kitchen table and then turned toward the stove where she helped herself to another cup of Paloma's fragrant coffee. She inhaled appreciatively before taking a cautious sip of the hot liquid.

"Umm. Delicious." Propping one slim hip nonchalantly against the edge of the work table, Callie cradled the cup in her hands. "Uh, Paloma, have you seen Logan around this morning? I guess I missed him upstairs. I . . . uh . . . thought I might make arrangements for the day's activities."

"Oh *sí, señorita*. I saw Señor Logan very early this morning. He and Señor Claymore were talking in the study when I served Señor Claymore's breakfast. I did not mean to eavesdrop." Pausing in her work, Paloma cast a hasty glance upward. Callie smiled her understanding of the situation and Paloma continued. "Well, you see, I couldn't help but overhear some of the conversation. Something about an errand *Señor* Logan should take care of."

"Oh." The word slipped out on a sigh of disappointment. Callie nibbled her lower lip, reluctant to drop the subject with so little information. "Did you happen to hear when Logan would return?"

"No, *señorita*," Paloma answered with a shake of her head. "All I know is that he left well over an hour ago."

Callie brightened a bit at that pronouncement. Perhaps Logan had only gone to town. If that were the case, and he'd already been gone for over an hour, then he might return before long. They could still have their outing.

For a moment Paloma ceased her preparations on what was obviously Mrs. Claymore's breakfast tray. "Too bad *Señor* Claymore has already left, too, or else you could ask him when Señor Logan might return."

Callie's last swallow of coffee threatened to go down the wrong way. The last thing she wanted this morning was to confront either of the Claymores. Last night was still too vivid in her mind.

Paloma, oblivious to Callie's discomfort, continued. "I doubt that *Señora* Claymore would know anything about it, but I could ask her if you wish." She motioned toward the tray she was putting the finishing touches to. "I'll be taking this to her shortly."

"What? Oh. No. That's quite all right, Paloma. I

146

wouldn't want you to bother her. It wasn't important anyway. I just thought Logan and I might take the children out for a while. You know, one of our usual little excursions."

Paloma pursed her lips and clucked her tongue in disapproval. "I do not think you should take the children out today anyway. Look out here," she said, pointing out the kitchen window. "See those clouds gathering over the mountains?"

Callie did as she was instructed, stretching up to gaze out the window. "Yes, what about them?"

"There's a storm brewing. Maybe a big one. It is a bad sign when the clouds are that heavy and rolling like God's own hand was stirring them up. No, you must stay in today. If a big storm comes to the mountains, then the water, it gushes through the gullies. Flash floods. Very bad. And sometimes it goes right through the middle of town. It is better that you stay here. We're high enough, there is no danger here at the house."

"Oh well, I suppose you know best," Callie agreed, avoiding direct contact with Paloma's sharp eyes and trying very hard to keep any hint of disappointment from creeping into her voice. She wasn't about to admit, even to herself, that her discontent was due more to Logan's absence than to the fact that she and the children would be stuck in the house all day.

With a suppressed sigh, Callie stacked her now empty cup atop the children's breakfast dishes and bade farewell to Paloma. There was still Betsy to dress, and the boys would need checking. Left to their own, there was no telling what they'd put on.

And there were the day's activities to plan. Perhaps they'd work on the alphabet, practice their letters. Maybe they could play some nice, quiet games, games that wouldn't disturb the people downstairs, Edith in particular.

Upstairs once again, Callie found that the boys had managed to dress themselves, although Richard's shirttail flapped over the waistband at the back of his pants. The washed-out blue of the shirt Thomas had chosen didn't quite match the trousers he had on, but they were certainly cleaner and neater than they had been when she first arrived. Callie had trimmed their hair and she'd managed to instill in them enough respect for soap and water that their faces, if not their knees and elbows, were shiny bright from scrubbing.

"Come over here, Betsy," Callie instructed after she'd passed inspection on the boys. "I'll help you finish dressing."

Betsy obediently walked toward Callie, the sash of the starched white pinafore she clutched in her arms dragging behind. Shadow, in a playful mood for once, stalked the garment, a wary paw occasionally reaching out to bat at the rippling fabric as it wriggled its way across the polished floor.

"Oh, no you don't," Callie said with a chuckle, rescuing the trailing sash with a jerk as the kitten readied itself for a serious assault on her prey.

Shadow's gaze bordered on disdain as she watched Callie gather up the full-skirted apron and drop the garment over Betsy's pale curls. When the intriguing sashes were secured within a bow at Betsy's back, taking the dangling ends far out of the kitten's reach, the ebony feline gave a haughty swish of her tail and marched out of the room.

"Turn around, sweetheart, so I can do up your buttons." With gentle coaxing Callie positioned Betsy and began to guide the little pearl buttons through their companion holes. "There," she said as she secured the last one. "That's lovely. Just the right touch."

Just as Callie bent to smooth a section of up-turned ruffle down over the skirt of Betsy's blue calico gown, footsteps echoed in the hall.

Logan! Callie thought with delight. She gave the stubborn ruffle one last pat and eagerly stood up. But the smile on her face quickly faded when Edith Claymore, not Logan, swept through the doorway, bringing with her an even heavier than usual aroma of "medicine." The young maid Consuela, looking sheepish and not at all happy about being there, hovered behind her.

"Mama!" Betsy piped in happy greeting. "Are you going to do lessons with us? If you'd like, I'll share my book with you."

Scampering to her mother's side, Betsy bestowed an excited hug just about knee-level. Her balance upset by the gesture, Edith was forced to reach out one hand and steady herself against the wall. The boys, older and more wary of such an unexpected event — they couldn't even remember the last time their mother had climbed the stairs to visit the nursery — edged closer to each other. Finally, after a stern look from Callie, they muttered polite hellos.

Edith acknowledged her children's greetings with little more than a nod of her head. Her eyes looked puffy, and the tender flesh beneath them was smudged bluish-plum, as though she hadn't slept well for far too many nights. The tight, pinched look about her mouth and nostrils made her look as though she'd just bitten into a green persimmon.

While Callie was still ruminating on Edith's unexpected visit and the rather disheveled state of her attire, Edith began to sway again, ever so slightly. Suddenly Callie wondered if something other than Betsy's exuberant greeting had been the cause of Edith's earlier, unsure footing. Once more Edith's hand fluttered upward until her fingertips grazed the wall. Almost immediately the barely perceptible weaving stopped.

Shaking off her bafflement, Callie hurried forward. "Welcome, Mrs. Claymore. What a . . . uh . . . a lovely surprise. I'm very pleased that you've come up to visit the children. Here, won't you have a seat?" She quickly pulled one of the small chairs from its place at the table and scooted it toward Edith.

Edith eyed first the chair and then Callie with obvious suspicion.

Callie gulped back her apprehension. "Would you like to sit in on some of the children's lessons? They know a good portion of their alphabet now. All three of them can recite—"

"I'm sure they can do all you say, Miss Nolan. However, there's no time for a demonstration now," Edith said, thrusting her chin upward and outward. "I'm here to discuss another matter. Consuela, please take the children outside. And remember what I told you."

"*Sí, señora.*" A recalcitrant Consuela sidled into the room and motioned for the children to follow her. Clearly reluctant to do so, the children moved forward in a slow shuffle.

"Outside?" Callie repeated in bewilderment. "But Paloma suggested that we remain inside today. She said there was a storm coming and—"

In response to Callie's statement, the children halted, their questioning gazes going instinctively to their governess for direction.

"Really, Miss Nolan," Edith snapped, drawing herself up stiff and straight. "One might think you were questioning my authority in this matter."

Callie's eyes grew saucer-big. "Oh, no, Mrs. Claymore. That's not what I meant at all. I just—"

"Then I'd thank you not to interfere with my instructions."

"Yes, of course." Dismay flooded Callie as she noticed the children hadn't budged another inch despite their mother's proclamation. Callie shooed them forward with a hasty wave of her hand. "Go on, now. Do as your mother says. And boys, be sure to keep an eye on Betsy."

"Yes, ma'am," Richard and Thomas said in unison. They each took one of Betsy's small hands and began to tug their less than enthusiastic little sister through the doorway.

With growing trepidation, Callie watched the children depart. She wondered what Edith wanted. Was the woman finally going to take an interest in the children's lessons? Perhaps she'd decided that she'd like to participate in their schooling in some way. Perhaps she had suggestions to offer. Well, her timing was certainly off, considering the fact that schedules had already been set up and lessons prepared, Callie thought with a touch of irritation which she quickly suppressed. After all, the woman was their mother, and, by all rights, she should have been involved from the start.

Better late than never, Callie decided. Whatever Edith wanted, Callie was determined to make the best of the situation.

As soon as the clitter-clack of the children's footsteps on the stairs had faded away, Callie squared her shoulders, pasted as pleasant a smile as she could muster on her lips, and turned to face Edith.

"Now," Callie said, forcing enthusiasm into her voice. "What is it you wished to discuss?"

"I regret to inform you that it's necessary to alter the plans for the children's schooling," Edith answered, shoving one hand into the pocket of her gown. "Here . . . this is for you."

Confusion washed away Callie's artificially-bright smile as she watched Edith withdraw a sheaf of bills from the pocket's recesses and thrust it toward her.

"Take it," Edith demanded.

Totally perplexed by now, Callie did as she was instructed. She accepted the bills, holding them lightly, almost cautiously, all the while waiting for some further explanation.

Edith gave a curt nod. "I believe that will be sufficient for your needs."

"Needs? Oh, yes, of course," Callie agreed,

thinking of books and papers and pens and whatever else Edith had in mind for the children's new lessons. "I'm sure there's plenty. What specifically would you like for me to purchase with this?"

"Why, a train ticket, of course. I thought you understood."

"A train ticket?" Callie questioned, her perplexed gaze ricocheting between Edith and the money clutched in her fist. "You want me to take the children on some sort of trip?" A terrible thought suddenly occurred to her. "Oh! Oh, dear, don't tell me you've received bad news from your family in Tucson?"

"No, of course not!" Edith snorted. "The ticket is for you."

"Me?" A new and total bewilderment filled Callie's voice.

"Yes. You shouldn't have any trouble booking a seat on tomorrow morning's train. Naturally, I've provided you with enough funds to pay for a night's lodging at the hotel across from the station and to take care of any other expenses you might incur while traveling—"

"Traveling?" Callie repeated blankly. Nothing Edith was saying made any sense. For one wild moment all she could think of was the Mad Hatter's Tea Party in the children's *Alice in Wonderland* book. "Traveling where?"

Her eyebrows arched high, Edith surveyed Callie as if she'd lost her mind. "Why, back to Boston, of course."

"Boston! But I don't understand."

Edith's sigh was filled with exasperation. "I don't

know how much clearer I can make myself. Your services are no longer needed."

Callie's mouth fell open. "You can't be serious," she stammered.

Edith's pale eyes speared Callie. "Let me assure you, Miss Nolan, I am very serious. Very serious indeed."

Dazed, all Callie could think to say was "but the children are doing so well. They're fond of me, and I know I've taken good care of them. Oh dear! Who will take care of the children if I'm gone?"

Color flushed Edith's face. "Consuela, of course," she answered. "She did just fine before you came. She can do so again."

"Consuela?" Callie protested. "Good heavens! How can she teach them their alphabet when she barely speaks English herself? And reading. What about reading? Richard and Thomas are starting to read whole sentences. And Betsy can pick out half a dozen words already. How will they ever learn?"

"That is no longer any of your concern."

Callie couldn't believe her ears. "It *is* my concern! You made it my concern when you hired me to take care of those children! And, besides, I *care* about them. Why are you doing this? Why?"

Edith swayed slightly. Taking a step backward, she edged toward the wall until one shoulder was snugged against it. Steady again, she drew herself up. "I don't owe you an explanation."

Raw, hot Irish anger flashed, thawing the icy numbness that had held Callie prisoner. She glanced down at the sheaf of bills, instantly calculating that it was nowhere near the balance of

154

payment due on her contract. Pictures of her family and all she'd hoped they could do with the funds she'd planned to send home during her term of employment seared across her mind.

She searched for a reason, one single, solitary, logical reason for her dismissal. There wasn't one. Not even one! She'd done her job. More than done her job! Well, she'd be damned if she'd let this woman cheat her out of her just dues!

"Owe me," Callie retaliated, her anger building like the thunder clouds over the mountains. "Owe me! Yes, you owe me. My contract was for one year. I can't stop you from dismissing me—even if you have no grounds at all—but I'll not go without my full payment. I've kept my part of the bargain, and I demand that you and Mr. Claymore keep yours?"

Fear sparked in Edith's eyes. Her tongue wet her suddenly dry lips.

Awareness dawned in Callie. "Mr. Claymore . . . he doesn't know, does he? Yes, of course. I remember now. Paloma mentioned that he was gone for the day. That's it, isn't it? You're doing this without his knowledge, without his approval. Aren't you?"

Edith shook her head in denial, but somehow Callie knew she was right.

"What were you going to tell him when he returned? That I quit? That it was my idea to return to Boston? Why? Why would you do this? I've done nothing to you."

Edith's face twisted bitterly. Her words dripped belligerence. "You can drop that innocent act any time you want, Miss Nolan. I'm not near the fool Owen thinks I am. Oh, I know, all right. Much more than he ever gives me credit for. I know about the business. I know about the women. And I know about you and Owen."

"Owen and me? *Owen and me?* Callie's voice faded to a shocked squeak as comprehension began to creep into her mind. She gawked in shock at Edith. "You can't possibly mean that . . . that . . . Good Lord!" Her hands flew to her inflamed face as she collapsed in the chair she'd so recently pulled out for Edith.

"You'll find, Miss Nolan, that I mean every word I said."

Callie stood in shock as Edith pushed herself away from the wall and swayed toward the doorway. Before leaving the room, she turned and surveyed Callie.

"You have one hour to pack your things and leave this house. Consuela has been instructed to keep the children away for that long. I see no reason to upset them. There's no one to take you to town at this time, but you've walked down before, on those little excursions with the children, so I presume you can do so again. When Logan returns, I'll have him bring your trunks to the hotel. Good day, Miss Nolan, and goodbye."

With that she was gone.

Logan! The name exploded in Callie's mind. Visions of deep brown eyes and sunlight caught in a halo of tousled tawny curls, a devil-may-care grin that could pluck the heartstrings of every female between nine and ninety. Memories of his strong

156

arms surrounding her, his soft words soothing her. His hands — big, square, strong hands that could swing an axe or tie a proper bow in the tiny pink ribbon on a little girl's gown.

She'd known that Logan was not for her. She'd known that the day would come when she would leave him behind, taking nothing but bittersweet memories with her. But she hadn't known until now just how much that leaving was going to hurt.

Dear God! What would Logan think when he learned about all this? Surely he wouldn't believe what Edith was accusing her of. He couldn't. She didn't think she could bear it if he did.

CHAPTER ELEVEN

The hem of Callie's traveling suit raised puffs of dust from the beaten dirt path as she marched ever downhill toward Bisbee's center. With each outraged step a large shopping bag loaded with the barest of necessities bumped against her leg. She'd met Edith Claymore's edict with righteous indignation and time to spare. And now the flood of tears that pride had kept dammed while she packed her belongings and changed her clothes threatened to spill forth.

A hot, salty lump lingered at the back of her throat. Callie swallowed hard and thrust her chin out. She'd given in to her emotions after that disastrous dinner and cried out her frustrations in Logan's arms, but she wasn't going to cry now, and never again if she could help it. Edith Claymore and her sick accusations weren't worth it.

But the children, a wee small voice cried. *What about the children?* And what Edith Claymore and her vicious tongue could not do, the thought of three towheaded urchins did. Droplets rushed to cling precariously to thick black lashes. The moisture blurred Callie's eyes and she misstepped on the rutted roadway, turning her ankle and emitting a small yelp of pain.

"Oh, damn, damn, damn!" she cried softly as the angry tears began to course down her cheeks. She dashed them away with the back of her free hand, righted the bonnet upon her head, and strode forth again.

Callie's anger was as black as the clouds hanging over the high peaks of the Mule Mountains. Her mind spun like a child's top, out of control and wildly erratic. Until this moment, she had thought no further than getting out of the Claymore house as fast as she could. But now, bits and pieces of the conversation with Edith came scampering back into her mind.

The paltry sum of money nestled in the bottom of her reticle added insult to injury. By damn, she was due the whole amount! She'd fulfilled her end of the contract, and somehow, some way she was going to make the Claymores stand by their part of the bargain.

She might be returning to Boston early—and under a disparaging cloud of totally unwarranted allegations—but if she could help it she wasn't going home without the balance owed her. She'd made the trip, gladly sacrificed a year of her life to ease the financial problems of her family, and they were going to have that money or she'd know the reason why!

Mr. Claymore, she thought suddenly. Edith had

deliberately made sure that Callie left the house while he was gone. Perhaps he possessed a bit more honor than his wife. After all, Callie rationalized, he did seem to like her well enough and he certainly gave all appearances of being pleased with the work Callie was doing with the children. If he knew the truth about what had happened, what had been said, then surely he would honor the contract.

Edith had managed to get Callie out of the house, but she couldn't force her to buy a ticket for the morning train. Callie would check into the hotel all right, but she wasn't getting on the train before she'd managed to get a message to Owen Claymore and he had a chance to right the grievous wrong his wife had done.

A tiny ray of hope peeped through the gloom of Callie's mind, but no such ray of sunshine probed the dark sky above. A gust of wind snatched at her hat, threatening to pluck it right off her head. She jammed the bonnet down and fought to hold it in place as the wind cavorted wildly. The short, coarse grass lining the path flattened to the ground; bushes and trees limbs whipped back and forth in a frantic, rattling dance.

Callie held her bonnet tighter and tipped her head back to glance up at the gun-metal sky and then toward the towering clouds that roiled and tumbled over the jagged mountains. A ragged flash of lightning flickered deep in the belly of one mammoth cloud. Two, three, four times the lightning flashed, growing brighter, nearer with each burst of sizzling incandescence. Thunder echoed its refrain, rolling and rumbling its way across the sky and through the steep mountain passes.

A huge raindrop fell from the sky, plopping upon her chin. Still another landed on the sleeve of her dress, leaving a wet spot as big as a two-bit piece. Another splashed upon her cheek. In fast progression a dozen more droplets peppered her gown. She knew there was little chance she'd make it to town before the torrents came.

"Wonderful. Just wonderful!" Callie moaned. "I'll be soaked to the skin in five minutes. A perfect ending to this blue-ribbon day."

She whirled, her eyes anxiously raking the landscape for some sort of shelter.

"Oh, thank heaven!" she exclaimed as she spied the corner of a house just beyond the next turn. One hand atop her head, the other clutching her bag to her chest, Callie scampered for the dwelling. She'd barely rounded the bend in the road when she realized whose house she was headed for.

Henrietta Winslow's.

There was but the barest hesitation in her pace. What choice did she have? Didn't sailors say "Any port in a storm?" Well, this storm promised to be a doozy and Callie had had all the aggravation she could stand for one morning.

So what if the widow was one of Logan's lady friends? Callie would soon be gone and what Logan did or who he saw was no business of hers. Besides, she had to admit that Henrietta had seemed very friendly the time they'd met. Unless Callie was doomed to disaster the whole day long, there was no reason why Henrietta wouldn't give

161

her shelter for a few hours.

The wind seemed to approve her decision. It poked her in the back with its chilly fingers and propelled her willy-nilly the last few yards to the porch. She stumbled up the steps and thumped into the door with a muffled "oomph!" before regaining her footing.

The door was yanked open before she'd even had time to shove her bonnet back in place.

"Hi, lady," a small voice piped. Callie's expectant gaze dropped several feet. A gap-toothed smile greeted her effort. The wind sent the child's cinnamon-brown hair churning.

"Who is it, Samuel?" came Henrietta's voice from within the house.

"A lady, Mama," the little boy shouted back over his shoulder. The door bucked in his hands as the wind rose again.

Henrietta appeared in the doorway. "Yes, what can I do for—" Her eyebrows flew upward in surprise. "Miss Nolan! Heavens above, come inside before you catch your death!"

She reached out and clasped Callie's arm, practically dragging her into the house. Within a second the door was secured again and Henrietta was turning back toward her unexpected guest.

"Oh, my," she said softly, one fingertip tapping against her cheek as she surveyed the havoc the wind had wrought upon her visitor.

Callie's hat leaned drunkenly over one eye; her ebony curls straggled down her back and stuck out this way and that around the brim of the bonnet and the hem of her skirt had caught on the last flounce of her petticoat, leaving a good foot of dust-spattered ruffle exposed to the world.

A carbon copy of the boy, one size smaller, appeared. With the innocence only a child possesses, the new arrival surveyed Callie from head to toe before casting a quizzical glance at his brother. Samuel answered his unspoken question with a shrug of his bony shoulders. Then, simultaneously, the little boys' hands flew to their mouths and trills of giggles trickled through their fingers.

Despite herself, the corner of Henrietta's mouth quirked upward. "Samuel, Joshua, you boys mind your manners!" she scolded softly, trying hard to stifle her own merriment. "Now, be off with you. Mother's busy now. Go play in your room for a while."

She gave them both a gentle push. Samuel reluctantly took Joshua's hand and began to lead him away. With one last look, the little boys exited the room trailing giggles behind them.

The women were left alone.

Wary blue eyes met welcoming hazel ones.

Henrietta raised her brows and spread her hands as if to say "I'm sorry. You know how children are."

Tentative smiles wreathed first one feminine mouth and then the other.

"Please," Callie said, her eyes rolling heavenward in unexpected amusement as she brushed a bedraggled tendril out of her eyes. "Warn me if there's a mirror anywhere near. I'm not sure I could take another shock right now."

Henrietta chuckled.

Callie's grin widened.

Suddenly the weight of the world seemed to lift a bit from Callie's slender shoulders as the fragile foundations of friendship were laid.

Outside, the heavens had opened up. Rain beat against the roof and water cascaded in fluid sheets down the windowpanes. Inside, Henrietta's kitchen was clean and cozy and warm. The pleasant aroma of the herb tea she'd brewed wafted through the room, and the tasty liquid was finally beginning to warm Callie's chilled body. Her hair brushed and tucked into place, her gown smoothed, there was now little evidence of her unconventional trip down the mountain.

"What a shame," Henrietta said with a mournful shake of her head as Callie finished her tale. "I was so glad to hear Claymore had finally hired someone proper to care for those children."

Callie's cup clattered softly against the saucer as she set it down. "I really like Betsy and the boys. I'm going to miss them," she said, leaning her chin upon her laced-together fingers in pensive reflection of the disastrous results of Edith's irrational behavior. "Henrietta, do you think there's anything peculiar about Mrs. Claymore's illness? I mean, the medicine and all. It really doesn't seem to work very well . . ." A bit ashamed of what was really on her mind, Callie let the sentence trail away.

"You mean, you wonder if Edith's tonic is something other than purely medicinal?" Henrietta asked with a wry chuckle. "Believe me, the thought has crossed more than one mind in Bisbee."

"Goodness," Callie said, blinking in surprise at Henrietta's bluntness. "I'd wondered, but I wasn't sure what to think. I've never known any ladies who partook of . . . of spirits. Oh, my."

What was it about Henrietta, Callie wondered, that made it so easy for a person to discuss such delicate subjects? Within minutes of her arrival, they'd been on a first-name basis, and then after a few well-chosen questions, much to Callie's surprise, her story had tumbled forth.

The telling had brought a reward of sorts; the hurt and anger seemed a little more bearable because she'd shared it with someone else. How lucky she was to have found someone who showed such kindness, such acceptance, just when she needed it most.

Henrietta had made it all so easy—even the difficult part about Edith's accusations. A flip of her head, a wave of her hand, and any fears Callie may have had about Henrietta believing the sordid lies were laid to rest. "Don't you pay any mind to what that woman said," she'd admonished sternly. "The people who care about you won't believe a word of it—and that's all that matters, isn't it?" Callie had fervently hoped Henrietta was right.

"Well, if we're right about Edith, then I sure feel sorry for Betsy and the boys," Henrietta said, bringing Callie's mind back to the present. "Seems like they've been bandied about from pillar to post the last year or so. Oh, the boys can be wild little Indians at times, but underneath they're good kids. I should know. They've spent many afternoon here playing with my boys. A little discipline, a lot of love—that's all it'd take to do the trick."

"Exactly what I thought," Callie agreed. "And they were doing well. I know they were!" A big sigh punctuated her statement. "But what will happen to them now? Unless their parents hire someone else who'll really care about them, they'll be right back where they were before."

"You were good for those kids, Callie. You did all you could."

"I guess," Callie said dejectedly. "It's all so confusing. Why did this happen? And how can the Claymores be so unconcerned about their children? I simply don't understand."

Henrietta snorted. "When Owen Claymore gets wrapped up in his business, he forgets he's got a wife and children. They've always played second fiddle to that mining company of his."

"That's awful," Callie declared, remembering how loving and attentive her own father had been.

"You know, I can still remember when they first moved here. Such an odd pair. Edith so quiet. Owen determined to hobnob with the rich and important men in the territory. He built the big house, hired the first governess, gave elaborate parties."

"But what happened?"

Henrietta shrugged. "I don't know. Claymore was gone more and more. Governesses came and went. Edith stopped coming to town to visit or shop. We started hearing talk about her illness. Oh, every once in a while Owen would throw some big soiree for business purposes and Edith would act as hostess, but before long most of Claymore's business associates quit taking their wives up to the house. Too many of them weren't exactly comfortable with the way things were."

"Oh, dear," Callie sighed, a surge of compassion blunting the edge of her anger toward Edith. "Well, I guess I should feel sorry for her. Sorry for them all actually, but mostly for the children. I just hate to think what's going to happen to them if they're left to Consuela's care for very long."

"You don't suppose Claymore would ask you to come back, do you? I'm shocked that Edith had the nerve to pull a stunt like this, she always seemed so cowed by him. Maybe Claymore will get things straightened out and you can have your job back."

Callie shook her head. "It wouldn't matter if he did. I don't believe anything would tempt me to return. I'll miss the children and I feel bad about leaving them, but I don't think I could ever go back."

"Well, I can't say as I blame you. More tea?" Henrietta asked, lifting the little china pot.

"Oh, thank you, no. I really should take a look at the road. It sounds as if the rain has let up. I should get on down to town before it starts up again. I can't thank you enough for your kindness."

Callie started to rise from the table but Henrietta reached out and laid her hand on Callie's arm to stop her.

"Wait a minute. I have an idea. One of my boarders recently moved out, so I have a spare

167

room. There's no sense in spending your money on a hotel when it's just sitting there empty. Why don't you stay here? I'd really like it if you did."

"Oh, Henrietta, I couldn't."

"Why not?" Henrietta demanded. "It's been a pleasure having a woman to talk to. My two borders are miners; they're gone all day. There's just the boys and me most of the time. It would be a pleasure to have a lady here even for a few days. Things have been rather boring since Logan moved out."

Logan. The name brought a million questions to Callie's mind. Had Logan returned from his errand? Did he know yet that she was gone? What had been his reaction? And, most of all, would he miss her? Heaven above knew she'd miss him. She already did.

"I . . . I don't know, Henrietta. Logan may have already taken my trunks to the hotel."

"In this downpour? I rather doubt it. More's the chance he's been waiting for the rain to let up just like you have. He can drop the trunks here just as easy as at the hotel, easier, in fact, since this is closer. Soon as one of my boarders gets home, I'll send him up to the Claymore house with a message for Logan."

"I'm really not sure it would be the wise thing to do." How would she feel when Logan brought her trunks? Just how badly would it hurt to see him and Henrietta together, to know that the small blond woman would be part of his life long after Callie herself was gone?

Her knuckles against her hips, Henrietta cocked

her head to one side and gave Callie a stern look. "Would you please get it through your head that you're not imposing on anyone? I'd *like* for you to stay."

"You're a very persuasive lady, Henrietta." Callie's voice was strong even if her smile was a bit trembly about the edges. "Thank you very much. I'd be pleased to accept your offer. But only for tonight."

All through the night Callie could hear the rain against the roof. Most of the night it had drummed a deafening cadence, but now it was falling in soft little pitter-pats upon the tin surface above her head. She turned her head toward the room's tiny window, but the small rectangle held no hint of light, no clue as to the time of day or night.

She'd spent a restless night, tossing and turning for the most part, dozing off and on, minutes here, an hour or two there. Callie's wakefulness wasn't so much due to the situation with the Claymores. She knew she was already doing all she could do about that. She had to believe that Owen Claymore would be a gentleman and honor her contract, and there was no sense agonizing over what would or wouldn't happen. There'd be time enough for that when she found an opportunity to talk with him.

No, what was worrying Callie right now was the fact that Logan had never shown up with her trunks. She sighed and flounced onto her stomach.

The trunks be damned. It was Logan not showing up that mattered.

Ben Cassadine, who worked the early shift at the mine, had gone up to the house as soon as he'd returned to the boardinghouse. He reported back that he'd left the message with Paloma. The little Mexican maid had assured Ben that she would relay it to Logan as soon as he returned. Callie had passed the afternoon in nervous expectation, but Logan had never come.

Sensing how tense Callie was, Henrietta had assured her that Ben or one of the other boarders would retrieve her trunks in the morning. Callie hoped she'd managed the proper amount of gratitude, but deep down inside she knew she could have cared less about those trunks.

What she desperately wanted to know was why Logan hadn't come. Was it because he believed what Edith said? Was it because he didn't want to see her again . . . ever? That thought hurt worse than anything Edith had said or done.

Flipping to her other side for what seemed like the hundredth time that night, Callie burrowed under the covers, pulling the quilt snug over her shoulders to chase away the cold. The night air, always chilly in the mountains, had taken on a particularly icy bite with the long onslaught of rain.

She snuggled deeper, squeezed her eyes shut, and prayed for sleep to come or the dawn.

Callie had finally begun the long, slow slide into deep slumber when a distant pounding broke the silence. The sound penetrated the cotton-batting of her sleep and became a part of her dream. It took the clatter of boot heels in the hall below and the discordant sound of a half-dozen voices raised in excitement to shake her awake.

Groggy, Callie pushed herself upright in the bed and tried to decipher what was happening. She could tell something was desperately amiss, but the words were too muffled for her to comprehend. She heard a woman's voice, the staccato beat of footsteps again, and then the sound of the door slamming shut.

Pushing the covers aside, Callie slipped from her warm bed and donned the wrapper Henrietta had loaned her. The floor was icy beneath her bare feet as she padded across the room and toward the stairs. A lantern had been lighted in the parlor. Callie's shadow spidered down the wall behind her as she clutched the robe to her throat and eased down the steps one by one.

Pausing on the bottom step, she peered over the banister. The hall was empty. She craned harder. So was the parlor. Her bottom lip caught between her small pearl teeth, she was wondering whether she should check out the kitchen when the front door was thrown open.

Callie jumped in fright as Henrietta hurried in, slamming the door against the wall and holding it in place with her body. The wind plucked at her sleep-tousled hair and whipped her damp gown and robe about her ankles.

"Hurry!" Henrietta urged to someone unseen. So intent was she on the task at hand that she didn't even notice the figure at the bottom of the staircase.

Callie's round-eyed gaze flew to the darkened doorway just as a man began to edge his way inside. Her first reaction was a disjointed thought about the strange manner the man was employing to enter the door—back first, stooped over as if under a heavy burden, his steps slow and shuffling.

"Easy there," he kept saying to someone still hidden by the darkness. "Just take it easy."

The words, the scene, nothing made any sense to Callie. Disoriented by lack of sleep, befuddled by the events of the day, she turned questioning eyes on her hostess.

"What is it, Henrietta? What's happening? Is something wrong?"

Henrietta spared Callie one quick glance before turning her worried gaze back to the figures emerging through her doorway.

"It's Logan. He's been shot."

CHAPTER TWELVE

"Oh, my God." The words slipped out on a sigh of anguish. "Is he . . . is he going to be all right?"

"I don't know," Henrietta said, her nostrils pinched and white with worry. "Time will tell."

Callie watched in horror as two burly, slicker-draped men eased through the doorway with a body supported between them. Logan was so still. Too still. His head lolled drunkenly against the second man's chest and his hanging arms swung like pendulums as his carriers lurched under the weight of their burden. Rainwater dripped from the men's slickers and from Logan's limp fingertips and puddled on Henrietta's polished floor.

Fear began to scamper and skitter within Callie's bosom as her gaze traveled back and forth along the length of Logan's motionless figure.

His denim pants were soaking wet and mud-splattered. His shirt was the same, and the right shoulder of the garment, once a pale robin's-egg blue, was marred by a huge reddish-brown stain — blood that had dried before the rains had come.

Dirt was caked here and there, and, where nature's torrents had diluted the blemish of life-sustaining fluid, the color had splotched and run rampant, painting the shirt in a macabre pattern of pale pinks and washed-out reds.

The sight sent Callie's heart swooping to the pit of her stomach. Dear God, it looked like he'd been bled dry. Could a man live after such a loss of blood?

But it was Logan's face, his dear, sweet, so well-remembered face, that almost stopped the beat of Callie's heart. Beneath the shading of red-gold stubble his flesh was the color of parchment, washed clean of all color, ashen, lifeless. His eyes were closed, the lids bruised and fragile looking. The biting cold of the night had edged his lips with blue. And, worst of all, an ugly, gaping gash marred the smooth skin at his temple. Blood had run and caked in the tangled mass of tawny curls. Lamplight shone in the raindrops caught in his hair, making them shine like a sprinkling of tiny diamonds.

"Wh-what happened?" Callie asked.

"Don't really know, ma'am," one of the men answered. "You know Ol' Zeke Conway?"

Callie shook her head. "No."

"I do," Henrietta said, shutting the door.

"Well, he was out prospecting this afternoon — you know how Zeke likes to roam around, always looking for that big strike. Well, he came across Logan laying out in the middle of nowhere . . . shot, that ugly slash on his head. Zeke weighs about ninety pounds soaking wet. No way he could

174

hoist Logan up on that ol' mule of his, so he covered him up best as he could and lit out for town. Trouble was, he was way up in the mountains and it took him hours to get here, what with the rain and all."

"Yeah," the other man grunted, "then we took a wagon and went after Logan. The trail was so bad we couldn't get the damn thing—pardon me, ma'am—the wagon up the last mile or so, so we had to hike up and carry him down to where we'd left it."

" 'Fraid we lost a lot of time gettin' him down that mountain, Henrietta," the biggest man said, apology in his voice.

"You did the best you could," Henrietta assured the two men.

"What about a doctor?" Callie questioned. "Didn't the doctor go with you?"

"No, ma'am," the first man answered. "Doc Pritchert was out delivering a baby when we left town. Ol' Zeke's over at his office now, though. He'll send the doc just as soon as he gets in."

"Let's hope he gets back soon," Henrietta responded. "Callie, would you get a lantern from the parlor, please. To light the way up the stairs."

Callie's head jerked up at the sound of Henrietta's strained voice. "Yes, of course."

Her teeth chattering as much from fear as the cold, Callie ran for the parlor, scooped up one of the glowing lanterns, and dashed back to the stairs.

"We'll take him to his old room," Henrietta instructed the men. "Up the stairs. Last door on the left."

175

"Yes'm." Logan's heavy body sagged lower as they struggled toward the steps. "Easy there, Dick."

"Hell, Roger, I'm going easy as I can," Dick replied with a grunt. Placing a supporting knee under Logan's back, he tightened his grip around the injured man's broad chest. "He weighs a ton!"

"Just don't drop him . . . aw, dammit, now look!" Roger exclaimed as a thin rivulet of crimson began to course down Logan's cheek. "All this moving around has opened up that wound again. Come on, let's get him settled as quick as we can."

One fist stuffed against her mouth to stifle the cry that threatened to escape, Callie held the light high and watched the men maneuver around until the one supporting Logan's upper body was backing up Henrietta's narrow staircase in a crablike crawl.

Her gaze locked on Logan, Callie followed the slow-moving men up the stairs, down the shadowy hallway, and into the room. Henrietta was hard on her heels.

Practically slamming the lantern down on a chest, Callie ran to the bed and jerked the bright patchwork quilt out of the way. With more grunts and groans and a few muttered curse words, Dick and Roger managed to place Logan catty-corner on the bed. Clutching the quilt to her breast, Callie watched Dick move around to the other side and take one of Logan's arms while Roger held the other. Together the two men lifted Logan's limp body while Henrietta placed his boot-clad feet on the bed.

"He looks pretty bad, Henrietta. I don't know if

he'll make it," Dick said, finally straightening up and rolling his shoulders to relieve the tenseness of abused muscles.

Callie's eyes flew upward. She bit back the angry retort that would have chastised the man for tempting fate with his negative words. The man had meant no harm. He was just stating the obvious.

But Logan would make it, Callie swore silently. He had to!

Drawing a shaky breath, Callie simply nodded her head when the man sent a curious glance her way. She couldn't trust her voice yet.

"Thank you for your help," Henrietta said.

"Sure," Roger answered. "We'll go back to the doc's and see if there's any word from him."

"That's a good idea," Henrietta said. "Just see yourselves out." With that she turned her attention back to Logan. "Mercy me, he looks chilled to the bone. First thing we need to do is get him warmed up. Help me get his boots off."

"Yes, of course." Callie hurried to the bottom of the bed. Within seconds Logan's boots had thudded to the floor. His soggy socks followed.

"My God," Henrietta said, her voice laced with worry. "His feet are like ice."

"Hot water—that's what we need," Callie interjected. "Oh! I know! Back home when we got a chill, my granny used to heat bricks or stones; then she'd wrap them up in old rags and tuck them under the covers so our feet would stay warm. We could do that."

"What a wonderful idea!" Henrietta said, a spark of hope in her eyes. "All right, then. First

177

thing we need to do is get him out of those wet clothes. There's a pair of scissors in the top drawer of the chest. You get started while I run down and get the stove going. I'll be back as soon as I can."

With a whirl of her nightclothes, Henrietta was gone, and Callie was alone with Logan.

Grabbing the scissors from the chest, she rushed back to the bed. Her ebony hair cascaded downward as she bent to the task. With an impatient flick of her hand, she brushed it out of her way and inserted one blade of the shears in the bottom cuff of one pant leg.

The handle bit into the tender flesh at the base of her thumb as she snipped away at the tough fabric. *Snick. Snick. Snick.* Up one leg she went and then the other. After several minutes of determined hacking Callie managed to split the garment into several pieces. With persistent tugging and jerking she freed Logan's legs. Her first inclination was to leave the union suit that clung damply to his body.

"Don't be stupid," she muttered vehemently. "Those drawers are sopping wet. They've got to go."

Throwing modesty to the wind, she attacked the garment. Sections of faded red wool began to fall away, revealing long legs slabbed with rock-hard muscle and peppered with rough-textured hair the color of autumn wheat.

She snipped and tugged and discarded until there was but one ragged piece of material left. Callie hesitated, then gulped hard, barely moving the lump in her throat.

178

What was wrong with her? For the love of heaven, Logan might be dying and she was worrying about something as foolish as propriety.

Taking a deep breath, she reached out with trembling fingers and snatched away the last piece of material, revealing the blatant masculinity that nestled between his thighs. Crimson flooded Callie's face. She jerked the quilt up to his waist and applied herself diligently to the blood-soaked shirt.

Soon the stained blue garment was nothing more than a scattered pile of rags on the floor and Logan's chest was bare. Here the hair was thicker, and darker in color than the tawny curls on his head, reminding her of the amber stone in her mother's favorite locket. It blanketed bulging pectoral muscles, swirled around copper nipples puckered from the cold, and narrowed to a slim line that disappeared beneath the multi-colored quilt.

Callie eyed the wound on Logan's shoulder and wished desperately that she knew more about doctoring. She'd had plenty of experience with her younger brothers and sisters but it had consisted of such things as sore throats or scraped knees. Still, there had been the time Andy fell out of the tree and broke his leg. It had been a bad break. The bone had poked through, white and jagged, and he'd bled something awful.

Callie recalled bits and pieces of what the doctor had done, how he'd cleaned the wound and disinfected it before setting the bone. She sighed. It wasn't knowledge about gunshots, but it was something.

She didn't know what she'd expected—a huge

gaping hole, shattered bone, mangled flesh — but what she did find was a ragged-edged wound that slowly seeped a trickle of bright red blood.

Was the bullet lodged inside, or had it gone right through his body? She prayed for the latter.

With gentle hands, Callie rolled Logan to his side a bit so she could see his back. He groaned and Callie froze in place. It was the first sound he'd made and she didn't know whether to weep with joy at the evidence of life or leave him alone before she hurt him any more.

Her hesitation lasted only a moment. There was no choice. They had no way of knowing how long it would be before the doctor came and it was important to see how badly he was hurt.

"Hush, now, hush. It's all right. Everything's all right. I promise I'll be very careful," she soothed in a tone much the same as the one he'd used on her the night before.

Bracing him with one hand, she slid a plump feather pillow against his back to hold him in place so she could view the wound.

This time she felt a tiny ray of hope. The wound was small, red-rimmed, and puckered. Even Callie could tell that the bullet had gone in here and exited through the larger hole on his chest. Her relief died when she realized what that meant. Someone had shot Logan in the back!

An accident? Oh, please let that be so. She couldn't bear the thought that someone had deliberately shot Logan in the back and left him for dead.

The clatter of boot heels on the stairs put a stop

180

to Callie's shocking supposition.

"Dr. Pritchert's here," Henrietta called out as she rounded the doorway, a rotund little man in her wake.

"Oh, thank God!" Callie breathed. She quickly moved aside.

The doctor dropped his black bag on the small table beside the bed. He searched his pocket for a pair of spectacles, looped the bows over his ears, and then bent over Logan, his chubby little fingers gently probing the areas around the wounds.

"I'll be right back with hot water and bandages," Henrietta called over her shoulder as she swirled out of the room.

"Fine. Fine," the doctor said with a vacant nod. He never looked up as his fingers continued their delicate investigation.

"Umm," he murmured once, then twice again.

At the third "umm" Callie thought she would scream. Couldn't he say something? Anything? How long was he going to keep her in this agonizing suspense?

Callie took a white-knuckled grip on the bed's curved metal foot railing as the "umms" became equally indecipherable "uh-hums" when the doctor turned his attention to the ugly gash on Logan's head. He had just lifted an eyelid and was peering intently at Logan's pupils when Henrietta scurried in with a basin of steaming water and an armload of white cotton strips.

Callie could have hugged her when she demanded, "Well, Doc, how is he?"

"If you mean the gunshot, then I'd have to say

181

he was lucky. Damn lucky."

Henrietta dropped a handful of rags in the hot water, sloshed them up and down, and then wrung them out before she passed them to the doctor. As each compress turned scarlet from Logan's blood, she would hand him a fresh one. While he cleaned, the doctor continued his rambling discourse.

"Yep, I would say he was very, very lucky. Small caliber bullet. Passed clean through. Bones feel all right. Don't think it did any damage there. It appears the bullet missed anything vital."

Callie started to sag with relief, but the doctor's continuing words renewed her fears.

"But you take this lump on his head. Now that's a real nasty piece of business. Maybe the gunshot knocked him off his horse or maybe the horse spooked, but whatever happened, it appears Logan landed smack on a rock. Yep, musta took a hell of a wallop to knock him out cold like this."

The little doctor's thin gray hair fluttered with the slow shake of his head.

"But he's going to be all right?" Callie ventured timidly.

Over the rims of his spectacle, Dr. Pritchert shot a quick glance at her. His little round shoulders lifted in an eloquent shrug.

"Well, I reckon that depends. Now, you take that there head wound, Logan's tough so he'll probably wind up with not much more than a couple days of real bad headaches from it. And the gunshot . . . Well, he'll be sore for a while, but unless infection sets in, it should heal up just fine. No, little lady, what we really got to worry about here

182

is exposure."

"Exposure?" Callie echoed.

"Yep. Bad enough we got the head and the shoulder to worry about without him laying out in the cold and rain all day. Not good for a man, no sirree. Not good for a man at all. Especially one who's lost a lot of blood."

Callie's fear-filled eyes flew to the water in the basin. It was now tinted deep red from Logan's blood. Her heart lodged in her throat as the doctor continued his explanation.

"You got to understand, he's had a bad chill. 'Fraid it's gonna be a mite touchy for a few days. I expect we'll be fighting a fever before the day's over. Got to watch that closely. Can't let it get out of hand."

"No, of course not," Callie gulped.

"And there's always a chance of pneumonia in cases like this. Plus, we don't know for sure yet that the bullet didn't nick a lung on its way through. Yep, I'm afraid somebody's gonna have to watch him real careful-like for a while."

"Oh, I will," Callie said fervently. "I'll watch him every minute."

The rag Henrietta was wringing out stilled in her hands. Her probing eyes raked Callie for a long moment before she went back to her task.

Callie felt Henrietta's eyes upon her. Had her hasty words revealed too much? Would Henrietta want her there if she knew how Callie really felt about Logan? Would their budding friendship be crushed by jealousy? Callie couldn't bear to be sent away now — not until Logan was safe and well.

183

She'd be gone soon enough. She desperately wanted — needed — this last opportunity to be with Logan.

Callie spread her hands and smiled weakly. "I mean, what else could a friend do?"

CHAPTER THIRTEEN

High in the black velvet sky, the wind changed direction, blowing the ragged thunderclouds away. A thousand diamond-bright stars twinkled in the last dark before dawn. Feathery tendrils of light began to creep from behind the mountain peaks, painting the desert sky melon and fuschia, soft orchid and muted gold.

Inside the small second-story bedroom, Callie carefully unwrapped one of the warming stones and checked to see if it had grown cool. Finding that it had, she switched out several stones and placed the cold ones with a half dozen others lining a deep washbasin. It was time to replenish her supply.

Before leaving the room, she bent and made sure the quilt was tucked securely around Logan's still figure. Satisfied, she hefted the basin, balanced it against the swell of one slim hip, and descended the stairs for what seemed like the hundredth time that night.

The kitchen smelled of fatback bacon and home-baked bread, evidence of the two boarders who had already eaten their breakfasts and left for work.

The clatter of the pan against the table drew Henrietta's attention from the pan of soapy water and stack of dirty dishes.

"Time for another batch?" she asked. She glanced at the tumbled rocks atop the old cast iron stove. "I'm sure those are plenty warm by now. Be careful. Don't burn yourself again."

Henrietta's warning set the two blisters Callie had already earned that night to throbbing. "I will."

She placed her hands in the small of her back and pressed against her aching muscles. "I think he's a little better, Henrietta. At least he feels warmer to the touch."

Memories of how Logan's long, lean body had felt under her fingertips when she checked to see if he was warm enough brought a sudden blush to her face.

"Well," Callie added brightly, grabbing up two thick rags and hurrying to the stove to cover her embarrassment, "guess I'd better get these exchanged and get back up there."

"How's his breathing?"

"A little shallow still, but I think it's okay. He's been fairly quiet the last hour."

"That's good. I'll be up to relieve you just as soon as I get the chores done down here."

"No," Callie said quickly, her grip on the speckled pan growing tighter. "I mean, that's all right. I know how busy your days are. Logan's care is an extra burden, one you certainly didn't expect. I'm happy to take a little of the strain off you. Besides, it's not as if I had anything else to do."

One pale blond brow edged upward. "What about your plans to talk with Owen Claymore?"

Callie shrugged. "I can do that any time. A few more days won't hurt. Who knows, it might even be better to let things calm down first. I really would like to do this for Logan. He was kind to me at a time when I needed it."

Henrietta eyed her guest speculatively. "All right. If you're sure."

"I'm sure."

"Call if you need any help."

"I will."

Callie scurried from the room, eager to return to Logan's side.

She didn't try to understand her desire to be with him or rationalize the intensity of her feelings. It was enough for the present to be close to him, to contribute something to his recovery, to be sure that he was going to be all right before she left.

Boston was a long way off and Callie suddenly knew that she'd carry with her the memory of a tall, tawny-haired, teasing man for the rest of her life. Was it so wrong to want to add a few more moments to the storehouse of her heart?

Through the long days and nights Callie cared for Logan, keeping the warming stones replenished until they were deemed unnecessary. She kept the quilts tucked tight about him, and a dozen times a day she lifted his head to spoon weak broth into

187

his mouth. In less lucid times, he thrashed the covers loose and mumbled incoherently and she wondered who the women were who peopled his restless dreams.

". . . pretty as a picture tonight, Della, honey. Sing another one . . . wish me luck, honey . . . now, do me right, honey . . . need a good card . . ."

Callie wondered if Della was the redhead she'd seen Logan with that first morning. His ramblings about Della brought a surge of jealousy.

". . . damn, Jasmine that water's cold! . . ." A deep chuckle of delight. ". . . get him, Jasmine . . . make him pay. No, you don't, Hezekiah. That's the way, Hawk! . . . get him again!"

Jasmine. Hezekiah. Hawk. Who were they? Relatives? Friends? Whoever they were, they had played an important part in Logan's life, a happier part in his life than the other name he called so often.

". . . we gotta hide . . . you gotta be still. Please, Sabra, please, don't move, don't move . . . the baby! Oh, God, Sabra, the baby!"

Callie dreaded the dreams of Sabra. Those were the times Logan became the most agitated, thrashing about, flinging his arms. Sometimes tears would creep from beneath the dark fan of lashes and run down his stubbled cheeks. Sometimes he'd try to get up, straining to rise until Callie would have to sit on the bed and hold him down. All the while murmuring soft words, gentle, soothing phrases.

Callie soon learned to go to him quickly when the memories of Sabra began. Her nearness, the sound of her voice seemed to calm Logan. Within minutes the panic would fade from his voice, the tears would dry, and his chest would lift with a deep sigh.

More than once Callie considered asking Henrietta who the people were, especially Sabra. But she never could quite bring herself to do so. What if Sabra had been—still was—his wife? What if the baby he anguished over was his?

Had he belonged to someone else, loved another woman, held her in his arms and whispered the sweet words that Callie longed to hear? She didn't want to know.

And so the days crept by.

"Hide, Sabra, hide . . . don't let them see you!"

Callie's head jerked upward. The big double bed was cast in shadows; the soft golden glow of the small lantern burning low on the chest across the room did little more than light its own immediate area. Quickly she unfolded herself from the rocking chair where she'd been dozing and hurried to Logan's side.

Downstairs the mantel clock chimed faintly. One, two, three times it chimed. Three o'clock in the morning. He'd made it almost a whole night without the dreams.

"Hush, now, my sweet—" Endearments had crept into her litany without her even knowing it. "Shh, shh. It's all right, dearest, it's all right. You're safe. I'm here. You're safe."

Her fingers lightly stroked his brow, brushing

189

away the fine sheen of moisture. Her hands skimmed the red-gold stubble on his cheeks, down the corded column of his neck, across the slope of muscled shoulder. Long, satin-soft strokes that always seemed to quiet him.

The quickened beat of Callie's heart slowed as Logan sighed and grew still. She waited for him to sink back into the depths of sleep, but to her surprise he turned his head toward her and his dark lashes fluttered up. For the first time, his eyes didn't hold that faraway expression that bespoke the haze of semiconsciousness.

He blinked twice, trying to focus on the shadow-wrapped figure perched on the side of his bed.

"Oh, Logan, you're awake," Callie whispered, her joy at his state obvious in her voice.

"Callie," he murmured.

No question. No confusion. Just utter acceptance that it was perfectly right, absolutely correct for her to be by his side.

"Oh, thank heaven. You had me so worried."

"I'm flattered," he said in a voice just barely above a whisper. A teasing smile, a heartbreaking shadow of its former self. "Must have been a hell of a party. I haven't felt this bad in years. But . . ." There was a faint sparkle of mischief in his eyes. "I'd do it all again if it meant waking up to find you in my room."

Something in Callie's face must have triggered his first glimmering of awareness. Logan frowned. Then his head rolled upon the pillow. His gaze fell upon the swath of white bandage padding his shoulder. For a long moment he perused the bulky dressing as if he couldn't quite comprehend what it was, then his eyes slowly swept the room.

"Henrietta's," he said in surprise. "We're in my old room at Henrietta's."

"Yes," Callie confirmed.

Logan shook his head. "Don't tell me. That damn White Rabbit's been at it again."

The small jest drew a smile from Callie. "Something like that."

"What happened?" Logan asked, his gaze locked steadfastly on her face.

"You got shot. Some prospector named Zeke found you, and then two men—Roger and Dick, I think their names were—brought you here. I guess they knew Henrietta would take care of you."

"Well, that explains what I'm doing here." Confusion furrowed Logan's brow. "But I sure don't understand what you're doing at Henrietta's. Don't tell me the Claymores had you come down here?"

"No," Callie said, her eyes sliding away for an instant. "Not exactly."

Logan's frown deepened. "Not exactly? What does that mean?"

Callie's chin inched upward. "It means that I'm no longer working for the Claymores."

"What?" Logan demanded in surprise. Forgetting his wound, he made an attempt to sit up. "Ouch! Dammit to hell! That hurts."

"And well it should," Callie scolded. She placed her hand on his chest and exerted a gentle downward pressure. "Now lie still before you start bleeding again."

Weak as he was, there was nothing Logan could

do but obey. "All right, all right," he grumbled. "I'll be still. I promise. But I want to know what happened."

"Mrs. Claymore and I had a small disagreement. She asked me to leave so I did."

Logan blinked in surprise. His eyes were beginning to look bleary and his words were becoming slurred. "Disagreement? About what? I don't understand how she could do that."

"Well, neither do I," Callie said gently, eager to put an end to the conversation. She could tell how tired he was, and, truth be told, she had no desire to discuss the issue any further. There was no way she could tell Logan what Edith Claymore had accused her of. "But that's exactly what she did. And that's the end of the subject for now. You've been up far too long already. You don't have your strength back yet. You need your sleep."

Logan recognized the stubborn tone in Callie's voice. He thought about pursuing the matter, but he realized he didn't have the energy.

It was becoming a struggle to keep his eyes open, and his limbs felt heavy, almost as if they were anchored to the bed. He sighed with resignation. Maybe she was right. A few minutes rest. Just a few, and then he'd find out what had happened.

"I'll see you in the morning," Callie whispered as Logan's eyes drifted downward.

She waited until his breathing had become slow and even. When she thought he was sound asleep again, she started to rise. The bed springs creaked with her movement and Logan's eyes flew open.

"Callie?" he rasped, his voice laced with apprehension. His sleep-blurred eyes searched frantically.

"Shh. It's all right," Callie soothed as she had so many times before. "I'm here. Everything's going to be fine."

"Don't go," he whispered. "Not yet." Logan's hand groped its way across the quilt until it found hers. He gave a small sigh as he laced his fingers through hers. "Please."

"I won't," she managed to say around the sudden lump in her throat.

His lashes feathered downward, but his fingers never loosened their hold. "Callie . . ." he whispered one last time. Her name was but a sigh. His breathing slowed. His broad, hair-roughened chest rose and fell with the regularity of his breathing.

CHAPTER FOURTEEN

Through slitted eyelids Logan followed every move Callie made as she tiptoed into his room and quietly placed a stack of clean bandages atop the dresser. Even dressed in faded calico, her hair held back with a three-cornered kerchief, she was the most beautiful thing he'd ever seen.

Logan lay very still. Callie didn't know he was awake yet, and with a little play-acting on his part he hoped to watch her for a few more minutes.

When exactly had she become so important to him?

That first day at the train station when she squared her slim shoulders and bravely stood her ground at a stranger's approach?

Later that afternoon when she weathered the episode with the snake with such aplomb, and refrained from giving the Claymore boys the stern lecture they so richly deserved?

When he found out that a good portion of her wages were promptly dispatched each month to Boston, that she'd willingly sacrificed a year of her life to help her family?

When he shared the day-to-day routines with her, saw the infinite patience she displayed with three little hooligans, experienced the dedication she possessed while she strove to teach them to appreciate nature, to show kindness to one another, to look for the small joys in life?

When he realized that it had been Callie who'd been by his side through the long days and nights after he was wounded? When he knew how much he'd come to depend upon her, how much he missed her when she quietly slipped from the room, and how eagerly he awaited her return? When he finally realized that Callie's gentle touch and sweet voice had been far more effective in chasing away the shadows and the pain during his convalescence than any medication Doc Pritchert had prescribed?

Yes, all those times and more.

Somehow, some way, because of all the little idiosyncrasies that were Callie's and Callie's alone, she'd managed to kindle a fire in his heart as well as in his loins.

Now what was he going to do about it?

For the life of him, he didn't know.

Logan was all too aware that time was running out. In her usual candid manner, Henrietta had apprised him of some of the circumstances pertaining to Callie's dismissal and subsequent arrival at the boardinghouse, as well as Callie's plan to confront Owen Claymore about the balance of her wages. Since then, Callie and Logan hadn't done much more than skim the surface of the situation in their conversations. Callie was reluctant to discuss her falling out with Edith, and Logan didn't want to say or do anything that might spur her to act upon her vow to contact Owen. Eventually, it simply became easier for both of them to ignore the whole thing.

Despite his outward nonchalance concerning Callie's dismissal, a slow anger flared within Logan whenever he thought of how unfairly she had been treated, and even the smallest mention of her eventual visit to Owen Claymore sent his usually good spirits plummeting. Callie might believe Claymore honorable, but Logan knew better. A man of honor would have stood by his obligation and sent the money immediately. Gossip was alive and well in Bisbee; Claymore was bound to know where Callie was.

So why hadn't he sent the payment? Claymore certainly wasn't hurting for money. Did he actually believe that Callie would leave without those funds? Or did he have something else in mind? The thought of what might happen when Callie went to see Claymore sent Logan's mind whirling. Warranted or not, he didn't want Callie anywhere near the man.

Oh, he admired her spunky attitude and, if asked, he would have agreed without reservation that she deserved the money. Why, if he hadn't been flat on his back in bed when he first found out what happened, he'd probably have stormed into Claymore's office himself to demand the full payment of Callie's wages.

But time had passed while Logan's body healed,

and somewhere deep within his subconscious he began to realize that every day that went by without her obtaining the money meant another day that Callie stayed in Bisbee.

Rationalization became a way of life with Logan. It hadn't been difficult at all for Logan to decide that he couldn't do anything immediately about obtaining Callie's funds without jeopardizing the promise he'd made to help George and the independent miners.

So, deep inside his secret soul, he hoped that Claymore would continue to do nothing. Meanwhile, he indulged in unconscious sabotage at every opportunity. He stretched out his convalescence longer than necessary, and his continued dependence on Callie kept her busy throughout the hours of the day, never quite allowing her enough time to take that trip to town.

Logan never dissected what he was doing—or why. All that mattered was the end result. Without the money, Callie couldn't leave and Logan wouldn't have to face the truth about the situation, about himself. He couldn't bring himself to make the kind of commitment that would stop Callie from leaving forever, but he was human enough to take advantage of anything else that would keep her in Bisbee.

No, he didn't know what he was going to do about the situation when time finally ran out. All he knew right that moment was that he couldn't wait one more minute to hear her voice, to see her smile, to touch her.

"Callie." Logan's heart leaped as she looked up

with instant pleasure in her eyes.

She hurried to his side, and the sunbeams spearing through the window set aflame with a blaze of blue-black fire the long hair swirling about her shoulders.

"Good morning," she said, perching on the edge of the bed and laying her cool hand against his brow as she had done each morning for the past two weeks. "Wonderful. No fever. And you slept the whole night long. How do you feel? Are you hungry?"

"A little." He started to push himself into a sitting position. The movement brought a twinge of pain to his shoulder and a grimace to his face.

"Logan, you know you aren't supposed to exert yourself," Callie scolded softly, tiny worry lines etched between her brows. "That wound isn't fully healed yet. You'll tear it open if you keep wallowing around like that. Let me help you."

"Well, if you insist," he said, faking a sigh of resignation.

"Put your arms around my neck."

He did as he was told, looping long, strong arms around her as she scooted closer and slipped her left arm around his back.

"Hold on."

With pleasure, Logan thought, tightening his hold and drawing Callie so close that the soft fullness of her breasts flattened against his chest. The pain in his shoulder seemed insignificant when compared to the exquisite agony he was experiencing in other parts of his body.

As she lifted him, the starched fabric of her

bodice rasped gently against his flat male nipples and they hardened instantly. Each breath he drew seemed to screech to a halt halfway to his lungs, and his heart began a crazy staccato beat. Frissons of excitement licked through his veins, setting each and every nerve ending atingle.

"All right, just hold tight while I get the pillows in place."

Steadying him, Callie used her free arm to stuff the extra pillows behind his back. When she eased him down against the fluffy feather nest she'd fashioned, he maintained his hold and took her with him.

The hand that had been fussing with the pillows grew still, hesitated, then slid down the bulge of his arm and came to rest against his chest, her fingertips tangled in the tawny curls. For a long moment she lay against him, glorying in the rough scratch of his beard against her cheek, the tom-tom beat of his heart beneath her palm. The temptation to stay there, to give herself up to the pleasure of being in his arms, was almost overwhelming.

She nuzzled her face into the curve of his shoulder, inhaled deeply, enjoying the clean, masculine scent that was Logan's alone. Her fingers tightened their hold in the springy coils of hair, the rounded tips of her nails rasping ever so lightly against his sensitized skin.

Logan felt an immediate explosion of heat in the pit of his stomach. The muscles tensed, the blood pumped. He forgot that it was morning-bright. He forgot they were not alone in the house. All he knew was he wanted this woman more desperately than he'd ever wanted anyone or anything in his life.

Callie felt as well as heard Logan's sharp gasp. Afraid she'd done something to hurt him, she raised her head and started to pull away.

"No . . . don't," he pleaded, his whisper hoarse and laced with need.

"Logan—" But Callie's protest was lost beneath his kiss.

His lips found hers, tenderly, reverently, touching, tasting, claiming, conquering. His kiss was everything she'd ever dreamed of—and more. A thousand butterflies went wild in her stomach. Her heart went galloping after them.

With one hand splayed against her spine and the other cupping the back of her head, Logan continued his devastating assault. His mouth, so soft yet so firm, angled across hers. He rolled his head, his big hand holding her securely in place, as he increased the pressure of the kiss. Each change of angle, each small adjustment of mouth against mouth, added fuel to the flames building within him.

Logan couldn't get enough of Callie, couldn't hold her tight enough, taste her enough. A sweet, wild need—utterly devastating, wholly consuming—drove him onward.

Flicking the tip of his tongue out, he traced the seam of her lips, eliciting a small moan of surprise that quickly became pleasure. Her lips parted beneath his and he plundered the sweet recesses, stroking the satin lining, gliding over her pearly teeth, dueling gently with her velvet-textured tongue that timidly parried his thrusts.

A groan, half agony, half ecstasy, rumbled in his chest and he locked his fingers in the cascade of long black curls, chaining her to him.

"Uncle Logan, Uncle Logan!" Little-boy voices accompanied the clatter of little-boy feet upon the staircase.

Henrietta's aggravated shout from somewhere below them overlapped the sounds of both. "Samuel! Joshua! I told you to peek in and see if Logan was awake. Good heavens above! There'll be no doubt about it now!"

Callie and Logan jerked apart just as the boys rocketed into the room. She was out of his arms and standing beside the bed before he could move.

Clasping her trembling hands tightly together in front of her, Callie gulped once and managed to say, "I'll . . . uh . . . I'd better go help Henrietta with your breakfast."

Her blue eyes, huge and filled with confusion, connected once with his smoldering brown ones before quickly looking away.

With a whirl of calico skirt, Callie scurried for the door, passing the two eager little boys as they skipped toward Logan's bed.

"Callie!" Logan called after her, but she was gone before the boys screeched to a halt beside him.

"Whatcha doing, Uncle Logan?" the boys piped in unison.

Logan groaned. His head fell back against the pillows and he quickly cocked one knee upward, forming a concealing 'tent' over the blatant results

201

of what he'd been doing. *Not one-tenth of what I'd like to,* his inflamed mind retorted.

"Mama wants to know how you feel this morning," Samuel intoned gravely.

"Fine," Logan mumbled between great gulps for air to quench the heat in his blood. "Just fine." *Just fine if you enjoy feeling like your insides are on fire and you know damn good and well that you can't do a thing about it.*

"Oh, yeah," Joshua chirped. "Mama said to ask you what you want for breakfast."

It isn't on the menu.

"So, how's our patient feeling this morning?" Henrietta questioned as Callie rushed into the kitchen.

"Feeling?" Callie echoed blankly. *He feels wonderful. If he felt any better, I don't think I could stand it.* "He . . . uh . . . seems fine. Just fine."

"Is his shoulder giving him much pain? He was up quite a bit yesterday. I was hoping he hadn't overdone it."

It certainly didn't appear to be. "No," Callie said with a hard shake of her head. "No, I don't think so."

"That's marvelous. Doc Pritchert is very pleased with his progress. He said Logan could come downstairs for a little while this afternoon, if he felt like it. Why, before we know it, he'll be well again."

And gone again. The thought made Callie realize what a short time she might have left to spend

202

with Logan. He'd go back to work and back to his women.

"I wonder if he's up to some flapjacks this morning?" Henrietta mused.

I almost wish he wasn't. "Here," Callie said with forced brightness as she took the big iron griddle out of Henrietta's hands and placed it on the stove to heat. "Let me help you."

"Thanks." Henrietta relinquished the griddle and turned back to the table where the bowl of batter waited. "There's plenty left. I'll fix a batch for you, too."

"Thank you," Callie croaked, wondering if she'd be able to swallow even one bite.

Henrietta paused in her vigorous stirring of the batter to look up at her new friend. "Is something wrong? You're not getting sick, are you?"

Callie's startled gaze flew upward. "Sick? Me? Heavens, no." She forced a laugh. "Whatever gave you that idea?"

"I don't know. Your eyes are overly bright— rather glassy-looking. And there's a rash on your cheek."

"Rash?" Callie repeated, her hand flying to her face. That was no rash. All too well she remembered the wonderful, raspy feel of Logan's stubbled beard against her cheek.

"I'm not so sure." Henrietta wiped her hands on the tail of her apron and bore down on Callie. "I'd better see if you're running a fever." She pressed her hand against Callie's forehead in the same gesture Callie had used earlier on Logan. "Umm. Peculiar. Your temperature seems normal."

"I told you, I'm fine. Really." Callie quickly bobbed out of Henrietta's reach. "Oops! I'd better see to the griddle. It'll be too hot."

"Very well. But if you start feeling bad, you let me know."

"Oh, I will," Callie readily agreed. She suppressed a heartfelt sigh of relief when Henrietta went back to her batter.

In far too short a time, Logan's breakfast was ready to carry upstairs. Callie wasn't ready to face him again this soon, but there was no way to avoid the encounter without making Henrietta suspicious. She picked up the tray, squared her shoulders, and marched up the stairs.

Carefully avoiding any eye contact with Logan, Callie entered the room and positioned the tray across his blanket-clad lap. She was grateful to find that the boys were still perched, one on either corner, at the bottom of Logan's bed.

Callie had planned to make a speedy exit but Logan was too quick for her. She'd barely released her hold on the tray when his fingers encircled her wrist.

"Thank you . . . for everything."

Callie's "rash" disappeared in the flush of color that suffused her face. "Y-you're welcome." Timidly her eyes met his.

"You are going to stay and change my bandage after I eat, aren't you?"

"Y-yes, of course." What else could she say? It was their standard routine; it would seem decidedly peculiar if she varied it now.

"Can we stay and visit while Uncle Logan eats?"

204

Samuel inquired.

"N—" Logan began.

"Yes!" Callie said. "But you have to sit still and don't shake the bed. Understand?"

"Yes'm!" the boys chorused.

Callie puttered nervously about the room while Logan ate. Little tingles ran up and down her spine, making her positive he was watching her. With great determination, she resisted the temptation to turn and see for sure.

By the time he finished his meal, she'd rearranged the bandages and ointments atop the dresser at least a half dozen times.

When Logan was through eating, Callie moved his tray to the side table by the bed and made preparations for changing the dressing on his shoulder. Fully expecting denial, Samuel and Joshua made a halfhearted plea to be allowed to stay and view the process—an activity endlessly fascinating to the two small boys when someone else was on the receiving end of the doctoring. Much to their surprise, Callie agreed.

A chance encounter with Logan's eyes made her wonder if he knew exactly what she was doing. She waited for one of his usual teasing comments, but he simply grinned that wide, white, devastating smile of his and gave himself up to her ministrations without a word.

"Does it hurt, Uncle Logan?" Joshua asked, his eyes big as saucers as he viewed the puckered red scar on Logan's shoulder.

"Right now, I'd say that shoulder wound is the last thing on my mind," Logan replied.

Callie's blush returned.

"Miss Callie's a good nurse, isn't she?" Samuel commented sagely. "I heard Doc Pritchert tell Mama she was. Gee, you're lucky she was here, aren't you?"

"I couldn't agree more," Logan said.

Thanks to the constant banter between Logan and the boys and her own vivid recall of what had transpired such a short time before, it took Callie almost twice as long as usual to complete the dressing change, and by the time she did her nerves were all ajangle.

As soon as the bandaging was done, the boys lost interest. Like rats deserting a sinking ship, they scurried for the door and the beckoning delights of the outdoors. The dismay Callie felt as she watched them scamper from the room was quickly dispatched when Henrietta arrived at Logan's door.

"You've got a visitor, Logan."

Relief surged through Callie. She'd been wondering what to say, how to act when she was once again alone with Logan. The prospect of postponing that confrontation was infinitely appealing. Without further ado, Callie began to gather up her supplies.

"Logan, darlin'!" In a whirlwind of blue taffeta, the woman Callie had seen with Logan on her first day in Bisbee rushed into the room.

"Della!" Logan exclaimed. "What a . . . a nice surprise to see you. How kind of you to come visit me."

All of a sudden, the thought of escaping Logan's room lost all its appeal to Callie.

"Oh, sweetie! That looks positively awful!" Della exclaimed, plopping herself down on the side of the bed and running one long nail down the edge of the white bandage that marred Logan's bronze skin. "Does it hurt, darlin'?"

"Oh, just a little now and then."

Callie glowered. The darn thing hadn't been hurting thirty seconds ago!

"Well, don't you worry, sugar, I know just what to do. I know a cure-all that'll fix anything."

Della leaned forward and pressed her full red lips to Logan's. The ointment tin Callie was holding fell to the floor with a clatter and went spinning across the polished wood planks. Pure, raw jealousy surged through Callie and she fought the urge to grab a handful of the bright red curls that hung down Della's back and yank her right off the bed.

Instead she first retrieved the jar and then Logan's breakfast tray and marched out of the room without a backward look. The sounds of three chattering voices followed her down the stairs.

When Henrietta returned to the kitchen, she found Callie on her hands and knees scrubbing the last quarter of the floor.

"Good heavens, Callie, I don't expect you to do that kind of work!" Henrietta protested.

Callie grimly shook her head and kept on scrubbing. "Don't be foolish. I did plenty of his kind of work at home. Besides, I earn my own keep, Henrietta, and I've already been here much longer than I planned to."

"Well, as far as I'm concerned, you've more than paid your way by caring for Logan. It would have

207

been quite a burden on me if you hadn't been here."

Callie dipped her rag in the pail of soapy water, sloshed it up and down several times, and then wrung it out. The actions kept her from having to meet Henrietta's gaze.

"You know I was happy to help Logan, but he's almost well now. He doesn't need me. Uh . . . he doesn't need constant care anymore. I think it's time for me to finish up my business here and go home."

Perceptive as always, Henrietta noticed the huskiness in Callie's voice. When a rumble of laughter from upstairs jerked Callie's attention from the floor, her blue eyes troubled, her mouth a grim, thin line, Henrietta knew her intuitions had been correct.

"Tell me, Callie, does it bother you that Della Maxwell came here?"

"Bother me?" Callie questioned as she renewed her vigorous attentions to the floor. "Heavens, no. Why should it?"

"I can think of several reasons. One, I rather doubt that you ever had a lady of Della's . . . uh . . . particular standing in the community come to call in Boston. I can see where that might make you a bit uncomfortable. But she's really not a bad sort."

Callie rocked upward and steadied herself upon her heels. "Really, Henrietta. Do I appear such a blue-nose? I'm not prejudiced, and it certainly isn't my business how the lady makes her living."

"What I meant was—"

208

"Believe me," Callie continued, ignoring any hint that Henrietta's question might have had more to do with Della's relationship with Logan than the lady's profession. "If I didn't understand before why a woman might be forced into pursuing certain avenues of employment, I assure you I do now." She laughed mirthlessly. "Having limited funds and no job is a great eye-opener to the harsh realities of life."

"If it's any consolation, I don't think she's the least threat where Logan is concerned."

Callie's eyes grew guarded. "I'm sure I don't know what you're talking about." She gave the far corner one last swipe with the rag and rose to her feet.

Henrietta watched Callie tiptoe across the still damp floor, open the back door, and heave the dirty water out. She met Callie at the door as she returned, laying a gentle hand upon her arm.

"I'd have to be blind not to know how you feel about Logan," Henrietta said softly. "And, if I'm not sorely mistaken, he cares for you."

Callie smiled bravely and shook her head. "No, I don't think so. Oh, not that he's not fond of me. I'm sure he is to some extent. But then again, Logan's fond of anything female."

Henrietta shook her head. "I think you're wrong about that. I've known Logan for a long time and I think there's something special in the way he feels about you."

Hope flared briefly in Callie's eyes, but she quickly shook the foolish thoughts away. "It wouldn't work, Henrietta. Logan and I are like oil and water. Oh, there's no denying he's the most charming, appealing man I've ever met, but I knew from the first that he wasn't the kind of man who was looking for a home and family and that's all I've ever wanted. I can't be something I'm not and neither can Logan."

"Are you so sure he couldn't change?"

"I'm sure. He doesn't want to be tied down and I don't think he could ever be satisfied with one woman. Good Lord, Henrietta, half the women in town are in love with him! Why, at first, I even thought you—" Callie's eyes grew wide with embarrassment as she realized what she'd been about to say. "Oh, dear. I'm sorry."

Henrietta smiled. "It's all right. I understand. But let me assure you, Logan and I have never been more than good friends."

"I've known that since the night they brought him in," Callie said. "If he'd meant more than that to you, you wouldn't have relinquished him to my care." Irony edged her smile. "That's how you knew, isn't it?"

Henrietta nodded.

"Well," Callie said with false brightness, "there you have it. If you guessed that easily, then it won't be long until Logan begins to suspect. I don't think I could bear to see pity in his eyes. No, the sooner I return to Boston, the better. It'll save both of us from embarrassment."

CHAPTER FIFTEEN

The clerk looked up from the long row of figures he was tallying. Replacing his pen in its well, he gave Callie a speculative glance. "May I help you, miss?"

"Yes, thank you," Callie replied. Her fingers tightened on the reticule clutched in her hands. "I'd like to see Mr. Claymore, if it's convenient." She prayed her voice wasn't as shaky as her insides.

"May I say who's calling?" the clerk asked, giving his paper cuffs a fastidious brushing as he rose from his place behind the desk.

"Miss Nolan. Callie Nolan."

With a curt nod, Claymore's clerk slipped through an ornately carved door at the side of the room.

Callie drew a deep breath to still her quivering stomach. The distant whistle of a train beckoned her gaze to the window opening onto Main Street, and she fervently wished the encounter with Claymore was over. As soon as she had her money, she was getting on the first train headed east.

The thought was bittersweet. It would be wonderful to see her family again, but deep in her mind was the memory of Logan Powers and the knowledge that, while he'd be out of her life, he'd never be out of her heart.

"Miss Nolan, is there something I can do for you?" Owen Claymore's terse inquiry snapped Callie out of her reverie.

Callie stiffened her spine and turned to face her former employer. "Yes, there is, Mr. Claymore. I hope you'll agree when you hear what I have to say."

Claymore studied Callie for a long moment, his amber eyes unreadable. "Very well," he finally said. With a nod of his leonine head, he moved aside so that his bulk no longer blocked the entrance to his office. "Won't you come in?"

"Thank you."

Callie brushed past the curious little clerk who was back in place at his desk. As she swept through the door, she heard Claymore tell his employee that he didn't wish to be disturbed until further notice.

Claymore's private office was large, the furnishings impressive in an overabundant sort of way. As Callie waited in front of the massive oak desk, she fleetingly wondered if all that opulence was for the benefit of those who called upon Owen Claymore—or the man himself.

"Won't you be seated?" Claymore asked, taking his place behind his desk. He leaned against the tall, padded back of his chair and tented his fingers. "Just what can I do for you, Miss Nolan?"

Perched primly on the edge of her chair, Callie clasped her hands tightly in her lap to keep them from trembling. She managed to meet Claymore's gaze with unwavering eyes. "You can correct a grievous wrong, Mr. Claymore."

"I'm afraid I don't know what you're talking about."

Her head dipped in a tiny nod of acceptance. "I didn't think you would. If you'll be kind enough to listen to my side of the story, perhaps I can clear up some misconceptions."

Bravely, Callie began her tale.

"And so," she finished, long minutes later, "as you can see, the breach of contract was none of my doing. I would hope that, under such circumstances, a gentleman such as yourself would see fit to honor his obligations."

Owen Claymore had scarcely moved throughout Callie's recital, but now he placed his big hands upon the polished surface of the desk and leaned toward her.

"Please accept my apologies, Miss Nolan," he said, his face a study in earnestness. "I had no idea. I must admit I was quite vexed with your seeming lack of responsibility when I returned that evening and found you gone. When Paloma repeated the story Edith had told her, how you'd been so terribly unhappy with us and had insisted on returning home immediately, well, I suppose I let my anger at your abrupt departure get the best of me. I should have known better."

"Please, sir, don't be too harsh on yourself," Callie said, relieved that her story had found acceptance. Evidently she'd been too severe in her earlier considerations of Owen Claymore. "I can understand how you must have felt."

"Yes, but I should have made an effort to contact you. It was remiss of me not to do so. My only excuse is that the house was in such a turmoil. Edith was quite . . . uh, incapacitated. And Consuela was functioning in her usual incompetent manner. That blasted cat of Betsy's had managed to get itself stuck in a tree and she had climbed up after it."

"Oh, dear!" Callie responded, her face etched with concern. "Betsy didn't get hurt, did she?"

"Oh, no," Claymore assured her. "She's fine. I managed to get child and cat down safely, although I must admit I was sorely tempted to let that damned feline stay right where it was. But Betsy would have none of that." A fond smile tipped one corner of his mouth. "Got a mind of her own, that one does. I rather think she takes after me."

Callie smiled politely. She fervently hoped young Betsy would turn out to be nothing like either of her parents.

Claymore continued his excuses. "And, of course, there was the added problem of Logan's absence. I didn't learn about his accident until the next day." One long finger absently stroked the pale mustache rimming his lip. "I do hope he's getting along all right."

"He's doing splendidly," Callie answered. "Dr.

Pritchert told us yesterday that he should be his old self in just a few more days."

"That so? Well, I'm certainly glad to hear that he's doing so well. Such a shocking incident. I suppose you've heard the whole story. I mean, about what really happened . . ." The sentence trailed away.

Callie shook her head. "Actually I know very little about it. I don't think anyone does."

Claymore frowned. "Come now, Logan must have some idea as to who shot him?"

"No," Callie said, wishing Claymore had never brought up Logan's name. It just served to remind her again of the problems she faced. "He doesn't remember a thing."

"Umm. What a shame. Well, at any rate, you must tell Logan that he'll have a job waiting just as soon as he's fully recovered."

"Yes, of course," Callie agreed quickly, knowing it was time to get back to the subject she'd come about. "Mr. Claymore, I don't wish to seem impatient, but I was wondering about the contract. I mean, rightfully . . . uh . . . don't you think — "

"Tsk, tsk, my dear, put it right out of your head." Claymore fairly beamed at her. "You're quite right. There should be an adjustment of your severance pay, that is, unless I can persuade you to return. The children do miss you."

Callie squashed down her feelings of guilt. "It's kind of you to offer, Mr. Claymore, but I don't see how I could ever return."

If it were just the situation at the Claymore

house, Callie knew she might reconsider. But there was still the problem with Logan and her own feelings. Feelings she could no longer deny.

No, her thinking had been correct from the beginning. They'd both be better off if she was gone.

"Very well," Claymore said with a sigh. "I won't press you at this time."

"I appreciate that," Callie said, positive that there'd be no next time.

"And now, on to the issue at hand."

Callie waited expectantly. But instead of counting out cash or writing a bank draft, Claymore rose and rounded the desk.

"I keep a private suite at the hotel next door. I have some extra funds in a safe in the suite. Would you mind accompanying me there and I'll see if I can't do a little something to correct this situation."

"Oh," Callie said, a bit flustered by the unexpected turn of events. But why shouldn't she do as he asked? It would speed up the process considerably. "I suppose that would be all right."

"Fine."

Claymore extended a hand to help Callie rise. They stopped in the outer office while Claymore held a whispered exchange with his clerk, and then they were on their way.

It was a short walk to the hotel. Claymore ushered Callie into a richly appointed lobby and then up a curved staircase to a door at the end of the hall on the second floor.

Callie couldn't help but be impressed when Claymore escorted her inside his suite. The room was lush beyond belief, the heavy mahogany furniture upholstered with rich green silk plush. Satin drapes of a deeper hue lined the windows. Through an archway Callie spied a bedroom, beautifully furnished with a large brass bedstead and a massive chest.

"Won't you have a seat, my dear?"

Callie's first inclination was to say no. She had thought no further than a hasty completion of the transaction and a quick leavetaking. But there was no sense offending Claymore at this point. He had, after all, agreed to her request. A few more minutes and the uncomfortable encounter would be over. With an accepting inclination of her head, she took a seat on the edge of one of the massive chairs.

Claymore crossed to a large breakfront, where he unstopped a crystal decanter and held it up for her to view. "With your permission?" he said.

Callie knew that anything but an affirming nod would be rude.

"Would you care to join me?" Claymore asked, as he poured the burgundy liquid into a sparking goblet. But before Callie could answer, he continued. "Ah, but I forget. You don't care for spirits, do you?"

"No," Callie said, watching Claymore saunter over to a matching chair and sink into it.

"Ah," Claymore said with a sign of pleasure as he sipped the wine. "Delightful bouquet." He crossed his legs, ankle to knee, and settled his big frame more comfortably. Waving his glass expansively, he asked, "How do you like the suite?"

"It's lovely," Callie answered truthfully, resisting the temptation to squirm with impatience.

"Did you notice the ladies' parlor and the dining room as we crossed the lobby? Exquisitely appointed, and the food is excellent."

"I'm sure it is."

His amber eyes pinned Callie as securely as a mounted butterfly. "You know, Miss Nolan, something just this moment occurred to me. I keep this suite for the convenience of visiting businessmen, but I'm not expecting anyone for several months. I feel a real responsibility concerning the circumstances in which you find yourself. After all, it was my bidding that brought you to Arizona."

"Yes?" Callie responded when he hesitated, wondering where the conversation could possibly be heading.

"I hate to think of you staying in that cramped boarding house when these spacious accommodations are sitting here empty. It would go a long way to salving my conscience if you'd make use of the suite until we can settle our little situation."

Callie's mouth dropped open. "But . . . but I thought you were going to settle the matter now."

Owen Claymore gave a sad shake of his massive head. "Would that I could, my dear." He uncrossed his legs and edged forward in the chair, his elbows on his knees as he cradled the fragile wine-filled goblet between his fingers. "Let me explain. Business expenses have been astonishingly high lately.

I'm afraid I've sunk all my ready cash into current projects. Oh, not that I don't have a small sum that I can advance you at this time."

Apprehension began to ribbon through Callie. "Just exactly what do you mean, Mr. Claymore?"

"Please be assured, Miss Nolan, I have only your best interests at heart. I'm simply suggesting that you avail yourself of the comforts and services of the hotel until I can obtain the funds to pay off your contract."

"But I couldn't possibly—"

"Oh, dear." Claymore's brow wrinkled in consternation. "Perhaps I didn't make myself clear. Are you worrying that the expenses accrued during your stay will be your responsibility? Now, you put those foolish worries aside, my dear. Let me assure you that I will take care of all your expenses. You need not lift a finger. The staff of the hotel is excellent. You'll be well cared for. And, in the meantime, I will of course furnish you with a reasonable amount of funds to cover any needs not furnished by the hotel."

Flabbergasted, Callie could only stare in shock as Claymore rose from the chair and hurried across the room to unlock the top drawer of the sideboard. His broad back blocked Callie's view, but when he returned to her side he had a small bundle of bills in his hand.

Claymore placed the bills in Callie's hands and she gawked first at the cash and then up at Claymore. Her fingers ruffled the edges of the bills and she realized that what he had handed her amounted to approximately one-tenth of what he owed her. Her mouth thinned with indignation.

"You can't be serious—" she began.

"But of course I'm serious," Claymore intoned, his voice oozing earnestness. "Haven't I given you my word that I'll take care of everything? The suite is all yours, for as long as you like."

Anger surged. Deep, dark, utterly righteous anger. Clutching the bills in her hand, Callie lurched to her feet.

"You misjudge me, sir."

Claymore spread his hands. "But, Miss Nolan—"

"I don't want to hear any more."

Her spine rigid, her chin titled at an angle that bespoke no further discussion of the subject, Callie stormed to the door and jerked it open. Her hand on the handle, she turned and gave her former employer a scathing look.

"When you have the balance of what you owe me, you may send it to Miss Winslow's boardinghouse. I expect it to arrive expediently."

The door slammed shut.

CHAPTER SIXTEEN

"Pardon me, ma'am, but could you tell me if I'm anywhere near the Winslow boardinghouse?"

The deep, rumbling voice brought Callie up short. She looked up in surprise to find that she'd traversed almost the entire distance back to Henrietta's and had come very close to running smack into the man who had just spoken to her. Her anger at Claymore had been so intense that she'd scarcely been aware of her furious march through town and up the rutted road leading to the gray frame house.

Striving to gather her wits about her, Callie shaded her eyes against the blaze of the sun and gazed upward . . . and upward . . . at the largest black man she'd ever seen.

Almost immediately Callie's initial apprehension faded away. For all his bulk, there was an unmistakable gentleness to the man's demeanor.

"Begging your pardon, ma'am. I didn't mean to frighten you," he said in reaction to the scowl on Callie's face.

He carefully backed away until he was up against the sideboard of an old wagon. The woman atop the wagon's plank seat reached out a slender hand and laid it reassuringly upon the man's shoulder. The battered hat clutched against his huge chest began a slow, nervous rotation in his ham-sized fists.

Realizing that the man thought her anger was directed at him, Callie quickly offered a conciliatory smile. From the looks of the wagon and the couple's travel-rumpled clothes, she assumed they'd been on the trail for quite some time.

"I'm sorry," she said contritely. "My mind was on something else. Can I help you?"

"Yes, ma'am," the man answered with a polite bob of his woolly head. "We're looking for the Winslow boardinghouse. I was hoping you might give me directions."

"Next house up the hill," Callie informed him, surmising from the well-bred tone of the man's voice and the careful enunciation of his words that he'd received far more education than most black men of the day. "This is quite a coincidence; I was headed there myself."

"Is that a fact, ma'am?" His pearly white teeth gleamed against the deep chocolate of the man's face. He cast a quick glance up at his lady. "Maybe our luck's about to change, sugar."

Callie took her first good look at the woman, and experienced a moment of awe at what she saw. The lady atop the wagon was the most beautiful black woman Callie had ever seen.

Even sitting down, it was obvious she was tall and willow-slim. There was a grace and dignity to her carriage that Callie had witnessed in few women of any color. She wore her rich brown tresses plaited and pinned atop her head like a crown, and her flawless skin was the rich creamy color of café au lait.

Pure love shone in the woman's dark slanted eyes as she gazed at the big man beside the wagon. Her lips turned up in an answering smile to the man's comment. Finally, she turned her attention back to Callie.

"Perhaps you know the gentleman we're looking for," she said. "A Mr. Powers? Logan Powers? It's very important that we talk with him."

Callie's jaw dropped in surprise. "Logan? You're looking for Logan?"

"Yes, ma'am." The man's head bobbed again and his eyes grew hopeful. "I'm Hezekiah Kane and this is my wife, Jasmine."

"My, oh, my," Callie said softly, remembering Logan's fevered mumblings. Her hands on her hips, she swung her head from side to side in bemusement. "I know this sounds strange, but I feel like I already know the two of you."

The couple exchanged a perplexed look.

Callie gave a dismissing flip of her hand. "Oh, never mind that for now. Just follow me. Something tells me Logan's going to be more than pleased to see you."

* * *

Callie's pronouncement proved to be a serious understatement. From her place just inside the door to Logan's room, she watched the joyous greeting of the three old friends, positive that she'd never seen such exuberant hugging and kissing and chattering in all her life.

"Callie," Logan called when the revelry had died down a fraction. "Callie, come on over here, girl. And hurry."

Obediently, Callie went to his side, worrying that Logan's boisterous behavior at Hezekiah and Jasmine's arrival had broken something loose again.

"Is something wrong?" she queried, concern evident in her voice. "Does your shoulder hurt?"

"Good Lord, no." Logan dismissed the thought with a wry grin. He quickly claimed her hand and drew her down to sit beside him on the bed. "I want you to meet my friends. Hezekiah, Jasmine, this little lady is Callie Nolan, the finest and most beautiful nurse a man could ever wish for. Callie, meet two of my dearest friends. Hezekiah and I served in the Army together."

Beaming from ear to ear, Logan glanced from Callie to his friends and back again. He missed the sudden knowing look that Jasmine and Hezekiah exchanged.

Callie missed it, too. Rolling her eyes heavenward, she gave an amused shake of her head. "Logan, I believe that fall from your horse did some damage after all. Have you forgotten? We've already met. *I'm* the one who brought them in."

"Oh." A sheepish look stole over Logan's face.

"So you did." He chuckled at his own foolishness. "Well, all I can say is, this is better than any medicine ol' Doc Pritchert could have prescribed. I can't tell you how glad I am to see the two of you."

Hezekiah's smile was enormous. "We feel the same way."

"Well, don't just stand there. Sit down and get comfortable," Logan instructed. "Hezekiah, pull that rocker up for Jasmine. You can sit here for the time being." Logan patted the bed as he scooted his legs to one side of the mattress.

Hezekiah positioned the rocking chair beside the bed. With casual grace, Jasmine settled herself in its seat. As soon as he was sure his wife was comfortable, Hezekiah perched on the corner of the bed. It sagged significantly under the big black man's weight.

"Excuse all this," Logan said, waving his hand at the bed. "I'd entertain you in the parlor but I've got strict orders from Henrietta. She says I have to rest for a little while since I'm going downstairs for supper."

"Don't worry about such nonsense, Logan," Hezekiah chided. His eyes turned dark and broody as he scrutinized the bandage on Logan's shoulder. "Say, what happened? Did you do that when you fell off your horse? I thought the Army taught you better horsemanship than that, or were you trying to tame a bad bronc?"

Logan laughed. "Don't you worry, I can still hold my own on a horse. I had a little help falling off this time. A bullet through the shoulder plays hell with your balance."

"A bullet!" Jasmine gasped, her gaze flying to her husband's face and then back to Logan's. "You mean someone shot you? Do you know who?"

"Nah. I'm sure it was just a crazy accident. Probably some jackass hunter thinking he'd heard a deer," Logan assured them. "I don't remember anything except riding out on an errand for Claymore. Next thing I knew, I woke up here. But let's not discuss that now. Lord, we have more important things to do like catch up on what's been happening the last few months."

Callie's voice interrupted his musings. "There's another chair in my room, Logan. Why don't I bring it in here for Hezekiah? It would be much more comfortable."

"Good idea. Thanks Callie." He waited for her to rise, his expression of expectation turning decidedly sheepish when he realized he was still holding tight to her hand. Logan gave a muffled cough and quickly released his grip.

Her attention momentarily yanked away from the shocking news of her friend's accident, Jasmine watched the episode with keen interest. Despite Logan's sudden preoccupation with rearranging the bed covers, his gaze kept returning to Callie as she crossed the room.

Well, well, Jasmine thought with surprise and pleasure. The impossible had happened. The high and mighty Logan Powers had finally fallen. Of that, she had no doubt. What she didn't know was whether he was aware of it yet.

"Can I help, Miss Nolan?" Hezekiah called after Callie as she neared the door.

"Callie, please," she called back brightly, earning a grateful smile from Logan. "And no thank you; just stay here and continue your visit with Logan. I'll be back shortly."

With that, she was gone.

Jasmine pushed the tip of her toe against the floor and the rocker began to move. "Have you known the lady long, Logan?"

"What?" Logan responded, dragging his eyes from the now vacant doorway. "Oh, you mean Callie?" He shrugged with forced indifference. "A couple of months, I guess. She was governess for the Claymores' children. The same man I've been working for."

Two lines formed between Hezekiah's bushy brows. "Working for? I thought you came to Bisbee to work your claim?"

"You're right. I did. But something came up. It's a complicated story."

Callie's arrival with the ladder-back chair put a halt to Logan's explanation. She handed Hezekiah the chair and stopped by the iron bedstead's high footrail.

"I'll leave you three alone for now. I need to change clothes, and I told Henrietta I'd be down to help in the kitchen. Oh, by the way," Callie said, turning to Hezekiah and Jasmine, "Henrietta insists that you two stay here at the boardinghouse."

Callie's comment about changing clothes drew

227

Logan's attention to her attire. For the first time, he noticed she was wearing the same blue serge traveling suit she'd worn the day he picked her up at the train station.

Sudden apprehension flared within him. Obviously she'd been out. But where had she gone?

Damn! Logan swore silently. What could he have been thinking of? Sure, he had enjoyed seeing Della. Wouldn't anyone be glad to see an old friend? Wouldn't any man enjoy the company and attention of such a beautiful woman? But, truth be told, Logan had to admit that the best thing about Della's visit had been the satisfaction of seeing Callie's reaction. Lord, how smug he'd felt, assuming her sudden frosty attitude had been due to a healthy dose of jealousy.

Logan squirmed in discomfort at his own stupidity. He knew he'd let Della stay too long. While he was feeding his ego, Callie had been free. He'd blithely assumed she was downstairs with Henrietta. And when she'd didn't come to his room after Della left, he'd smugly decided she must be pouting. He'd never considered that Callie might have used the time he spent with Della in a way that made his blood turn cold when he thought about it.

Dear heaven, had she been to see Claymore? And worse, much worse, had Claymore given her the money?

The alarming thought and all its portents whirled like a dervish in Logan's head. He was almost grateful when Hezekiah's continued protestations once again snared his attention.

"Please tell Mrs. Winslow thank you kindly, but we don't want to put anyone out."

"Hezekiah," Logan interrupted, his voice so gruff that his friend eyed him with surprise. "Will you quit worrying? Henrietta's a woman with a mind of her own. She wouldn't offer if she didn't mean it."

Hezekiah exchanged a quick glance with his wife. Jasmine nodded ever so slightly.

"Well, all right," Hezekiah relented. "If you're sure."

"I'm sure."

"Good," Callie said with a smile. "I'll tell Henrietta it's all settled."

Once again, Logan's eyes followed Callie as she left the room, only this time there was obvious worry mixed with the hunger. With great reluctance, Jasmine squelched her avid curiosity about Logan and Callie's relationship. She'd make time for that later. There were more important things to discuss now.

"I think you'd better tell him, Hezekiah," Jasmine said as soon as the three of them were alone again.

"Tell me?" Logan asked with a frown. "Tell me what? Is something wrong?"

"I'm afraid so. Jennings escaped."

Logan's jaw dropped in shock. "He *what?*"

"Escaped," Hezekiah repeated. "About two months ago. He's been free as a bird ever since."

"Dammit, how'd he manage to get out of a

federal prison?"

"Killed a guard, stole a horse, and disappeared. No one's seen him since."

Logan lurched bolt upright in bed, his eyes wide with sudden fear. "Oh, my Lord! Sabra! And Hawk! You don't think he's headed to Arkansas, do you? You don't think he's going to try to carry out that crazy threat he made at the trial? Good God, Hezekiah, we've got to do something!"

"Now just calm down and think a minute, Logan. Didn't you get a letter from Sabra and Hawk about their trip to Europe?"

"That's right," Logan rasped, sagging back against his pillows like a rag doll. "I'd forgotten. Thank God. It'll be months before they're back. Surely they'll catch that bastard before then."

"Logan, it's not Hawk and Sabra I'm worried about," Jasmine interrupted. "It's you and Hezekiah. A couple of weeks ago, he was almost the victim of the same type of accident you've had."

Logan's head snapped upward at Jasmine's words. "What? You mean, you think—"

"Yes, I do," she stated emphatically. "Jennings threatened all three of you. And look what's happened. Jennings is loose. He could find out easy enough that you two are still here in Arizona. And now, these two accidents, so much alike. That's too much for a mere coincidence, as far as I'm concerned."

"Maybe—"

"Don't you 'maybe' me, Logan Powers!" Jasmine scolded. "We all know what I'm saying is true.

230

Hezekiah was lucky. The bullet missed. Another inch or two and he could have wound up just like you. And look at you! How many inches would it have taken for you to be a dead man? We've got a problem here, and I want to know what you two are going to do about it?"

Logan struggled with the implications of what Jasmine had said. He speared Hezekiah with a worried look. "I don't guess you got a look at who fired at you, did you?"

"Nope," Hezekiah answered. "And the sheriff scoured the countryside afterward. He didn't find a thing."

Logan raked long, lean fingers through taffy curls. "Well," he said with a sign of resignation, "what do you think we ought to do?"

"I think we ought to hightail it out of here as soon as you're up to traveling," Jasmine declared. "You and Hezekiah risked your lives enough when you were in the Army. Let the law do their job. They'll find Jennings eventually. When he's locked up safe and sound again, you can always come back."

"Nope," Hezekiah said, his close-cropped head swinging back and forth in a slow arc. "I'm not running like a coward. I agreed to come here and warn Logan. But that's as far as I go."

Jasmine's head jerked toward her husband and her heart skipped a little beat when she saw the determination in his eyes. She knew him to be gentle and kind to a fault, an ebony giant with the heart of a lamb. But she also knew that when

Hezekiah really set his mind to something, there was no changing it.

"He's right, Jasmine," Logan said. "You can't let scum like Jennings put you on the run. Besides, I couldn't leave now anyway. I've got friends here who are in a passel of trouble themselves. Several of them have already died because of one unscrupulous man. I gave my word to help them. What kind of man would I be if I turned tail and ran when they're fighting for their very lives?"

Jasmine sighed. She knew when she was beaten.

CHAPTER SEVENTEEN

"I want supper to be really special," Henrietta said. "Even though Logan assured Hezekiah and Jasmine that they're welcome, I'm afraid they feel a bit uncomfortable being here."

Callie bent and peeked into the stove to check a pan of biscuits. The tops were just beginning to turn golden brown and their warm, yeasty smell permeated the kitchen. "It's kind of you to welcome them the way you have. Most people wouldn't bother to be so gracious to people of color."

Up to her wrists in flour, Henrietta grimaced. "Well, I'm not 'most people.' I don't tolerate prejudice of any kind in my house. The world is too small and life is far too short. It's difficult enough without judging people by such nonsense." She gave Callie a quick grin. "Oh, by the way, I know Logan is very pleased that you've taken to his friends so readily."

Callie blushed. She couldn't help but be glad that she'd done something to please Logan, but he'd had little to do with her response to Hezekiah and Jasmine. They appeared to be exceedingly nice people, and as far as Callie was concerned, that's all that mattered.

"There," Henrietta said, dusting her hands off. "That should be enough. If you'll pop this last pan of biscuits in when that one comes out, I'll get the boys ready for bed."

"Of course."

"Heavens, weren't we lucky?" Henrietta continued happily. "Ben and Dexter couldn't have picked a better time to go up to Tucson for a visit. It worked out perfectly. Now we have an empty room for the Kanes. And, since I've already fed the boys, tonight we're going to have something I seldom get to enjoy—a blissfully quiet, all adult meal shared among friends."

The two women exchanged happy smiles.

While Henrietta oversaw Samuel and Joshua's nightly ablutions, Callie put the finishing touches on the table and kept a close watch on the pots and pans atop the stove. A festive bouquet of wildflowers and the warm glow of fat white candles ensconced in matching brass candlesticks—a long-ago gift on Henrietta's wedding day—added the perfect touch to Henrietta's rather humble crockery and cutlery.

Logan escorted his friends into the dining room just as Henrietta and Callie carried the last bowls of food to the table. Callie's heart skipped a little double beat of pleasure when she saw the quick flare of appreciation in Logan's eyes.

The evening was a complete success. Hezekiah lived up to all the stories Logan had related regarding his friend's prodigious appetite. Callie was pleased to note that Logan himself did ample justice to the meal. Another sign of how close to being healed he was.

Two trains of thought warred within Callie at her discernment. She wanted him well again. Well and whole and healthy. But she knew without a doubt that each step toward that goal widened the gap between them.

She thought of those first days after Logan had been brought in, and the nights when she'd sat by his side through the long, dark hours. Those days and nights had been frightening at times, and unbelievably tiring, but somehow utterly wonderful. Those had been the times when she'd allowed herself a small moment of fantasy, when she had pretended, if only for a little while, that he did belong to her.

She had poured a lifetime of love and caring and commitment into those hours. Logan would never know the true meaning of the gentle words she'd whispered to him as he struggled in delirium's fevered clutches. That if he had listened with his heart, things like "hush, hush, my dear, it's all right" and "no more bad dreams, Logan. They're gone. I'm right beside you and they can't come back as long as I'm here to watch over you," those utterances said "I love you" as surely as if the words themselves had been spoken aloud.

No, he'd never know. And no matter how much

it hurt to realize that, Callie knew it was for the best.

Maybe Henrietta was right. Maybe Logan did care for her just a little. But Callie also knew that, once she was gone, it wouldn't take long for her memory to fade from his mind.

There were a dozen other women waiting to take whatever small place she might have had in his heart. Eventually she'd just be "that little governess from Boston . . . what was her name?" and he'd go on with his rowdy, reckless, devil-may-care life, charming the ladies with his teasing laugh and dancing eyes, leaving a trail of broken hearts behind him as he sailed blithely through life.

Deep inside Callie, there was a secret relief that Owen Claymore hadn't given her the balance of her money that morning. For, if he had, she'd have no more excuses to stay in Bisbee. And she desperately wanted just a few more days, just a few more memories to take home with her, because memories were all she'd ever have.

So, she'd donned one of her prettiest dresses and arranged her hair the way she knew Logan liked it. Then she'd labored side by side with Henrietta to prepare the finest meal possible. She was determined to live to the fullest every moment, every second of the few days she had left with Logan.

She would soak up all the things that made Logan who and what he was. The tousled dark gold curls that forever spilled onto his broad forehead. The mischievous sparkle of his deep brown eyes. The chiseled line of his jaw, and how the stubble of his beard was red-gold rather than dark like her father's. The characteristic little shrug of his massive shoulders accompanied by the quick flash of his devilish smile. The rumble of his deep, delighted laughter—a sound that could set her stomach aquiver.

But most of all, she'd remember his kiss. The unexpected softness of his lips. The way his mouth on hers had sent heated shivers dancing through her blood. The shock and ensuing pleasure of his velvet-textured tongue dueling with her own.

And the unbelievable, utter rightness of being in his arms.

By the time supper was over and the table had been cleared, darkness had descended. Jasmine and Henrietta were putting the finishing touches to the kitchen, and Callie had been elected to take a fresh pot of coffee and clean cups to the parlor.

As she walked slowly down the hall, carefully balancing the heavy weight of the tray she was carrying, she could hear the men talking.

"You do understand what I was saying about the situation here, don't you?" Logan was saying. "Somebody's got to do something about the independent miners. I agreed to do a job, and I'm going to follow through with it just as soon as this damn shoulder is healed."

"Sure, I understand. And you know you can count on me to do what I can to help you. Just don't say anything to Jasmine. You know how she gets if she thinks I'm getting into anything sticky."

Logan chuckled low. "Why she ever set her heart on a big galoot like you, I'll never know. Good thing you got out of the Army right after you two married. With her peaceful nature, I don't think she'd ever have been happy as a soldier's wife."

"Yeah, I think you're right. All Jasmine's ever wanted is a little house of our own and a few acres to farm."

"Maybe this won't be a wasted trip after all," Logan interrupted.

"What do you mean?"

"You haven't forgotten the silver, have you?"

"What about it?"

"Well, I think there's going to be plenty of it. No reason why you can't go in as a partner with me on this deal. Chances are you can come out with enough money to give Jasmine what she wants and still have a nice little nest egg. What do you say?"

"Sounds good to me."

"Then it's a deal, partner," Logan said.

Callie had almost reached the entrance to the parlor when she heard footsteps in the hall. A quick glance over her shoulder confirmed that Henrietta and Jasmine were only a few paces behind her. By the time she'd eased the half-closed door open with her shoulder, the two women had caught up with her.

Logan and Hezekiah rose as the three ladies entered the parlor. There were several busy moments while the coffee was being poured and served, and then everyone settle down. In the ensuing revelry of the evening, the nebulous questions that had started to form in Callie's mind as she accidentally eavesdropped on Logan and Hezekiah's conversation were forgotten.

Eventually the women settled on the sofa, a large album of photographs spread across their laps. Callie knew few of the people in the pictures but she found the backgrounds fascinating. She could pick out some of Bisbee's landmarks and she was amazed how much the boom town had grown in the past few years.

"Oh, look!" Jasmine said in surprise as another page was flipped. "A bear!" She squinted at the faded photo. "But what's it doing?"

Henrietta grinned. "Drinking beer."

Jasmine and Callie dissolved into giggles at the thought of such a thing.

"Say, I want to see that," Logan exclaimed, coming over to take a look at the album. "I've heard tales about Joe Mulheim's bear for years. I always wondered if the stories were true."

"Oh, they're true, all right," Henrietta declared. "Joe got it when it was just a cub and it grew up in his saloon. The bear took a real liking to Joe's special brew, but that fondness proved to be his downfall. Joe used to chain him to a tree at night. He'd climb up and settle in the crotch of the tree limbs to sleep. I guess he had a bit too much one night, because he fell out of his tree and hanged himself."

"Oh, the poor thing!" Callie exclaimed.

Henrietta shook her head sadly. "Those crazy

miners mourned that old bear like he was one of them." She turned another page. "Now, take a look at this one. There's a story here, too."

And so the evening progressed.

The next ten days were some of the happiest of Callie's life. Logan seemed to feel stronger by the hour. He no longer required afternoon naps and he began to take an occasional ride with Hezekiah.

At first the men were only gone an hour or so, but as Logan's strength returned, they started to roam farther afield, disappearing into the wilderness that sloped away behind Henrietta's house. Shortly thereafter they began to make trips to town, returning with purchases that were always carted away on the next trip up the mountain. Jasmine knew they were stocking Logan's mine so Hezekiah could start working it; Callie and Henrietta simply accepted the explanation that Hezekiah had a hankering to do some prospecting on his own. Claymore could hardly complain if Hezekiah decided to do a little mining. As long as Logan's name wasn't connected to the undertaking, he should be able to complete the job George hired him to do.

The patterns set that first evening prevailed. Jasmine now helped Callie and Henrietta in the kitchen, and the men even offered an occasional hand at clearing the table and cleaning up. The hours after supper were spent in pleasant companionship and whatever activities might take their fancy.

Henrietta dug an old stereoscope out of the closet and they spent one evening viewing its accompanying box of photographs, intrigued at how the optical instrument could bring fuzzy pictures into sharp focus.

Another night, Logan prevailed upon the ladies to let him teach them the finer points of poker. Once Callie overcame her initial feelings of wickedness for playing a game which involved gambling, she surprised them all by excelling in the newly learned skill. Before the night was over, she had won almost as many matchsticks as Logan and Hezekiah.

Even the weather cooperated. The warm, balmy days lured Joshua and Samuel outside from sunup to sundown and sent the thoroughly worn-out boys to an early bed each night.

The pleasant days also brought several bittersweet visits from the Claymore children.

Callie felt a tug at her heartstrings each time the children, in search of playmates, appeared at Henrietta's front door. She was overjoyed to see them, but each subsequent departure left her feeling moody and helpless. The obviousness of Consuela's haphazard attention to the children was a continual source of irritation to her. She had no way of knowing whether the little Mexican maid had given them permission to come or if they had wandered off on their own, but either way they weren't receiving the supervision Callie thought they should.

It touched her heart to see that the boys hadn't

forgotten all her lessons in cleanliness. And Betsy had learned a few more letters of her alphabet, so they were getting lessons of some sort. For that, Callie was grateful.

She tried to ignore the multitude of small things that told her the children weren't getting the same careful supervision she'd given them. One time there was a rip in Richard's trousers, and all too often Thomas's socks didn't match. Most days Betsy's pinafore needed a good pressing. And from the lopsided condition of the bows in the little girl's hair, Callie suspected Richard was more responsible for their placement than their current nursemaid.

Knowing there was nothing, absolutely nothing, she could do about the situation, Callie did her best to push the worrisome thoughts to the back of her mind and simply let herself enjoy the pure pleasure of seeing the children again. But each time they left to return home, there was a bigger lump of tears at the back of her throat.

"Those kids are sure crazy about you and Logan," Jasmine remarked to Callie one day after the children had finished the milk and cookies Henrietta always provided and had gone outside to play with Joshua and Samuel. "It's obvious that they miss you a lot."

A tremulous smile tipped Callie's mouth. "I miss them, too."

"Looks like Logan feels the same way," Jasmine commented as she peered out the window. The children were gathered around Logan, waiting to be lifted one at a time and swung round and round. Giggles and shrieks of delight filled the air.

Callie stopped clearing the table long enough to take a look. "Oh, dear," she said, worry filling her eyes. "I hope he isn't overdoing it."

"I think that shoulder's well enough by now," Henrietta assured her. "I doubt Logan would be dumb enough to do anything to hurt it again."

Callie sighed. "I suppose so." She turned away from the window and went back to her cleaning.

Jasmine continued her perusal. "He's sure got a way with those kids," she remarked with an amused shake of her regal head.

"Not just the Claymore children—*any* children," Henrietta said. "He works the same kind of magic on my boys."

"You're right," Jasmine said. "He was the same way with the kids at Fort Huachuca. It didn't matter if they were the children of the officers or the Indian scouts, Logan always managed to find time to show interest in their small treasures, to praise them for their accomplishments, or simply to listen to what they had to say. And more often than not, he had a pocketful of penny candy to distribute among them. Believe me, he was a great favorite among the fort's children."

A small frown puckered Henrietta's forehead. "You'd think, as fond as he is of children, that he would have married long ago and had a whole houseful. I can't understand it."

The mug Callie had been washing slipped from her hands. It hit the washbasin with a thump and then fell to the floor.

"Oh, dear!" Callie exclaimed as she gazed at the shattered pottery. "How clumsy of me. Just look at this mess. I'm so sorry, Henrietta."

"Oh, pooh!" Henrietta said. "It was just an old mug. I don't want to hear another word about it. I'll get the broom and we'll have it cleaned up in no time."

Callie bent to pick up the bigger pieces while Henrietta went after the boom.

Jasmine's gaze swung from Callie to Logan and back again as she pondered what Henrietta had been saying before Callie's accident. Jasmine had wondered the same thing about Logan — until Hezekiah confided something about Logan's past.

That first afternoon, when she'd watched the way Callie and Logan looked at each other, she had hoped he'd finally been able to put those old memories behind him. But she'd soon realized that wasn't the case. Things weren't right between Callie and Logan. Not by a long shot. And Jasmine couldn't figure out why.

There was no doubt in Jasmine's mind that, for the first time in Logan's life, he truly cared about someone. His actions and the look in his eyes bespoke the depth of his feelings, so why hadn't he declared those feelings to Callie? Was he still so afraid of loving that he was unable to admit how he felt even to himself?

Jasmine was equally sure that Callie cared just as much for Logan. No woman looked at a man like that if she didn't love him with all her heart.

So why was Callie still planning to return to Boston? And why hadn't Logan told her he didn't want her to go? The man would be a fool, a pure fool, to let Callie slip away. That kind of love didn't come around but once in a lifetime.

Her natural matchmaking instincts aquiver, Jasmine continued to ponder the confusing situation while Callie and Henrietta disposed of the broken mug.

Men! Jasmine thought in disgust. They could be so darn stubborn. Why did they have to complicate something as simple as falling in love? Why couldn't they be smart enough to recognize what was best for them instead of running away like scared little boys?

But, frustrating as it was, it looked as though Logan wasn't seeing any plainer than Hezekiah had before they married. If she hadn't had the help of Logan and his sister, Jasmine knew she might still be waiting for Hezekiah to make his first move. Thank heavens for friends.

Friends. Sudden inspiration blossomed.

Because he was her friend, Logan had provided his unsolicited help when she needed it. Well, she was Logan's friend, wasn't she? Didn't she have the right—no, the obligation—to help him if she could? Perhaps a private talk with Logan would help push him in the right direction. It was worth a try.

Now all she needed was the opportunity.

CHAPTER EIGHTEEN

"Dammit! Nothing's gone right lately. Not one damn thing." Owen Claymore stopped his furious pacing and glared at the man sprawled casually in one of the deep leather chairs in front of the desk. A spot on the lapel of his coat marred Claymore's usually immaculate appearance, and his tie was more than a little askew. "I want something done about it. Now. You guaranteed you could deliver, and that's exactly what I expect."

The man known as Lee Jenkins slowly crossed one long denim-clad leg over the other and took a sip from the crystal tumbler in his hand. "Calm down, Boss. I've got everything under control."

Claymore snorted in disgust. "Control, my ass! If you're so much in control, why are Jud Kirchman and Dennis Miller still working their mines? What happened to all the big boasts about scaring them so bad they'd be willing to sell out for a song?"

Sitting low on his spine, Jenkins balanced the drink against his flat stomach and watched the syncopated swing of his booted foot with mild interest. "Don't worry, they will. You just have to have patience. I've got a little surprise planned for them in the next few days. After that, I don't think they'll be interested in hanging around anymore."

Owen stormed to the chair behind the massive desk and dropped into it. "They damn well better not," he muttered. Once again he pinned Jenkins with a piercing scowl. "I'm paying you top dollar to see that things are handled the way I want. Time is running out. I don't like all these delays. And I damn sure don't like failures!"

Sparks flared in Jenkins's dark eyes, and his knuckles grew white as his fingers tightened around the delicate crystal glass. Taking a deep breath, he forced his anger down and deliberately relaxed his stranglehold on the tumbler.

Jenkins reminded himself there's be plenty of time to deal with Claymore later—after he'd served his purpose. And, besides, Claymore was right. He was paying top dollar, and Jenkins had every intention of padding his stash as much as possible while he had the opportunity.

No more scrimping and running and hiding for Lee Jenkins. No sirree. As soon as he settled some old scores, he was hightailing it up to Canada to live the good life.

"I suppose you're referring to Powers," Jenkins said when he was finally sure no anger would show in his voice.

"Hell, yes, I'm talking about Powers!" Claymore exploded.

One brow quirked high as Jenkins eyed his boss. He was beginning to feel like a man perched atop a high wire. The cool-headed businessman who'd hired him was fast becoming unstable. It was getting to be a real challenge to weather the man's increasingly frequent tirades and unreasonable expectations, but Jenkins knew he had no choice. He was almost ready to put into action the nebulous plan that had been brewing in his head, and Claymore would play a key role.

Meanwhile Jenkins was obliged to continue playing his own role, part of which was to keep Claymore believing that his business ambitions were coming to fruition. But all the while, Jenkins would be gently fueling the flames of anger which would allow him to fulfill his own goals.

"Don't worry about Powers," Jenkins said. "He'll be taken care of. I give you my word. And Boss, you might think about holding it down a little bit. If that prissy little clerk of yours comes back early, he'll be able to hear every word you're saying."

"Damn," Claymore said softly, slumping into the depths of his big, padded chair. "Sorry, Jenkins, it's just that the last few weeks have been pure hell. Edith's been acting so damn peculiar lately.

248

It's got to the point I don't even like to go home anymore. She just sits there and looks at me with those wounded cow eyes and I don't have the slightest idea what's going on in that head of hers." Claymore ran a shaky hand through his hair. "And, thanks to Edith's stupid interference, the kids are running wild. Consuela is worthless when it comes to watching them."

Lee Jenkins took another sip of his drink. "Can't you hire another governess or offer that Nolan girl more money so she'll come back?"

A muscle ticked in Claymore's clenched jaw. "Hell! I don't want to hear Callie Nolan's name. She's what got Edith all riled up in the first place."

"Ah-ha," Jenkins said, a wicked grin belying the innocent boyishness of his face. "The wife catch you two fooling around?"

"Of course not!" Claymore retorted angrily. "What makes you think that?"

Jenkins shrugged his broad shoulders. "Didn't you entertain the lady in your private suite at the hotel one afternoon?"

"Believe me, there wasn't a damn thing entertaining about that afternoon."

Claymore's angry words confirmed Jenkins's suspicions. "What's the matter? Didn't the lady want to play?"

Claymore's amber eyes snapped upward as his mouth thinned into a hard line. "No, the lady didn't want to play. She wasn't even interested in staying in the suite. Self-righteous little bitch. If she'd played her cards right, she could have had anything she wanted and I'd have eventually sent her back to Boston in style."

"That's too bad, Boss."

Claymore's eyes darkened with irritation. "You can save your condolences, Jenkins. I don't need them. There are plenty of other women in this town."

"Aw, come on, Boss, don't get all pissed off," Jenkins said in a placating tone. He slid upward in the chair, then leaned forward and balanced his elbows on his knees, his face a study in sincere concern. "I just thought I might be able to help you out. I've known all along that you had a special yen for the little lady. Can't say I blame you either. She's a real looker. And I always said, if a man has an itch, he ought to be able to scratch it."

"Yes. Well . . ." Claymore cleared his throat to cover his discomfort. "No sense dwelling on that now. I might have considered such a . . . a meeting of the minds once upon a time, but not now. Believe me, Callie Nolan isn't interested in such activities."

Jenkins feigned shock. "Don't tell me you're going to back off and let Logan Powers have that little morsel all to himself?"

"Just what are you implying?" Claymore asked, his eyes narrowing dangerously.

Jenkins spread his hands in a gesture of innocence. "Why I figured you already knew." He slid back to his original position in the chair, the perfect picture of total nonchalance. "Well, all right," he said, recrossing his long legs. "If that's the way you want it."

"Quit talking in riddles, Jenkins," Claymore snapped. "Just what exactly is it that you thought I already knew?"

"About Callie Nolan and Logan Powers."

Claymore's contemptuous snort interrupted Jenkins. "Don't be ridiculous. The lady's got ice water in her veins. If she wouldn't lift her skirts for me, I hardly believe some dirt poor nobody like Powers is going to win her over."

"If you say so," Jenkins said with a shrug. "But that's sure not what it looks like to me."

"Listen, Jenkins, I've heard about all of this nonsense I care to today. If you have something worth saying, then say it. Otherwise take your stupid suppositions out of here and take care of Kirchman and Miller like you were hired to do."

"Sorry, Boss. My mistake. I guess I'd better fill you in on what's been happening the last few weeks."

"I'd say that might be a wise move," Claymore said. He replenished his glass with a hefty dollop of whiskey, purposely ignoring his guest's almost empty tumbler.

"Well, it's like this," Jenkins continued. "I've been thinkin' about you catching Powers in your study and all, and I decided it might be wise to

251

find out exactly what he was up to before I put the fellow out of his misery once and for all, if you know what I mean?"

"I know that was what you were supposed to do in the first place," Claymore replied in a frosty voice.

Jenkins ignored the stinging comment. "Anyway, I had this kinda hunch. So I've been keeping an eye on that boardinghouse pretty regular the last couple of weeks. I've seen some interesting things, and one of them has to do with Powers and that little ex-governess of yours."

"Will you get to the point?"

"Sure, Boss. What I've been trying to say is I'm almost dead positive those two have got a hot thing going."

The tick in Claymore's jaw beat double-time. "Go on."

"It didn't take any effort at all to find out she's the one who nursed him after his . . . uh . . . little accident."

"So?"

"Oh, there's more," Jenkins assured. "I found a real good look-out place. I can see both of the back bedrooms with no problem. Didn't take long to put two and two together when there's seldom a light in one of the rooms. And let me tell you, an oil lamp throws a right pretty silhouette on the curtains Miss Winslow has up in those rooms. Would it surprise you to learn that Callie Nolan has spent many a night in Powers's room?"

"Good Lord, Jenkins," Claymore retorted. "The man had a gunshot wound. It's not likely that he was able to take advantage of the . . . uh . . . situation in that kind of shape."

Jenkins nodded. "You're absolutely right. But . . ." He cocked his head to one side. "Powers has recovered quite nicely from that bullet wound. He's been getting around just fine lately, even gone back to riding again. And don't forget all those weeks when they were both living at your house. Who knows what was going on then?" Jenkins left the titillating thought shimmering in midsentence.

"I see," Claymore said testily. Lee Jenkins's words were like salt in the wound of his frustrating failure to bed Callie Nolan. "Well, you've certainly been busy lately, haven't you? Perhaps if you spent less time checking up on Powers's imaginary love life and more time working on your job, we'd have a few more of those miners run out of town by now."

Jenkins played his hole card. "Maybe so, Boss, but if I hadn't been watching the boardinghouse, I wouldn't have found out another little tidbit of information I think you're gonna find very interesting."

"And what might that be?" Claymore asked with a weary sigh.

"Oh, just this big black buck who showed up a couple weeks back. Fella's name is Hezekiah Kane. Well, Kane and his wife have been staying at the boardinghouse ever since they got into town—"

"So what?" Claymore snapped. "I can't say that I approve of letting colored folks stay in a decent home, but Henrietta Winslow's always been more than a little unorthodox."

Jenkins stilled a swift jab of exasperation. "Hell, that wasn't what I meant!"

"Then what did you mean?" Claymore demanded. "Damnit Jenkins. Will you quit dancing around the subject and get to the point?"

"Whatever you say, Boss." Jenkins grimaced. This was going to be harder than he thought. It was time to lay his ace on the table, time to taunt Claymore with the most threatening thing he could think of. "Maybe this will interest you. I've heard a few rumors down in Brewery Gulch the last couple of days. Powers and his friend have been making a lot of purchases lately. And guess what they've been buying?"

"I have no idea."

"Mining supplies."

Claymore's mouth gaped open. "What?"

"Yep. Seems like Hezekiah Kane has decided to do a bit of prospecting. Gossip is, he's found himself a hot little claim somewhere up in those mountains. 'Course, Powers is the one who's been paying for all the supplies. I guess a man might grubstake an old friend, but it sure makes me wonder about what's going on—and whether this Kane fellow is in it by himself, after all. They're trying to keep it hush-hush, but you know how this town is. Not much happens but somebody

254

sees or hears about it."

Claymore's fingers drummed nervously on the desk as he contemplated this unexpected bit of news.

"Even if Powers doesn't have an interest in the mine, it seems kinda funny to me that he'd help another independent miner get started when he's supposed to be working for you. He knows how you feel about those people." Jenkins took a deep sigh and tried to look perplexed. "Makes me wonder if the man has been double-crossing you all along."

Jenkins didn't give a damn if what he said was true or not. All he cared about was revenge. If Owen Claymore fell for his scheme, Jenkins would soon have the help he needed to pay back a long overdue debt.

"Logan Powers and the independents," Claymore muttered with a shake of his head. "That sneaky son of a bitch. And I thought he was just helping Edith." He glanced quickly up at Jenkins. "Well, never mind that. If you're right, we've got to do something about those two, and fast."

Jenkins smiled smugly. "I couldn't have said it any better myself, Boss. I've been ponderin' the situation for several days now, and I think I've come up with a plan."

"I'm listening," Claymore said grimly.

"Like I said, I've been watching Powers and Kane, trying to figure out exactly what's going on. Just about every afternoon they ride off up into

255

the mountains. I followed them a couple of times until cover got too scarce. Figured finding out where they were heading wasn't worth putting them on the alert right now."

"Good thinking," Claymore said with a sage nod of his head.

"My guess would be they're up at that claim."

"That bastard," Claymore muttered, his face pinched with righteous anger. "One of these days he's gonna pay for double-crossing me."

"I couldn't agree with you more, but this is gonna take some careful planning and a little patience. I want to get rid of Powers and Kane as bad as you do, but if we kill them off now we might never find that mine. Wouldn't it be worth it to wait a couple of days and see if we can find out where that mine is located?"

"Yeah, but soon as we know that, they're dead men."

"Agreed." Jenkins slung one arm across the back of his chair and grinned with satisfaction. "Then you can take over the claim, and I'll settle for a nice fat bonus. Who knows? With Powers out of the way, you just might get another chance at Callie Nolan. How does that sound?"

"Perfect."

CHAPTER NINETEEN

"Mr. Logan! Mr. Logan! Come quick! You gotta help us!" Richard's almost hysterical voice shattered the silence of the serene afternoon.

Callie dropped the mending she'd been working on and hurried outside just as a white-faced Richard slid from the elderly horse reserved especially for the Claymore children's use and stumbled up the steps to Henrietta's front porch.

"Good heavens, Richard!" Callie exclaimed as the boy almost collided head-on with her. Quickly she reached out to steady the gasping boy by both arms. "What's wrong?"

Between great gulps for air, the towheaded youngster managed to stammer a few words. "It's Betsy. She's stuck . . . up on Castle Rock."

"Stuck?" Callie repeated. "On Castle Rock?" Her eyes grew huge with sudden understanding. "Oh, no! You can't mean that gigantic boulder up on the mountain? You children were told never to go near it!"

Richard ducked his head in shame. "Yes'm, I know. But we . . . uh, kinda did. And then Betsy got stuck, and I couldn't reach her, so I came to get Mr. Logan to help."

Callie's hands flew to her face, and her voice grew husky with alarm. "Logan's not here. Oh, dear! I don't even know when he'll be back. And Henrietta and Jasmine have gone to town!"

Stunned at that unexpected news, Richard turned big blue eyes up to his former governess. "But we gotta have help, Miss Callie. We gotta! I tried real hard, really I did, but I couldn't get to her."

"Well, then, I guess I'll have to be the one to help you, Richard."

The boy's head moved in an emphatic shake, and tears of frustration gathered on his pale lashes. "I don't think you can do it, Miss Callie. It's high. Real high. And I know you don't like high places."

"Never mind that," Callie said, pushing the words through lips that had suddenly lost all their color. "There's got to be a way. I'll think of something."

"I don't know, ma'am," Richard said forlornly. "Maybe you better have a look before you decide. Come on, we can see Castle Rock from that bend in the road."

His skinny legs pumping, Richard charged across Henrietta's bare dirt yard and then a dozen yards

258

up the dusty, double-rutted trail that hugged the mountainside. Callie hiked her skirts knee-high and followed as fast as she could.

Richard ran straight to the outer side of the hairpin curve in the road while Callie skidded to a halt well back from the edge. Then, with grim determination, she forced herself to cover the remaining distance to where the road fell away in a heart-stopping slope. Carefully, she inched up behind the boy and peered forward. There, laid out before her in all its terrifying splendor, was a panorama of overlapping mountains and deep gulches.

Her heart fluttering like the wings of a captured wild bird, Callie made a half-turn to the side and forced her frightened gaze upward until it finally fastened on the huge craggy chunk of limestone jutting impudently from the scrub-dotted mountainside. Larger than many of the miner's cabins clinging precariously along the switchback trails that climbed the Mule Mountains, the bulk of the great stone behemoth hung in midair over a sheer drop to the floor of Tombstone Canyon.

An uneven ledge circled the outer face of the jagged gray boulder, and there, mere feet from eternity, was a doll-like figure that must be Betsy Claymore.

Callie's heart leaped into her throat. "Oh, my God," she moaned softly. "How on earth did Betsy ever get out there?"

"It was Shadow, Miss Callie." Richard's words

259

tumbled over one another in his hurry to explain. "We were playing by the rock—not on it, cross my heart we weren't on the rock—and Shadow was chasing a butterfly. Then the butterfly flew away and Shadow went after it. That stupid cat scampered right out onto Castle Rock, and before I knew what was happening, Betsy had followed it. Honest, Miss Callie, she was out on that ledge before I even knew she was gone."

Callie gave Richard's thin shoulder a consoling pat. "It's all right, Richard. I'm sure you didn't mean for this to happen."

"I told her to sit down and be still, and I had Thomas stay up there and keep talking to her. See," Richard said, pointing to a high shoulder of rock close to where the jagged stone bulged from the mottled brown mountainside. "You can see his head pokin' up over the top."

Squinting hard, Callie was able to see someone peering over the jagged stone crest. "Yes, you're right. I can see him. That was good thinking, Richard. Very good."

Richard's smile was trembly and just the tiniest bit hopeful.

"All right, let's just pray that Thomas keeps talking to Betsy and that she stays calm and quiet. We'll think of some way to help." Callie cast one last desperate glance toward the speck of periwinkle blue that was Betsy and turned away. Too much time had been wasted already. She had to do something and quickly. "Come on, Richard, let's

260

get back to the house."

Callie hurried down the road to Henrietta's with Richard hard on her heels. The horse, still standing patiently in the yard, raised its head and rolled its eyes at the two figures barreling toward it.

Desperate, Callie made the only choice she could think of. "Richard, listen to me. I want you to run for town as fast as you can. Get help. Anywhere. Anybody. Do you understand?"

"Yes'm." Richard's head bobbed up and down like a cork.

"Good." Callie's mouth thinned into a stubborn line as she snatched up the horse's trailing reins and led it toward the steps so she could mount it.

"You gonna ride Sugarplum to town, Miss Callie?"

"No, Richard," Callie answered, keeping her voice as calm as possible. Hoisting her skirts, she slung one leg over the horse's broad back. "I'm going up to Castle Rock." She gulped hard as a mental picture of the awesome boulder and the bottomless abyss below it slid through her mind. "And, Richard, please hurry as fast as you can."

"Yes, ma'am, Miss Callie. I will."

Richard raced across the yard and down the lane as fast as his legs could take him. Giving a sharp jerk on the reins, Callie headed the horse in the opposite direction—up the narrow mountain road.

Reins clutched tightly in her trembling fingers, she nudged her mount's brown velvet flanks with her heels. The horse ambled forward. Callie groaned in despair. "Come on, you ol' bag of bones, let's go," she implored, slapping the reins hard against the horse's muscular neck.

Sugarplum gave a startled whinny and broke into a lumbering, bone-jarring trot. Holding on for dear life, Callie hunched over the mount's neck, urging the animal onward and upward. Her heartbeat matched the uneven thunder of the old horse's pounding hooves.

Heedless of the twisted limbs and thorny shrubs clawing at her wind-whipped skirt, Callie held Sugarplum as close as possible to the rising wall of earth on her right side. With grim determination, she refused to think about the steep drop-offs and often perpendicular precipices that passed in a blur on the other side. The ride seemed endless, and yet far too swift as the towering mass came nearer and nearer.

A soft sob of half relief, half escalating fear bubbled from Callie's lips when she finally reached the plateau at the back of Castle Rock. She was there, but what was she going to do? Besides pray that Richard found someone to help — fast.

Barely taking time to loop Sugarplum's lines over a bush, Callie ran for the mammoth outcropping of rock. Overjoyed at her arrival, Thomas hopped down from his lofty perch and hurried to greet her. The momentum of his thigh-high hug nearly knocked Callie off her feet.

"There, there, Thomas, it's all right," she soothed, bending to wrap her arms around his bony shoulders in a reassuring embrace.

Turning his worried face upward, Thomas immediately began babbling. "Boy oh boy, am I glad to see you, Miss Callie. Richard said he'd find someone, but I didn't know if he could. I've been talking to Betsy, just like he told me to. She's just sitting there, her and that dumb old cat of hers."

"That's fine, Thomas. You did a marvelous job." Callie gently disengaged his arms and took hold of his hand, leading him toward the back of Castle Rock. "Now, you stay right here while I . . ." There was an audible gulp. ". . . while I climb up where you were and have a little chat with Betsy."

"Yes, ma'am, Miss Callie." Thomas obediently plopped himself down on the grassy knoll mere inches from the massive lump of rock.

Callie closed her eyes for a second, blinked them open, and then took a deep breath. Placing one foot gingerly upon the rough rear slope, she began to inch her way up and onto Castle Rock. She found that, if she was very, very careful and kept her eyes strictly on the rise of gray limestone in front of her, she could pretend that all that open space surrounding the other three sides of the boulder didn't exist.

Step by careful step, Callie crept forward until her hands found purchase on a slab of wind-hewn stone. The crest that Thomas had been peering around and over sloped upward on her left, joining with the uppermost bastions of Castle Rock.

263

To her right, the ridge tapered off and melted away to almost nothing where the encircling ledge began. Callie's heart gave a sickening thud against her breastbone as she realized how very near the edge Betsy had to go to climb out onto the lime-stone lip.

Inches, mere inches, were all that existed be-tween the child and a drop of hundreds of feet. A slip of the foot and the little girl would have plummeted to her death.

Hugging tight against the rising rock face, Callie edged around an outward curve of rock. Craning her neck, she peered around the stony curl, her breath catching in her throat when she spied Betsy sitting cross-legged on a ledge not more than three feet wide. Cuddled in her arms was her dearly beloved Shadow, looking utterly relaxed and satis-fied with the whole situation.

Callie's breath stopped altogether when she saw the jagged slash cut into the living rock—a gaping V-shaped cleft that split the ledge in two. Brack-eted by the ragged edges of the opening was a slice of open space. Callie could see straight down to the floor of the canyon.

Dear God in heaven! How had the child man-aged to cross that terrifying fissure?

Callie pressed her face against the sun-warmed surface of the rock and prayed for strength and courage. Then, her fingers clinging mightily to the cracks and crevices of Castle Rock, she leaned out enough for Betsy to see her.

"Hello there, Betsy," she said softly, not wanting to startle the little girl.

She turned to gaze up at Callie, a cherub smile ringing her face, her huge blue eyes sparkling with delight. The movement of her head sent pale, baby-fine hair rippling in the breeze.

"Hi, Miss Callie! Did you come to play with us?" Betsy's chubby baby fingers endlessly stroked Shadow's soft black fur.

"Yes, darling, I suppose you could say that."

"Richard told me to sit down and be still," Betsy related in a self-important voice. "I'm mindin' him real good, just like he said to do."

"I'm very proud of you, sweetheart. You're being a very good girl." *Please hurry, Richard. Please.* "You keep doing exactly what Richard told you to do. All right?"

Betsy's cupid-bow lips turned down in the beginnings of a frown. "I guess so, Miss Callie, but—"

"Now just sit still, darling. I have to ask Thomas something. I'll be right back."

Callie maneuvered the few inches necessary to allow her to turn her head toward Thomas without losing her deathlike grip on the rock wall.

"Thomas!" she whispered loudly. "Do you see anyone coming up the road?" *Please, please, let someone be coming.*

Without a thought, Thomas leaped to his feet and trotted to the drop-off point. Callie closed her eyes to block out the frightening scene. *It's all right. He's played on these mountainsides since he was a baby*. She forced her eyes open in time to watch Thomas shade his face and peer intently for a few moments. Finally he turned toward Callie and gave a negative wag of his head.

Callie's heart sank.

"Miss Callie?" Betsy's baby-lisp voice floated through the air.

Callie took another fortifying breath and edged forward again. "Yes, dear, what is it?"

"I'm tired of this game, Miss Callie. Me and Shadow are ready to get up."

Alarm raced through Callie. "Can't you play the game just a few more minutes, sweetheart? For me?"

Betsy's bottom lip thrust forward. She shook her head and white-gold ringlets danced in the wind. "We don't want to, Miss Callie. Shadow's getting hungry." Her voice had taken on a whine, and her little face was all pinched up like she might cry at any moment. " 'Sides, if I don't go potty pretty soon, I might wet my britches and then Consuela'll spank me."

Oh, no! "No, she won't, Betsy," Callie quickly assured her. "I won't let her, honey. I promise. Just wait a little while longer, all right?"

Betsy's lip stuck out further and started to tremble. "I don't wanna. Even if Consuela didn't spank me, I'm a big girl now and big girls don't have wet britches. I'm ready to get off this ol' rock. Right now."

Betsy started to rise and Callie bit back a

scream. "No! Betsy, don't do that, honey! Please!" *Oh, dear God! What am I going to do? What am I going to do?*

Deep down inside Callie was terrified at what she knew she was going to have to do.

Betsy's voice grew shaky. "I want off this old rock, Miss Callie. Now!"

Callie's voice was quivering more than Betsy's. "All right, darling. Just sit still. I'm coming to get you."

"Mr. Logan!"

At the sound of Richard's joyous shout, Logan pulled his horse to a halt. He propped one muscular forearm on the saddlehorn and leaned toward the little boy, a wide grin tilting his mouth.

"Hey, Richard. How are things goin', son? What are you doing so far from home?" Logan's eyes swept the brushy roadside. "And where's Thomas and Betsy? It's not like you to be out without them."

"Things ain't good at all, Mr. Logan," Richard blurted. "That's why I was comin' after you. But you weren't there and then Miss Callie told me to come on down to town."

"Callie sent you to town? Why? What's wrong?"

"That's what I been tryin' to tell you, Mr. Logan. We're in a heap of trouble for sure this time. Betsy's stuck up on Castle Rock and Miss Callie's gone up to get her."

Under his breath Logan muttered a string of curses. The harness jingled wildly as the big bay stallion sensed his master's agitation and tossed his head, crabbing sideways. Logan quickly jerked the horse to a standstill and reached down to scoop Richard up behind him.

"Hold on tight," Logan said grimly, kicking his horse into a gallop.

"Yes, sir." Richard's words were lost in the wind. He clung tight as a tick on a hound's ear as Logan headed up the mountain.

Never in her life had Callie been so frightened. She could feel the beat of her heart in the back of her throat and her fingertips gouging their way into the unyielding rock. Every nerve in her body quivered like the strings of a banjo strung too tight.

She knew if she stopped to think about it, she'd never go. So she simply closed her mind to everything but Betsy and started moving.

With her body pressed as tightly as possible against the face of the rock, she lifted one foot over the knee-high barrier of the stone crest and then the other. Her right hand, then her left, scrabbled for each new grip. Inch by agonizing inch she made her way around Castle Rock's perimeter until the only thing that separated her from Betsy was that awesome cleft in the rocky ledge beneath her feet.

One tiny glimpse downward was all it took to set her head whirling. Callie gasped and clung tighter to the rock's craggy face. *Don't look. Don't look. Don't look.* The words pounded with each beat of her heart.

"Can I get up now?"

Betsy's pitiful little voice broke through Callie's paralyzing fear. She tried to smile at the child, but her lips felt frozen.

"No, Betsy, not just yet. Hold on. I'll be there in a minute."

Callie's breathing was shallow and raspy as she stretched her right hand out and clutched at a jagged protrusion. She forced herself to look at nothing but the gray granite her foot was reaching for. Then with a push and a prayer, she shifted her weight and crossed the chasm.

If she'd had the privilege of a few free seconds when she safely reached the other side, she would have cried or laughed or both. But there was still Betsy to consider.

And the return journey.

They had passed Henrietta's when Richard cried out, "Look, Mr. Logan! I can see 'em!"

Fear exploded in Logan's dark eyes as his gaze swept upward in response to Richard's cry and he saw what the boy had seen—Callie and Betsy teetering on the windswept ledge of Castle Rock. And below them, hundreds of feet of nothingness

269

all the way to the canyon floor.

Logan jerked the reins hard and the stallion rose on his haunches, pawing the air with wildly slashing hooves before Logan finally got him back under control. Richard, his arms locked tight around Logan's waist, somehow managed to keep his seat. Mindlessly, Logan calmed the agitated animal as his stricken gaze stayed locked on the drama being played out on the side of the mountain.

He knew there was no way he could reach them in time to help. No way in hell. All he could do was watch—and pray—as Callie picked the little girl up and began to inch her way back.

Something slid and lurched deep in Logan's gut as he watched the terrifying scene. A fear so ingrained, so visceral, that for a moment he thought he might be sick to his stomach. Memories flashed through his mind—disjointed, all too vivid memories of another time, another place, when all he could do was wait and watch and die a little inside.

Memories of an afternoon long, long ago.

Memories of the words his father had spoken to him before riding away that fateful day.

I'm leaving you in charge, Logan. Get your chores done, and, remember, no playing until you're through with all of them. You're old enough to take a little responsibility around her. I'm depending on you to take care of your mother and your sisters.

The shameful memory of disregarding his father's admonitions, of playing hide-and-seek in the barn with his sister, Sabra.

And worst of all, memories of the bloodthirsty renegades who'd swoop down on his family's farm, catching them unaware, unarmed. Memories of watching his mother and baby sister being hacked to death by those savages.

We gotta hide. You gotta be still, Sabra, be still . . . please don't move. Mama! Oh, the baby! Don't look, Sabra, don't look! Oh, God, they've got Mary. Hide, Sabra, hide . . . don't let them see you . . .

Memories that had tormented him. Memories that had frozen his heart against any thought of caring, of needing, of loving.

If you loved, you could lose. And that hurt too much ever to bear again.

"Oh, sweet Jesus!" Logan sobbed as Callie and Betsy disappeared around the edge of Castle Rock. "I can't see them anymore! Did they make it? Dear God, Richard, tell me they made it!"

"Hang on, Betsy, we're almost there."

Somehow, some way, Callie managed to hold the little girl and work her way back around the craggy face of the rock. She didn't remember re-crossing the gaping chasm; she was barely aware of easing over the top of the crested barrier and getting down the final rear slope to blessedly solid ground.

For a moment, all she felt was jelly-kneed relief. Then a blinding, mind-searing anger swept through her, and she knew what she was going to do.

Her chin jutted skyward, her blue eyes blazing with righteous fire, Callie hoisted the children atop Sugarplum. Fueled by an all-consuming rage, she then took a tight hold on the reins and stormed off in the direction of the Claymore house, Sugarplum following behind.

"What are we gonna do, Miss Callie?" Betsy piped.

"I'll tell you what *I'm* going to do," Callie muttered vehemently. "I'm going to say something I've been wanting to say for a long time."

CHAPTER TWENTY

In response to Callie's persistent knocking, a very startled Paloma opened the front door. Her round-eyed gaze took in the wild look in Callie's eyes, her disheveled appearance, and finally the two apprehensive children peeking from behind their ex-governess's skirts.

"S-*Señorita* Nolan," the little Mexican maid stammered. "I did not think to see you again."

"I'm sure you're not the only one." Callie squared her shoulders. "I'm here to see the Claymores."

Paloma's eyes grew even larger at the sharp tone of Callie's voice. "Oh, I'm sorry, *señorita,* but *Señor* Claymore is not at home now."

"Then I guess I'll have to settle for his wife," Callie retorted, sweeping through the door and inside before Paloma knew what was happening.

Without another word to the gape-mouthed maid, Callie stomped across the foyer, Thomas and Betsy following in her wake. Paloma reluctantly trailed half a dozen steps behind, her fingers plucking nervously at the hem of her apron.

Callie gave three sharp raps on the door to Edith Claymore's parlor and walked in. She was immediately enveloped with memories of her first visit to that room.

As before, Edith Claymore's private domain was shrouded in gloom, and the lady herself was in her usual place, ensconced on the chaise in the far corner of the room. A vague sense of change tugged at the corners of Callie's mind, but her sense of outrage was far too strong to give much consideration to such contemplation.

Given another opportunity, when her hot Irish temper wasn't ruling her head, Callie might have noticed that there was something different about the lady she faced. Edith's eyes no longer held the glassiness they once had; it had been replaced with a more rational look which Callie would have interpreted as haunted. Or she might have realized that, for the first time, the room lacked its usual medicinal aroma. But Callie was a lady with a mission, and at the moment all she could think of was saying what she'd come to say.

Edith's head jerked up at Callie's sudden entrance, her eyes filled with surprise and then anger. "What . . . what are you doing here? How dare you—"

"Oh, I dare, all right," Callie replied in precise clipped words. "You have nothing to hold over my head now, Mrs. Claymore, and you're going to listen to me—like it or not."

With that, Callie turned and motioned to Betsy and Thomas, who had been huddling by the doorway. Though obviously disinclined, they shuffled forward and sidled up as close to Callie as possible. She placed one arm over each child's shoulder.

"I want you to take a good look at these children," Callie demanded. "I want you to see—really see—how blessed you are. I want you to see what you almost lost this afternoon . . . what you will lose, one way or another, if you don't wake up!"

Edith lurched to her feet. "Just who do you think you are, barging into my house like this, talking to me in such a manner?"

Callie ignored Edith's indignant remark long enough to stoop and hug each child. "Paloma," she called over her shoulder as she gave the children a gentle nudge toward the foyer. "Will you take the children upstairs, please? And see that they're entertained until Mrs. Claymore and I finish our little chat."

"Sí, señorita." Her dark brown eyes huge with astonishment, Paloma fairly leaped to obey. With fluttering gestures and little clucking sounds, she shooed the children from the room. The closing of the door cut off a stream of muttered Spanish.

"Now," Callie said, her chin held high as she once again turned to face her opponent. "I'll tell you exactly who I am. I'm the person who pulled your little girl off the ledge of Castle Rock a few minutes ago."

"What?" Edith's mouth dropped open.

"That's right," Callie affirmed. "One misstep and that child could have tumbled to her death! Do you understand what I'm saying? That precious little girl would have been gone—gone forever. Tell me, Mrs. Claymore, how long are you going to ignore your responsibility to the children you brought into this world? Are you going to wait until it's too late? Until you actually lose one of them? Well, lady, let me tell you, if you don't wake up, and soon, that's exactly what might happen!"

"But . . . but . . ." Edith sputtered. "Consuela was supposed to be watching them."

Fists jammed on her hips, elbows akimbo, Callie gave a snort of disgust. "Consuela doesn't have the brains God gave a goat when it comes to taking proper care of those children. Having a governess is well and good, but you're not supposed to relinquish all responsibility to the children God saw fit to give to you. Good heavens, woman! Where has your mind been?"

Edith bristled. "How dare you—"

"Yes, I dare!" Callie hissed. "I dare because no one else in this house dares. Not Consuela. Not you. And certainly not the children's father. He's too busy worrying about his mines and his money to take an interest in his own flesh and blood. And speaking of Mr. Claymore, let me assure you that I wouldn't have the man on a silver platter!"

276

Edith gaped in shock.

"It's just too damn bad if your husband isn't trustworthy," Callie railed. "But that doesn't give you the right to accuse other people of things they haven't done. Especially when your stupidity reflects on the well-being of Richard and Thomas and Betsy!"

Edith drew herself up straight, the tilt of her head stiff and proud. "Have you quite finished?"

"Not quite. I don't know what your problem is or why you changed so much. I do know you're not the person my headmistress told me about. Maybe you're willing to waste your life away feeling sorry for yourself, but if you're any kind of a mother at all, you'll start thinking about your children. *Now* I'm through."

With that, Callie turned on her heel and left.

Callie's fingertips had barely touched the brass knob on Henrietta's front door when Logan's horse thundered into the yard. The big bay stallion's hooves sprayed plumes of dust as his rider sawed desperately on the reins. Leather creaked in protest as Logan swung out of the saddle even while the horse was still moving. He ran for the porch and charged up the steps two at a time, his boot heels pounding against the weathered wood.

"Dammit to hell, Callie Nolan!" Logan yelled, grabbing her arm and swinging her around. Fear and anger sparked in eyes beneath a sweat-beaded forehead. "Don't you ever stay in one spot long enough for a man to catch up with you?"

"What are you talking about?"

"I'll tell you what I'm talking about," Logan exploded. "I like to have run that poor horse to death getting up to Castle Rock and when I did, you were gone! And then I rode all the way down to the Claymores' to drop Richard off, and guess what . . . you'd already been there and gone again! I've been chasing you up and down this damn mountain for what seems like eternity!"

Logan barely took a breath before continuing his tirade. He was too far out of control to recognize the rekindled flicker of anger in Callie's eyes.

"And what's more, I'd like to know what in hell you said while you were at the Claymores! That whole house was in an uproar. Consuela was bawling. I couldn't get a thing that made any sense out of Paloma. And poor Edith, she looked like she was in shock or something. Hell, I didn't think I'd ever get them all calmed down!"

That did it. She'd just had the most frightening experience of her life, and there was no way some big lout of a man was going to take her to task for anything! Callie's eyes narrowed menacingly, as very deliberately she reached up with her free hand and pried Logan's fingers from her flesh.

"I said exactly what had to be said. If you want details, then go back and talk to your poor, precious Edith. You shouldn't find that difficult, you have such a *winning* way with women." With a

278

contemptuous glare, Callie reached for the door-knob again.

"I'm not through talking to you!" Logan fairly roared.

"I don't think I care to hear anything else you have to say."

Bright spots of color flared on Logan's cheeks. "Is that so? Well, isn't that just too bad, 'cause I've got something to say about that little stunt you pulled up on Castle Rock! Jesus Christ, woman! I couldn't believe my eyes when Richard pointed you out to me up on that damn rock! Of all the feather-brained, idiotic—"

Outrage, fresh and furious, began to course through Callie. There was an ominous quality to the quiet words she spoke. "Don't you dare talk to me like that, Logan Powers—"

"Well somebody sure as hell needs to talk to you!" Logan retorted. "That was a stupid thing to do! Don't you know what could have happened? Do you even realize how dangerous it was to prance around on the goddam rock like you were at some garden party? You could have been killed!"

Callie lifted her chin, meeting Logan's furious gaze straight on. How dare he talk to her in such a manner after all she'd been through! "I believe I have a small idea of the danger." Her voice was icy with indignation.

"Then why in hell didn't you wait? Richard and I were on our way!"

"How very gallant of you." The words were like a blast of arctic air. "However, there were two small problems. I wasn't aware of your impending arrival, and Betsy had decided she didn't care to wait any longer—not one single, solitary second longer." She gave him a scathing look. "Now, if you'll excuse me, I'm going to my room. This conversation is finished."

With a toss of her head, Callie jerked the door open and marched toward the stairs.

Logan went slack-jawed with shock. How could she act so calm when he felt like someone had reached in and scooped out his insides? His teeth clacked like castanets and his mouth snapped shut. In a red mist of totally unjustified rage, Logan stormed the door and up the stairs.

Hearing the thud of furious footsteps behind her, Callie hiked her skirt higher and raced upward. She reached the top landing only a few steps in front of Logan. He lunged and made a grab for her, his fingertips barely brushing the fabric of her sleeve as she jerked out of reach. A side-step and a swirl of petticoats and she managed to reach the door to her bedroom.

"Callie Nolan!" Logan yelled as she twisted the handle and threw the door open. "You come back here!"

"Go to hell!" Callie shouted.

She whirled through the opening and turned to slam the door shut just as Logan caught up with her and braced his shoulder against the rapidly closing wooden panel. Even with all her weight thrown against the door, Callie couldn't budge it another inch.

Furious at her impotence against his greater strength, she suddenly relinquished her hold on the door, and it burst open, slamming against the wall. Taken by surprise, Logan fairly flew into the room. The heel of his boot caught the corner of a rag rug and he went skidding across the polished floor, his arms windmilling for balance.

With a startled squeal, Callie tried to get out of his way, but it was too late. One wildly flailing arm caught her around the waist and, in a vaude-villian shuffle, the two of them went stumbling across the room. In a topsy-turvy flurry of petti-coats and tangled limbs, they landed on Callie's bed.

"Son of a bitch!" Logan yelped as his head clanged against the iron bedstead. Tears sheened his eyes and, for the life of him, he didn't know if it was because of the pain in his head or the pain in his heart.

Winded and momentarily shocked into stillness by the unexpected molding of soft curves to hard muscles, Callie and Logan simply lay there. Little by little, a soul-searing awareness began to seep through each of them.

Logan lay half across Callie, her head cushioned on one of his arms. The other was wrapped se-curely around her body, the palm of his hand cupping the agonizingly tempting weight of one softly rounded hip. Each small, gasping breath she took brought the lush fullness of her breast into closer contact with his own laboring chest.

Her skirts were a tangled froth of fabric around her hips and her long legs were braided with his, the smooth warm expanse of one thigh snuggled tight against the bulge of his manhood.

Deep in Logan's heart, something cried out, taunting him, telling him how close he'd come to losing her, to having her snatched away before he'd ever even had a chance to hold her the way he longed to . . . to touch her the way he wanted to . . . to love her the way he had to.

Nerves strung tight and raw, senses more finely atuned than ever before, he gazed at the woman in his arms.

Suddenly he yearned to run his fingers through the midnight locks that fanned across the brightly colored patchwork quilt, to bury his face in the silken curls that caressed the delicate curve of her shoulder.

Her skin was as smooth and clear as fine porcelain. Beneath the flush of color on her cheeks he could detect a faint sprinkling of golden freckles — so pale he'd never noticed them. He longed to drop a kiss on each and every one of them.

He'd thought her mouth tempting before — lush and full and soft as satin — but now it near drove him to distraction. Even as he watched, the tiny pink tip of her tongue slipped out and nervously moistened lips the color of a blushing rose and

282

heat exploded deep in his gut.

Her ears, tiny and shell-like, seemed to beg for his attention. On the right side, one silken strand of hair had caught and curled ever so lovingly around a delicately shaped lobe. What would it feel like to take that tiny morsel between his lips? To nibble? To gently suck? Would tracing the delicate swirls with the tip of his tongue drive her wild the way simply thinking about it was doing to him?

The fragile line of her throat—long, slender, and as creamy textured as a magnolia blossom—led his eyes to the fluttering pulse at its base and then downward to the open vee of her bodice to the delectable shadowed valley between her breasts. If he dared to touch that secret place, would her skin be as cool as satin against his fingers, or would he feel a fire that matched the flames that were beginning to course through his own veins?

Beneath him, he could feel soft woman-curves, beckoning hills and valleys that fit as perfectly as the pieces of a puzzle against the hard ridges and hollows of his own body.

Their eyes met and locked. They were so close that Logan could have counted each delicate long lash rimming eyes of deepest blue—eyes that held the reflection of his own tormented face.

He hung suspended between heaven and hell, knowing he should move away from her, knowing he could not.

Locked within Logan's strong embrace, Callie

felt the ragged tendrils of fear begin to drift away. Little by little, she began to think she might survive the whirlwind of emotions she'd been feeling since she faced Castle Rock and her age-old fears. The harsh injustices and cold realities of the world dimmed and faded from her mind, and an aura of peace surrounded her. Logan's very nearness worked a gentle magic, and she knew that within his arms she'd be forever safe and secure.

Mesmerized, Callie stared into Logan's eyes. Starburst flecks of gold and umber danced in irises rimmed with darkest brown. Her grandmother had always said that eyes were the window to a person's soul, and now Callie knew why. Desire radiated from those dark orbs, but also mirrored in the midnight-black pupils were sorrow and hurt and heart-wrenching fear. What awful thing had left him such a painful legacy, she wondered.

She could feel the coiled-spring tension in Logan's body, see it in the rigid cords that stood out on each side of his neck.

Suddenly she longed to soothe the tiny worry lines from around his eyes, to brush the tousled curls from his furrowed brow, to drive the fear from his eyes.

With trembling fingers Callie reached to touch Logan's face. One butterfly-light brush of fingertips down his cheek, then a gentle cupping of her palm against the rigidity of his tight-clenched jaw and Logan was lost.

Utterly and hopelessly lost.

"Heaven help me," he moaned as he tightened his hold on the woman in his arms. Dipping his head, he captured her lips. His mouth plundered hers in a frenzied kiss as he strove desperately to fill the aching void within himself.

Callie's heart went cartwheeling. Logan's kiss was wild and wicked and wonderful. A reckless fever began to race through her veins as his tongue traced the seam of her lips and went gliding over her pearly teeth before searching out the sweet recesses of her mouth. Logan devoured her, consumed her soul with the sweet agony of a kiss that molded, savored, blended, bonded.

In a reflex as old as love itself, Callie lifted her arms and threaded her hands through Logan's tawny hair. Her fingers splayed across the base of his skull, exerting an infinitesimal pressure that locked his mouth to hers as surely as any chain.

He groaned with desire as her tongue timidly responded to his rapier thrusts. White-hot fire flamed deep in his belly when she instinctively arched against him. The hand beneath her hip flexed and he pulled her hard against him, seeking, needing greater contact with the heated velvet of her body.

With a peppering of tiny kisses, he traced a line from her mouth to her ear, where he allowed himself to do all the delightful things he'd been imagining. His heart leaped with joy as she writhed beneath him in response to his ministrations.

A string of love nips down the side of her throat elicited delicate shivers of ecstasy. Then Logan's tongue flicked the wildly beating pulse at the base of her throat and blazed a searing trail downward. He buried his nose in the hidden valley, glorying in the sweet woman-scent that was Callie's and Callie's alone.

At last he turned his attention to flesh that ached for his touch. Each lush breast received a bevy of encircling kisses. Callie's nipples swelled and tightened, straining pebble-hard against the fabric of her bodice. Beneath his lips, Logan could feel the fierce beating of her heart.

Her hands skimmed up and down his back, caressing the muscles that bunched and slid beneath the cotton fabric of his shirt. Callie's questing fingers found that tempting opening where his shirttail had pulled free of his pants and tugged the restricting material upward.

The feel of her hand on the bare flesh of his back was sweet agony. Shivers of delight coursed through Logan as her fingers stroked him. The gentle rasp of her nails against his heated flesh created the most exquisite of tortures.

Shifting his weight slightly, Logan freed one hand. His fumbling fingers found the tiny pearl buttons that fastened the bodice of her dress. One by one, he slipped them from their holes, dipping his head to press a kiss upon each delectable morsel of flesh exposed by his actions.

His fingers trembled even more as he brushed aside the edges of her bodice, and his breath caught in his throat at the tantalizing sight of dusky aureoles and pearled nipples straining against the gossamer cotton of her chemise.

"Callie," he whispered, his agony-filled eyes melding with hers. "Please, Callie. Let me touch you. I think I might die if I don't."

There was no turning back for Callie. She saw his pain, felt his need, and deep within she knew that she and she alone could give him surcease.

Her hand slid from Logan's back, trailing across the curve of his ribs, coming to rest at the lace-edged top of her chemise. With expert ease, her fingers loosened the first of the tiny blue bows that marched down the center of the garment. And then the next. And the next.

Inch by inch, the fabric fell away. Inch by inch, ivory flesh was revealed to Logan's hungry eyes, a feast for his starving soul.

And when Callie's hands reached out to bracket Logan's face and gently pulled his head down to her breasts, he truly thought he might die — but this time, of pleasure.

Callie gasped with rapture as Logan's mouth, wet and warm and demanding, closed over her sensitive flesh. Something deep within her vibrated like the plucked strings of a harp as he suckled gently at her breast. Frissons of pulsating need bloomed deep in her belly, radiated outward, and sang through her veins, setting afire every nerve, every fiber of her being.

Could anything ever give her greater pleasure than this? How wonderful to feel the gentle weight of the man she loved snug against her own body. How marvelous, his mouth upon her breast. Surely, surely, there could be no greater ecstasy.

But there was.

Once again Logan stamped his mouth across Callie's with delicious abandon, his tongue stroking, caressing, urging the flames within her to greater intensity. Then his hand swept downward, gliding over her tiny waist and softly rounded hip. He tugged her tangled skirts even higher. With infinite gentleness, he stroked the curve of her leg, the exquisitely sensitive skin of her inner thigh, the flat plane of her stomach, and then his palm cupped against flesh that ached with desire.

Callie whimpered, a tiny, mewling sound halfway between fright and rapture. She tilted her head back, rolling it slowly from side to side, leaving her neck exposed . . . vulnerable . . . irresistible.

Relinquishing her mouth, Logan rained butterfly-soft kisses across the curve of her jaw, down the ivory column of her throat, ever downward until he could press a gentle kiss upon the wildly beating pulse-point in the delectable shadowed hollow of her throat.

"Callie, my Callie. Sweet Jesus, but I want you." With each whispered word, Logan's breath, fever-hot with his desire, fanned against her throat. "Please, please, don't turn me away. I need you so much."

Logan's deft fingers inched upward, plucked loose the ties of her pantalets, and then crept beneath the prim cotton fabric. His touch branded her flesh as his fingers blazed a downward trail. And when Logan found the treasure he was seeking, Callie gave a soft little cry. She moaned and rocked against him, answering the heated tempo of his touch with a rhythm as old as time.

His breath rasped hot and heavy. His hungry mouth ravaged first her lips and then each taut peak of her breasts. With expert finesse, Logan gently laved her pouting nipples, drawing a string of small, passion-filled whimpers from her parted lips.

But he wanted more. Much more. Everything.

With a groan of frustration, Logan surged upward.

"Oh, Logan, no! Don't go. Don't leave me," she cried when he moved away.

"I won't, darling," he murmured. "I couldn't. Patience, my love. Just a little patience and it will be better still."

Clasping Callie by both arms, he lifted her up until they were standing face to face. In mere seconds, her clothes lay in jumbled heaps on the floor.

Logan's breath wedged in his throat as the last garment fell away. Callie's cheeks blazed with rosy color, but she stood quiet before him while his eyes worshipped the beauty of her body. He loved her all the more for her gentle dignity, her proud acceptance of his visual homage.

His heart pounding madly within his rib cage, Logan reached to unfasten the buttons of his shirt.

"No," Callie protested.

Logan's gaze flew upward in confusion. She took a step toward him and raised her hands to his chest.

"Let me do it," she whispered.

Joy, hot and sweet, leaped within him when he heard her plea. He didn't trust his voice, so he simply nodded his head. His eyes never left her gaze as she slowly stripped his clothes away.

She'd seen his body before. She'd washed away the blood and the dirt. She'd tucked the covers around his cold flesh. She'd bathed away the sweat of his fevers. But nothing she'd done or seen or thought prepared her for what she felt when Logan finally stood naked before her.

It was quite one thing to view a man's body when he lay wounded and still as death; it was something else entirely when the man vibrated with good health and desire.

He was magnificent.

A slant of late afternoon sunlight caught and lingered in the tousled curls that fell across Logan's forehead. Beneath sun-tipped swirls of hair, his broad, muscular chest rose and fell with the rapidity of his breathing. Beneath desert-bronzed skin he was all layers of muscle, angular ridges and hollows. And nestled in the vee of his legs was undeniable proof of the passion she aroused in him.

With utter tenderness he eased her down on the bed, and with exquisite care he positioned himself over her.

"Callie." Her name was a sigh, a plea, a prayer. Into that one word Logan poured all the emotions, all the feelings he'd tried so hard to deny.

With an eager, upward arch, Callie met the thrust of his body and gave to Logan the rare and treasured gift that could only be given once.

CHAPTER TWENTY-ONE

The thunder of hooves brought Lee Jenkins bolt upright in bed, the gleaming revolver in his hand aimed straight at the door of his rickety cabin. His finger tightened on the trigger as footsteps thudded across the minuscule porch. The door flew open and the flimsy wall vibrated as the wooden panel slammed against it.

Owen Claymore was half a heartbeat from death when Jenkins recognized the figure silhouetted by the coming dawn in the doorway of the old mining shack.

"Goddammit, Boss, you're gonna get yourself shot doing that one of these days," Jenkins complained as he gently released the pressure of his trigger finger and slipped from the rumpled bed.

Claymore never even acknowledged what had been said. He stormed into the room, his eyes wild, his hair disheveled. His suit looked as if he'd slept in it.

"Get up!" He shouted at Jenkins. "We've got work to do."

Scarcely giving Jenkins a second look, Claymore stalked to the table and poured himself a tall glass of liquor. By the time Jenkins had pulled his boots on, Claymore had emptied the glass.

Christ, Jenkins thought sourly. *If he isn't drunk now, it won't be long till he is.*

"Somethin' up, Boss?" Jenkins inquired as he reached for his gunbelt and buckled it around his slim hips.

The glass slammed against the tabletop. Claymore whirled and glared at Jenkins. "You damn right something is up! Edith is leaving me and it's all thanks to that little bitch Callie Nolan and our good friend, Logan Powers."

The gun Jenkins was reholstering hung in midair for just a moment before sliding as smooth as butter into its accustomed place. "What happened?"

Claymore ceased his agitated pacing long enough to throw Jenkins a scathing look. "Hell if I know. I've never seen Edith act like this before. When I got home last night, she had trunks packed for herself and the children. Said she was taking this morning's train—going back to Tucson where the kids'll have a decent life. And that's *all* she said."

"I don't get it," Jenkins said with a frown. "What makes you think Powers and the woman had anything to do with it?"

"Consuela," Claymore answered bitterly. "She

293

told me Callie Nolan and Logan Powers had been to the house yesterday. That's when all the trouble started. Edith started packing right after Powers left. I don't know what they said or what they did, but I promise you they're going to pay for this! Do you understand?"

"Sure, Boss. Whatever you say."

"I want Powers dead. Now. Immediately. But I have other plans for Miss Nolan." Claymore's laugh was mirthless. "I'm going to enjoy the lady for a while . . . and when I'm through with her, she'll be glad to die."

"Listen, Boss," Jenkins said in a placating voice, suddenly worried that Claymore's erratic behavior was going to cost him the bonus money he'd been counting on to get away to Alaska. "I'm all for doing 'em in, you know that. But we gotta go about this the right way. You don't want people suspecting you had anything to do with their deaths. Hell, even a rumor to that effect could ruin your reputation and screw up those business deals you got going."

"Haven't you heard what I'm been saying? There won't be any business deals! Shit, there won't be any business at all if Edith leaves. Whose money do you think I've been using all these years? I don't have enough cash to bail out even one of those deals—much less all of them!"

Jenkins held his tongue while Claymore stomped to the table and poured himself another drink.

"I'm ruined, don't you understand?" Claymore

growled as soon as he'd downed the liquor. "Ruined! But if I'm going down, I'm not going down alone. I'm taking Logan Powers and Callie Nolan with me."

So this was it, Jenkins thought. The time had finally come.

He knew Claymore was too far gone to be of much use to him. But if he could get him to do just one last thing, then Jenkins would have enough money to finance his plans. All he had to do was convince Claymore that this last plan was workable. After that, Jenkins would be more than willing to close the books on those old debts and a few new ones.

Yep. Once Claymore had served his purpose, his bones could rot right alongside those of Logan Powers and Hezekiah Kane.

As for Callie Nolan, Jenkins had never killed a woman, but, upon examination, he found that the thought didn't bother him much. If he left her alive, she'd be able to identify him, testify against him — just like Powers and Kane had done before.

Well, not this time, Jenkins vowed with grim determination. When he was through, there's be no witnesses . . . not a single one.

"Fine, Boss, fine. You know I'll do whatever you want," Jenkins said in a soothing voice. "But I've got an idea that just might work. Nothing says that if you're finished here you can't go somewhere else and make a fresh start. All you need is a nice little nest egg. Right? And I think I know how you can get it."

"Oh, yeah? How? Claymore asked warily.

"Simple. It's doubtful that anyone in town knows about Mrs. Claymore leaving yet. Right?"

"I guess so."

"Good. All you got to do is go back home. Change clothes. Get all spruced up. Then go to the bank. Act like everything is all right. Draw out all the funds that you possibly can. Hell, get a quick loan. Use the house for collateral, the main mine, whatever it takes. Just get your hands on as much money as possible. You're a fine, upstanding man in this community. You've got a reputation. You've got contacts. You can charm that banker. Put on the right act and he'll fall over himself to give you anything you want."

"Umm," Claymore mumbled, one thick finger stroking his chin. "I suppose that might work."

"Sure it would," Jenkins insisted. "Then, once you've got the money, all you've got to do is keep up the act. Don't go back to the house after that. Don't pack anything. Don't do anything suspicious. Just put the money in a saddlebag and meet me back here. By then, I'll have done some scouting around and I'll know where Powers and the girl are."

"Then what?"

"We do Powers in fast and take the woman with us. When you're through with her, we'll get rid of her. We'll be clean out of the territory before anyone even suspects anything's wrong. And by then it'll be too late."

Jenkins knew by the gleam in Claymore's eyes that he'd swallowed the story—hook, line, and sinker.

"Well, good morning, Logan," Jasmine said in surprise. "You're up bright and early."

"Morning," he replied quietly, dropping into a chair and folding his arms on the tabletop.

Jasmine drained the last swallow from her mug. "The coffee's good and fresh. I think I'll have another cup. You want one?"

"Yeah, I guess so." With brooding eyes Logan watched Jasmine fetch another mug, fill the two, and bring them back to the table. "Thanks," he said as she handed him one.

"You're welcome," Jasmine replied, reclaiming the chair she'd been sitting in when Logan wandered into the kitchen.

He poured a dollop of milk into his coffee and began to stir. "Uh . . . where is everybody?" His wary eyes swept the kitchen but never quite looked directly at Jasmine.

Two tiny lines formed on her brow. This wasn't the Logan she was used to. She wouldn't have been surprised to see a measure of cockiness or maybe even a bit of lovestruck mooning. But that wasn't the case this morning.

Did he know she was aware of where he'd spent the night? Surely he did. But, of course! That was probably what was bothering him.

Good heavens! she thought in shock. Could Logan possibly be embarrassed? After all the rumors she'd heard about his many liaisons? Why, she'd never known him to be embarrassed by anything. Still, last night had to have been different from when he was simply slipping off with some gal at the local saloon. After all, he was obviously in love with Callie.

Jasmine took a sip of coffee and wondered what had precipitated last night's events. She'd begun to think Logan was never going to come to his senses regarding how he felt about Callie. But it certainly appeared that he had. Callie would never have let him spend the night with her unless something very special had happened. Logan must have confessed his love for her . . . or maybe even proposed!

Yes! Jasmine thought with delight. That had to be it! While everyone else was gone, Logan had told Callie he loved her and asked her to marry him. And about time, too!

Jasmine could almost see the scene in her head. Logan had proposed and Callie had said yes and then they'd . . . well, no sense dwelling on that, she thought, a flush of heat climbing her cheeks.

No wonder Logan looked so troubled. Under the circumstances, any man would be worried about the reputation of the woman he loved. And well he should be! Polite society hardly approved of a couple enjoying their honeymoon night before the wedding took place. How lucky that no one but Hezekiah and herself had been home — they'd certainly never tell!

Jasmine was tempted to give Logan back a little of the teasing he'd dished out over the years, but one look at his hangdog face put an end to the urge. He was her friend, and the least she could do was put his mind to rest.

"Everyone's out. Doc Pritchert asked Henrietta if she'd sit with Orie Clampett's wife — she's expecting a baby any day now and she's been kind of poorly. Actually . . ." Jasmine speared him with almond-shaped eyes of darkest brown. ". . . the doctor came by yesterday afternoon right after Henrietta got back from town. She took the boys and left almost immediately."

Hope flickered in Logan's eyes. "That so? Left yesterday afternoon, huh?"

"That's right. She was in a real tizzy to get out to the Clampetts'. I told her I'd take care of supper and let you and Callie know where she was. I don't think she gave any of us much thought after that."

Logan cleared his throat. "Probably not. And what about you and Hezekiah? I . . . uh . . . thought you might have gone on up to the mine with him, like we talked about the other day."

"No. We spent some time in the barn after Henrietta left — finished loading the wagon with the last of those supplies. But Hezekiah decided he wanted to take them on up to the mine himself

299

today so he can finish getting things organized. I'll go with him on the next trip."

"I see," Logan said with a slow nod of his head. "Then I guess you two were here for supper and all. I suppose you . . . uh . . . wondered where Callie and I were?"

Jasmine carefully placed her cup back in its saucer and looked squarely at him. "We didn't think much about if for a while, Logan, not until we went out to the barn and found your horse there, still saddled. Hezekiah thought we'd better check, so we came back in the house. Your room was empty."

"I see." Logan concentrated on his half-empty cup, turning it round and round and round on the table.

"I started to tap on Callie's door—to ask her if she knew where you were," Jasmine continued. "Well, the latch hadn't caught properly and it swung open just a little bit."

"What?" he gulped, his gaze flying upward.

"Oh, don't worry," Jasmine said quickly. "I closed that door real fast when I recognized the boots laying in the middle of the floor. Believe me, Logan, those boots were *all* I saw. It was real quiet and I guessed the two of you were asleep."

"Oh, Lord," he groaned, dropping his head into his hands. "How could I have been such a fool? How in hell could I have done something so stupid?"

Reaching across the table, Jasmine patted his

300

arm. "No sense crying over spilled milk, Logan. No one knows but Hezekiah and me, and you know we'll never say anything. Besides, you and Callie aren't the first people to let your hearts get the best of your heads. It'll be all right. It won't take long to arrange the wedding."

Logan's head snapped up. "Wedding?" His head began to shake emphatically. "No, you don't understand. There's not going to be a wedding."

"No wedding?" Jasmine stared incredulously. "What on earth are you talking about?"

The legs of his chair scraped harshly against the floor when he pushed it back. He paced the kitchen, raking his trembling fingers through his hair. "You understand how it is, Jasmine. You know I always said I'd never get married. I'm just not the marrying kind."

"Hummph!" she said, folding her arms across her bosom. "Not the marrying kind, indeed! That's pure balderdash, and you know it! All that talk was fine and dandy before Callie came along. But things have changed now."

"No, they haven't," he protested. "If anything, what happened yesterday made me more sure than ever."

Her eyes narrowed. "Is that so? Then I guess I didn't know you as well as I thought I did. My, my, you certainly had me fooled. Oh, I know all about your reputation with women, Logan Powers. I can't say that I approved, but at least the women you fooled around with were the willing kind."

Surprised by Jasmine's chastising tone, Logan stopped his agitated pacing and looked quizzically at his old friend.

She shook her head in disgust. "I just don't understand you. A woman like Callie falls in love with you, and you don't even know how lucky you are. And to think I actually thought you were in love with Callie, while all you cared about was having your way with her. And now that you have, you tell me she's not good enough for you to marry. Well, I have to disagree. In my book, you're not good enough for her." Jasmine's chin jutted toward the ceiling. "Lord, I hope you're real proud of what you've done."

"Good heavens, Jasmine," he protested. "You can't possibly think that's what I meant. I wasn't talking about last night . . . I was talking about yesterday afternoon when Callie climbed out on that damn Castle Rock to get Betsy."

Jasmine's eyes grew wide. "Castle Rock? You mean that big ol' chunk of granite that sticks out over Tombstone Gulch?"

"Hell, yes, that's exactly what I mean. Betsy was stuck out there and Callie went after her. I tried to get there to help, but I couldn't reach them in time. I was halfway up the mountain when I saw her climb out on that ledge, and I died a little inside while I watched her! One wrong step and she could have fallen! *She could have died!* Jesus, don't you understand? Don't you see what hell I went through? It just proved my point, all over again. I'm not going to love someone again and then spend the rest of my life being afraid that I'm going to lose them. I can't do it. I can't."

Jasmine rushed to his side. "Oh, Logan, I'm sorry for what I said. I just got so riled when I thought you meant— Oh, never mind that." She took his hand and pulled him toward the table. "Come over here and sit down. You've got to listen to me."

He followed meekly, sinking back into the chair he'd left earlier. Once again he dropped his head into his hands. "There's nothing else to say, Jasmine. Believe me. I've thought about this half the night. I couldn't even face Callie this morning. I just tiptoed out of that room before she woke up. Good Lord, she doesn't deserve any of this. I don't want to hurt her."

"Of course you don't," Jasmine assured him as she hastily dragged her chair closer so she could keep up the reassuring pats she'd been applying to his shoulder.

With eyes full of misery, he looked at her. "She deserves to be happy, Jasmine."

"Yes, she does. And so do you. Listen to me, Logan Powers. I know all about what happened to your family—Hezekiah told me. I know no one can really comprehend what a terrible experience that must have been, but please believe me when I tell you that I understand a little bit of what you went through. I lost my family, too. Oh, not like you did. I lost mine to cholera, but it hurt just

303

the same. And you've got to believe me when I tell you that having Hezekiah—loving him, being with him—makes up for a lot of the loneliness I felt after that. You can't throw this chance at happiness away, Logan. You can't let something that happened a long time ago mess up the rest of your life."

"It won't work."

"Of course it will. Just as soon as you and Callie are married—"

Callie reached the end of the hallway just in time to hear Jasmine's last sentence. She froze in place, her heart fluttering wildly within her breast. Her emotions had run the gamut from fright to euphoria, from doubt to hope since she'd awakened to find herself alone in the big bed. A hundred questions had swirled through her mind as she carefully dressed in a gown that was a particular favorite of Logan's.

When had he left her? And why? Had he done it to keep the others from finding out what had happened between them? Was he sorry, now that he'd had time to think about it? Or was his heart singing like hers?

She wanted so desperately for him to love her, for him to want to be with her as much as she wanted to be with him. She'd realized last night that neither Boston nor anything else mattered. She just wanted a life with Logan.

Oh, she knew it wouldn't be easy. He was wind and fire, where she was as solid as the ground beneath their feet. But it would be all right. It had to be. He couldn't have loved her so devastatingly, so tenderly, last night if he didn't care as much as she did.

Well, her wondering was soon to be over. Fate had stepped in — Jasmine Kane's words had cut right to the heart of the matter. Callie was about to find out exactly how Logan felt.

"I told you, Jasmine, there's not going to be a wedding. The best thing Callie can do is get on a train and go back to Boston where she—"

Callie's legs threatened to buckle under her as Logan's deep voice cruelly ended her dreams. She stuffed her fist against her trembling lips to stop the cry of anguish that threatened to erupt. Tears blurred her eyes and burned the back of her throat.

All she could think of was getting out of the house — away from the pain that was threatening to tear her apart — as fast as possible. Now. Immediately. Before Logan came out of that room and she had to face him.

With one hand still pressed tight against her mouth and the other clinging to the wall for support, Callie backed away from the entrance to the kitchen. Her careful, puppetlike steps carried her to the front door, where she groped for the doorknob with shaking hands. Finally, she managed to turn the knob and ease the door open, praying all the while that no one would hear the click of the latch or the telltale creak of the door.

305

She slipped through the opening and, with a half-swallowed sob, pulled the door shut behind her. With precise and careful steps she covered the short distance across the porch and down the steps.

When Callie's feet touched the hard-packed dirt, she snatched up her skirts and began to run, seeking the only source of solitude she could think of — the lonely mountain wilderness behind Henrietta's house. She had no goal, no plan. All she knew was that she had to flee, to escape the pain that threatened to tear her heart into shreds.

Heedless of the spiny cactus and thorny bushes that clawed at her pale-green dress, Callie ran until the house was lost from sight behind her, until a burning ache in her side demanded that she slow her pace.

Gasping for oxygen, blinded by the tears that pooled in her eyes and streamed down her face, Callie stumbled forward — and straight into the waiting arms of Lee Jenkins.

CHAPTER TWENTY-TWO

"I told you, Jasmine, there's not going to be a wedding. The best thing Callie can do is get on a train and go back to Boston where she can meet someone who deserves her. I want her to be happy." Suddenly Logan frowned. He cocked his head to one side and listened intently. "Did you hear something?"

"No," Jasmine answered. "Why?"

"I was afraid it might be Callie. I'd planned to be out of the house before she awakened. I . . . I just don't think I could stand to face her yet."

Frustration surged through Jasmine. She couldn't bear to let Logan throw away this chance at happiness. There had to be a way to convince him that he was making a mistake. She was determined to find it, even if it meant forcing him to face a past he'd fought long and hard to forget.

"Tell me something, Logan," Jasmine said softly. "Do you love Callie? Or have I been completely wrong?"

He sighed deeply and looked at his friend, his dark eyes full of misery. "Yes, I love her. I didn't want to, but I do. I don't know how it happened, or why. But loving her doesn't make any difference. I know I can't give her what she needs."

Jasmine gave a slow shake of her regal head. "I don't believe that. And I don't think you would, either, if you gave it some serious thought."

"It won't work."

"I don't want to hear you talk like that," Jasmine said, exasperation beginning to show in her voice. "When you're lucky enough to find true love, then there's nothing too tough to face in order to make it work."

"You can talk all day, Jasmine, but you're not going to change my mind. I believe Callie will be better off going back to Boston. I just want her to be happy. I can't give her the happiness and security she deserves and I know it."

"That's the coward's way out. Do you mean to tell me you're going to sacrifice Callie's happiness and your own rather than take a chance? Good Lord, man, that's what life is all about—taking chances. Something that's worth having doesn't come easy. You have to work at it. You have to take a risk once in a while."

Logan eyed his friend morosely. "I know you're trying to help, but you're wasting your time. I'm not going to change my mind."

"Well, I'm sorry to hear that. One of these days,

308

I think you'll realize that quality is more important than quantity when it comes to love. Look at Hezekiah and me—we don't know from day to day how long we'll have together. Something could happen tomorrow . . . an accident, an illness . . . who knows? Oh, I'm honest enough to admit it would hurt something fierce if I lost Hezekiah. But I also know I'd rather have a year, a month, or even one day with him than a lifetime with someone else. I'm telling you, Logan, you're going to be sorry if you pass up what you and Callie could have together."

"Maybe I will," he said with a shrug of resignation. "But I've got to do it for Callie's sake. In Boston she'll have the opportunity to find someone worthy of her. She needs someone to count on, someone who won't let her down when things get tough. She sure can't count on me. I proved that a long time ago."

"Oh, Logan, Logan," Jasmine moaned. "How long are you going to hug that old hurt to your heart? Why can't you realize that you did the best you could? You didn't let your family down. Good heavens! You weren't much more than a child. Do you really think anyone—even an adult—could have fought off those renegade Indians?"

Pain etched Logan's face. "I was in charge. I should have been paying attention. If I'd had a gun—"

"Listen to me. It wasn't your fault. It wasn't!

Why don't you give yourself credit for what you *did* manage to do? You saved yourself, and you saved Sabra. Doesn't that count for something? What more do you think you could have done?"

"I could have taken care of my mother and the baby like my father asked me to," he replied softly.

"Oh, Logan," Jasmine murmured, her heart breaking for her friend.

"Listen, I appreciate everything you've been trying to do. Honest. I just think it's time to let it alone."

Logan drew a deep breath and reached out one big hand to cover Jasmine's smaller one. The smile that barely tipped the corners of his mouth was the saddest she had ever seen.

"Enough of this, all right? I have a favor to ask of you."

"What is it?" Jasmine questioned, her mind still desperately searching for something else—anything else—that might make him change his mind.

"I have some money put away. It'll more than cover what Claymore owes Callie, but I know she won't take it if she knows it's from me. I want you to go to the bank with me. I'm going to withdraw the money and buy a ticket for tomorrow morning's train. Then I want you to bring the money and ticket back here and give them to Callie. You can tell her that Claymore had them delivered. Will you do that for me?"

Despair filled Jasmine. He was really going to

do it. He was going to let Callie walk out of his life.

"You could give it to her yourself," she said, desperately searching for anything that might throw Callie and Logan together, even for a few minutes. "Wouldn't it be more believable if you said you'd stopped by Claymore's office, and he'd given it to you to bring to her?"

"No," he said with an emphatic wag of his head. "I don't want to see her again. I can't. That's why I want you to go to the bank with me, so I won't have to come back to the house. As soon as I get the money and the ticket, I'm going up to the mine . . . probably stay for a couple of days. By the time I come back, Callie will be gone. It'll be best that way. Now, will you do a favor for an old friend, or not?"

"Yes, I'll do it," Jasmine answered reluctantly, her black eyes moist with tears.

Jenkins's plot had gone perfectly. The town's banker had been more than happy to fill Claymore's request. Obsequious as always, Jeremy Adams had been too busy bobbing and bowing to notice the gleam of madness in Claymore's eyes, and if he'd been aware of the alcohol on Claymore's breath, he had prudently ignored it. With scarcely a question, the little man had scurried off to gather the funds.

There had been only one short moment when

311

Claymore had been afraid the plan might go awry, and that was when Logan Powers entered the bank. Luckily, Powers had seemed preoccupied. He'd tipped his hat and nodded at Claymore and gone straight to the teller's window.

Adams had returned with the money almost immediately after Powers's arrival, and Claymore's nerves had vibrated like plucked strings as he'd packed his saddle bags with the bundles of banded bills. He had allowed himself one quick glance across the room as he left the bank, going weak at the knees with relief when he saw that Logan was too busy transacting his own business to notice what his erstwhile employer was doing.

In his hurry to quit the premises, Claymore had almost collided with a lady outside the bank's main entrance. Not even his anxiety to get out of town could keep a womanizer like Claymore from taking a second look at such a striking woman, quite the most beautiful Negress he'd ever seen. Hard on the heels of the thought that he'd have to find a way to get acquainted with the woman came the realization that he'd soon be gone from Bisbee and no such opportunity would ever exist.

Anger boiled within Claymore as he turned away and hurried on to his horse. All his fine plans. The house and the office. His business. The posh suite at the hotel. The mining empire he'd worked so long and hard to build. Gone. All gone. And it was all Edith's fault! And that damn Logan Powers!

Powers would pay for what he'd done. Oh, yes. He'd pay.

It wasn't until he was back on the road that Claymore recalled an earlier conversation with Jenkins and remembered his talking about a colored woman staying at Henrietta Winslow's boardinghouse. Bisbee had so few blacks that Owen knew it was highly likely that the woman he'd almost bowled over and the one Jenkins had mentioned were one and the same.

With a supreme effort, Claymore pulled his thoughts back to the situation at hand, doggedly trying to convince himself that things weren't so bleak after all. His saddle bags were filled with high denomination bills and he'd soon have his revenge on Logan . . . and Callie Nolan.

A zealous gleam lit Claymore's eyes as he considered Callie's many charms. It had been a long time since he'd traveled any way but first class, and he hadn't been looking forward to the arduous trip he and Jenkins had ahead of them. But now, thinking of the solitude and the hours he'd have to pleasure himself with Callie, he felt a rush of eagerness to begin their journey.

By the time the cabin loomed into view, Claymore was in considerably better spirits. The sight of Jenkins's horse tied out front elicited a small smile. Eager to show Jenkins what he'd accomplished, Claymore quickly dismounted. With hurried gestures, he hitched his horse beside Jenkins's and hauled the heavy bags from behind his saddle.

"Hey, Jenkins!" he called out as he stepped up on the porch. "Wait till you see what I've got!"

The door creaked open and Jenkins appeared in the dimly lit rectangle. "No, Boss," he said with a low chuckle, "wait till you see what *I* got." His grin was wide and wicked as he stepped aside and allowed Claymore to enter.

Jenkins closed the door just as Claymore gave a low whistle of surprise. In a chair across the room sat Callie Nolan. A frazzled rope crisscrossed the pale-green bodice of her dress, bracketing in the most delectable manner her breasts, which heaved from breathing that was rapid and shallow from fear.

"Well, well, what have we here?" Claymore asked, his amber gaze raking Callie's trembling form from head to toe.

Callie's struggle with Jenkins had shaken her long black hair loose from its pins. The wind and the wild ride to the cabin had whipped it into wild disarray. The gown she'd so carefully donned in an effort to please Logan was now rumpled and smudged with dirt.

"Mr. Claymore!" she gasped. "Oh, please, you have to help me."

"My, what a change a few weeks can bring. Right, Miss Nolan? If my memory serves me, it wasn't too long ago that I offered to help you. Don't tell me you've already forgotten?" Claymore smiled, but there was nothing reassuring about it. "A bit of poetic justice, wouldn't you say, Miss

314

Nolan? The tables seemed to have turned, and now you're *asking* me to help you."

With wide, frightened eyes, Callie watched Claymore saunter across the room. Each breath she labored to draw seemed to lodge halfway down her throat. With every step her former employer took toward her, her heart beat a little faster. By the time Claymore came to a stop mere inches from her, she could feel the accelerated thudding in every pulse point in her body.

"My," Claymore purred, "don't you look fetching this morning?" He reached out one thick finger and softly stroked the side of her face. Then slowly, tauntingly, he ran his finger down the slant of her jaw, down the vulnerable column of her throat and lightly over the slope of one firm breast.

Callie gasped with shock as his finger rasped across her nipple. Instinctively she pressed herself as tight as possible against the back of the chair she was bound to, but the millimeter of space her action provided did not hamper Claymore's teasing torment in the least.

Highly amused by Callie's futile efforts, Claymore softly chuckled. With gentle, stroking motions he ran his finger back and forth across the peak of her breast.

"Why, whatever is the matter, my dear? My good friend Jenkins tells me you're quite fond of such displays of affection."

Callie's frightened gaze darted to the dark man

across the room. Jenkins's salacious grin only confirmed what she already knew. No matter what Claymore chose to do to her, there'd be no help from the man who'd kidnapped her and brought her to this place.

Suddenly Claymore stopped touching her and stepped back a pace. Callie sagged with temporary relief. But as her former employer balanced his ponderous weight on the back of his heels and mockingly tapped his finger against his chin, she knew her suffering was far from over.

"A very convincing act, my dear. I'm quite sure I'd fall for that aura of maidenly shyness once again . . . *if* I didn't know that someone had been sampling those luscious charms for quite some time."

"What?" Callie gasped.

"I'm really quite wounded by your apparent lack of generosity, Miss Nolan. Tsk, tsk. And to think you turned down my generous offers. I find it hard to understand how you could have preferred the squalor of the Winslow boardinghouse to the obvious luxury of my hotel suite. And as for choosing Mr. Powers over myself —" He lifted beefy shoulders in a mocking shrug. "There's just no accounting for taste, is there? But believe me, my dear, before I'm through with you, you'll be quite convinced that my expertise far exceeds Mr. Powers's skills when it comes to pleasuring women."

Tears of embarrassment and rage sprang into

Callie's eyes and she struggled against the rope that bound her. Her efforts caused the chair to rock precariously. Only Lee Jenkins's swift action stopped it from toppling to the floor.

"You'd best settle down, Miss Nolan," he said, righting the chair. With seemingly little effort he scooted the chair and its occupant backward until it was braced against the ramshackle wall of the cabin. "There," he said, dusting his hands against the seat of his britches. "You'll be safer like that."

Jenkins crossed the narrow space to the table and poured a dirty tumbler full of whiskey and then held it out to Claymore.

"Here, Boss, why don't you have a little something to wet your whistle?" Jenkins was glad when Claymore accepted the proffered glass and quickly downed its contents. "Now, Boss, I know the little lady's very tempting, but shouldn't we take care of those other . . . uh . . . matters first? Namely, Logan Powers."

There was a hiss as Callie inhaled sharply. "What do you want with Logan?" she demanded.

"Oh. Yes. Quite right, Jenkins. Quite right," Claymore agreed, deliberately ignoring Callie's inquiry. "We do need to finish that business first, don't we? There'll be plenty of time for amusement later."

"Absolutely right, Boss."

Claymore hoisted his glass and gave Callie a questioning glance. "Would you care for a little liquid refreshment, my dear? No? Oh, that's right.

317

How forgetful of me. You don't care for spirits, do you?"

While Claymore refilled his glass, Jenkins snagged the remaining chair and placed it in front of Callie. Straddling the chair, he crossed his arms on the backrest and peered at Callie.

"We can all save ourselves a lot of time and unpleasantness if you'll just cooperate, Miss Nolan."

His quiet words were more frightening than Claymore's harsh blusterings. Callie stilled her useless writhing against the ropes and stared back at Jenkins. "Cooperate?" she said, her voice laced with trepidation. "Cooperate how? I don't understand any of this. I don't even know who you are, or why you brought me here."

"Don't worry about it, Miss Nolan," Jenkins soothed. "It's unimportant for the time being. First, I need a bit of information, if you don't mind. I didn't notice Hezekiah Kane around the house this morning. Do you happen to know where he is?"

"Hezekiah?" Callie repeated in confusion. "Well no, I don't. That is, not exactly. I haven't seen him since yesterday morning. But he did mention that he was going up to the mi—" Callie's mouth snapped shut as she realized what she'd been about to say. "No," she declared with an emphatic shake of her head. "I don't know where he is."

"Come, come, Miss Nolan," Jenkins urged, a puckish smile wreathing his boyishly handsome face. "Don't play games with us. You were about to say that Hezekiah had gone up to Powers's mine, weren't you?"

"No!" Callie protested. "I don't know what you're talking about. I don't know anything about a mine! I don't know where Hezekiah is. And I wouldn't tell you if I did!"

"We'll see about that!" Claymore snarled, lurching across the room and delivering a ringing slap which snapped Callie's head sideways.

Jenkins surged up from his chair. Grabbing Claymore's arm, he tugged the big man backward. "Now, now, Boss. Don't get yourself all riled up. You don't want to mark the pretty lady, do you? Why don't you let me handle this? After all, that's what you're paying me for."

As soon as he was sure that Claymore was going to keep his distance, Jenkins turned back to Callie. "Look, Miss Nolan," he said in a low voice, "you really have no choice. I suggest you cooperate. Otherwise, the boss here might get a little put out with you." Callie's frightened eyes see-sawed between Claymore and Jenkins. "I don't think you want that to happen, now do you?"

"I told you, I don't know where Hezekiah is." Panic was beginning to creep into Callie's voice.

Jenkins shrugged. "That's all right. I think I already have the answer I was looking for. Now, let's move on to the next little item on our list—"

"W-what?"

"Easy," Jenkins replied, spreading his hands

wide. "All I want you to do is write a note to Logan Powers asking him to join you at the mine."

"That's preposterous!" Callie protested. "Logan would never believe such a note. He knows I don't know where the mine is!"

Jenkins's eyes narrowed as he contemplated this latest bit of information. "All right. I believe you. We'll just have to think of something else."

"Wait a minute," Claymore interrupted. He swung his hand upward and whiskey sloshed from the glass onto the floor. "I saw Powers at the bank. Looked to me like he was drawing money out."

Jenkins frowned. "That so? Umm." He turned back to Callie. "You know anything about that, Miss Nolan? Is Powers planning a trip or something?"

Callie's mind spun. Tumbled memories of last night's rapture and this morning's agony whirled through her brain. She didn't know the answer to Jenkins's question, nor would she have told him if she had. "I don't know," she managed to say.

"Well, somebody's got to know."

"Jesus! That black wench!" Claymore's gleeful words interrupted Jenkins. "That *had* to be Kane's wife outside the bank. She was probably waiting for Powers. If Miss Nolan doesn't know, we'll simply go ask the Kane woman."

Jenkins grinned. "That's a great idea, Boss. Only this time, you'll have to go fetch the lady.

I'm afraid Kane's woman wouldn't be too happy to see me."

"Please," Callie begged, tears clogging her throat. "Leave Jasmine alone. She doesn't know anything, either! I don't know what you want, but I can't help you, and neither can she. Please, please, just let me go."

"Not hardly, Miss Nolan." There was a wicked twinkle in Lee Jenkins's eyes. "I got some big fish to catch, and you're the bait."

Once again, Claymore followed a plan laid out by Jenkins. With extreme care he slipped into Henrietta's barn. Sure enough, Powers's horse was gone, as was Hezekiah Kane's. Still, as instructed by Jenkins, he watched the house for several minutes through the partially cracked door. When he was reasonably sure that no one was home except Jasmine Kane, he eased through the opening and crossed the backyard.

A sharp rap on the back door brought Jasmine quick enough.

"Good heavens, girl, where have you been? I've been so worried— Oh!" Jasmine said in surprise. The man on the stoop was a stranger, and Jasmine stepped back a pace. "I'm sorry. I thought you were someone else."

Claymore hurriedly swept his hat from his head. "Pardon me, ma'am," he said. "I surely didn't mean to frighten you."

Jasmine's keen eyes took in the expensive cut of the stranger's suit, his distinguished bearing, and the gleam of anxiety in his eyes. She frowned. There was something familiar about the man, but she couldn't quite put her finger on it.

"No," she finally said, giving up trying to remember just where she'd seen him before. "You just startled me, that's all."

"I'm truly sorry, ma'am," the man said, bobbing his head in apology.

"It's all right. Can I do something for you? If you're looking for Mrs. Winslow, I'm afraid she's not at home today."

The man's face fell. "Oh, dear. That's too bad."

Tendrils of alarm began to creep through Jasmine. "Is something wrong? Can I do anything to help?"

The man hesitated for a long moment. "Dear me, I really don't know what to do. You see, there's been an accident."

"An accident?" Jasmine's eyes grew dark with apprehension.

The man nibbled his bottom lip. "I had really hoped to find Henrietta at home. After all, it's her friend who's hurt."

"Who?" Jasmine demanded. "Who's been hurt?"

"A Miss Callie Nolan," the man answered. His face brightened a bit. "Say, you wouldn't happen to know the lady, would you?"

"Of course I know her!" Jasmine said in exasperation. "Now tell me how badly she's hurt.

322

What happened? Where is she?"

Claymore's dour expression would have done justice to the town's undertaker. "Miss Nolan's injuries are quite extensive."

Jasmine pressed trembling fingers to her cheeks. "Oh, dear God! And everyone's gone. There's no one at home but me! Please," she said, clutching Claymore's sleeve. "You've got to take me to her. Now!"

Claymore frowned, as if giving her request deep consideration. "Well, I suppose that might be the best thing to do. If you *are* acquainted with Miss Nolan."

"Yes! Yes, I am," Jasmine assured him, frustration lacing her voice. "Now, will you please hurry? Where are we going? Is it far?"

"Several miles, I'm afraid," Claymore intoned gravely. "But have no fear, I brought an extra horse for Henrietta's use. Trying to save time, you know. It's tied back by the barn."

"Fine," Jasmine said, quickly jerking the door closed. In her worry over Callie's condition, she never gave thought to why the man had called at the back door rather than the front, or why he'd made the peculiar choice of leaving the horses at the back of the house rather than at the hitching post by the street. "Could we hurry, please?"

"My sentiments exactly, Mrs. Kane," Claymore answered, leading the way.

CHAPTER TWENTY-THREE

"Callie? Is that you?" Jasmine stared in shocked disbelief at the shadow-draped figure across the one-room cabin. What's going on? I don't understand. They told me you were hurt."

Jasmine started forward, but she froze in place when she saw the reason for her friend's stillness. "My God!" came her fervent whisper. "You're tied up." The horror-filled words barely made it around the sudden lump of fear in her throat.

"Oh, Jasmine," Callie said mournfully. "I was hoping they wouldn't find you."

"They?" Jasmine repeated, her eyes growing round and apprehensive. "They who?" she challenged, whirling to confront the man who'd brought her to the cabin.

For the first time Jasmine noticed that there was another man in the room. He must have been standing behind the door when she'd entered.

"Jennings!" The dreaded name fairly exploded

from Jasmine's lips as the man stepped from behind Claymore.

"None other, Mrs. Kane," the dark man said, moving forward and giving an impudent little bow. "How nice to see you again."

"Jennings?" Claymore's voice betrayed his confusion. "I thought you said your name was Jenkins."

Leroy Jennings gave an offhand shrug. "Jennings, Jenkins, what's the difference, Claymore? I'm getting the job done for you, ain't I?"

Claymore frowned as he contemplated this new bit of information. "Hell, I guess it's your business what name you want to use," he finally said.

Jasmine's befuddled gaze traveled from Claymore to Callie. "Claymore? This is Owen Claymore, the man you worked for?"

"Yes," Callie answered in a tired voice. "Oh, Jasmine, I'm so sorry you got pulled into this."

A bitter smile etched Jasmine's sculptured mouth. "Don't bother apologizing, Callie. I'm afraid it's the other way around. You got pulled into a situation because of us."

A frown puckered Callie's forehead as she tried to make sense of what Jasmine had said. "What do you mean?"

Jasmine whirled, her fierce gaze settling on the shorter of the two men. "Let her go, Jennings. She had nothing to do with this."

"Sorry, Mrs. Kane," Jennings answered with a mocking smile. "But the boss here has taken a shine to the little lady. I don't think he'd take kindly to your suggestion."

Jasmine's dark eyes speared Owen Claymore. "Why are you doing this?" she demanded. "Do you have any idea who you're dealing with? That man—" She jabbed an accusatory finger in Jennings's direction. "—is a murderer! He recently escaped from prison." Claymore appeared not to hear or not to care, if he had. Jasmine tried again. "You're going to have the blood of two innocent men on your hands if you don't do something to stop him!"

Leroy Jennings chuckled. "My, my, Mrs. Kane. Such eloquent oratory. But you can save your pleas. The boss here wants Logan Powers dead as much as I do." Callie's gasp echoed through the room. "And as for Hezekiah Kane, the boss could care less. What's one darky, more or less?"

"But why?" came Callie's anguished cry. "Why do you want to harm Logan, Mr. Claymore? He hasn't done anything to you. Please, please, you've got to think about what you're doing," she pleaded. "Think about Mrs. Claymore and the children. Good Lord, have you considered what it'll do to them if your part in this gets out?"

Claymore glowered. "It's really none of your business, Miss Nolan, but I'll tell you anyway. Edith and the children are gone. They left this morning for Tucson. You see what your meddling has caused? Yours and Logan Powers's? I don't know what you said or did yesterday afternoon, but whatever it was, it made Edith decide to leave

326

me. I'm losing everything that ever mattered to me—my business, my home, the respect and honor of this community. And now you're both going to pay for interfering in my life. Both of you."

Callie's eyes, dark with anguish, locked with Jasmine's. What could she say? She *had* talked to Edith Claymore, but never, never in her wildest dreams had she thought it might lead to this.

Jennings's sarcasm-laced words interrupted Callie's fearful thoughts. "And now, Mrs. Kane, if you'll have a seat in that other chair beside your friend."

Jasmine's chin rose impudently.

"No?" Jennings asked softly. "I think I can persuade you to cooperate."

With a slow, fluid movement he withdrew his gun and aimed it at Callie's head. Jasmine gave a gasp of fright and quickly sank into the chair. Jennings smiled.

"I thought you'd see things my way. Claymore," Jennings called, "I'll keep the gun on her while you get that rope over there in the corner and tie up our guest."

Claymore scurried to obey. His fumbling fingers dropped the rope several times but he finally managed to secure Jasmine in the chair.

"Now," Jennings said happily when Claymore stepped away. "Isn't this cozy? Just two old friends having a nice little chat."

"You're no friend of mine," Jasmine fairly spat at him. "If you'd ever been a friend, that was over the minute you killed Logan's father."

A broken sob of shock slipped from Callie's lips. Her anxious eyes ricocheted from Jasmine to Jennings to Claymore and back again as in desperation she tried to comprehend what was happening.

"Want to rehash old times, Jasmine?" Jennings asked softly. "Very well. Then by all means let's talk about the trial. Do you remember what I said that day after they sentenced me to life in prison?"

"Yes, I remember" came Jasmine's bitter answer. "Dear God, it should have been you and not Mortimer Henderson who died in that prison!"

"Aw, my old partner in crime," Jennings murmured, a sly smile tilting one corner of his mouth. "Poor Mortimer. Things never did go quite right for him, did they?"

"Jennings, don't do this," Jasmine pleaded. "They'll catch you! You've already got one murder sentence hanging over your head!"

"Precisely, Mrs. Kane," Jennings replied with a derisive snort. "Thanks to the testimony of Hezekiah Kane and Logan Powers. I swore at that trial that they'd pay for testifying against me." He pinned Jasmine with eyes full of hatred. "I've waited a long time to keep that promise and nothing's going to stop me, do you understand? Nothing."

A befuddled Claymore plucked at Jennings's sleeve. "Wait a minute. I'm confused. You mean to tell me you know Logan Powers, and you planned to kill him all along?"

Jennings shrugged Claymore's hand off. "Right, Boss, but so what? The end result is the same, isn't it? You want Powers dead. So do I. It's like I've said all along, just tell me what you want and I'll get the job done. Now, have I ever let you down?"

"Well . . . no," Claymore finally agreed.

"Absolutely right. So you just quit worrying. Everything's going to work out fine."

Jennings forced a smile to his face. He'd be glad when he no longer needed Claymore. The man was getting to be a real pain in the ass. But it wasn't time yet. Not yet. As long as Kane and Powers were alive, Claymore might still prove useful. First he had to get Claymore out of his hair, and then he had to find out where his enemies were holed up.

"Say, Boss, why don't you go outside and check my saddlebags? I think there's a couple more bottles in them. You might as well have yourself another drink, while I talk to the ladies here."

"Yeah. Sure. Good idea," Claymore hastily agreed. Somewhere, somehow, he seemed to have lost control of the situation, but at the moment a good slug of whiskey sounded much more appealing than staying in the cabin and trying to figure out what had gone wrong. With a hurried shuffle Claymore crossed the narrow room and departed.

Turning back to the women, Jennings gave them each a cool appraisal. "Now, Mrs. Kane, why

329

don't you make this easy on yourself? Just tell me what I want to know."

"Don't tell him anything, Jasmine!" Callie protested vehemently.

Jennings's eyes narrowed dangerously. "I suggest you keep your mouth shut, Miss Nolan or I'll call the boss back in here and let him deal with you while Jasmine and I finish our conversation. I don't think you'd like that too much, would you?"

Callie bit her lip to stop the flow of angry words that threatened to boil forth. There was no sense antagonizing Jennings any more than she already had.

"I thought you'd see things my way," Jennings said smugly as he squatted down beside Jasmine. "Now, Mrs. Kane, all you have to do is tell me where Logan is and give me the location of the mine. I already know that's where Hezekiah is, thanks to Miss Nolan."

Jasmine's disbelieving gaze flew to Callie's face.

"I didn't tell him, Jasmine! I swear I didn't!" Callie protested. "Don't believe anything he says. He'll try to trick you. I told him we don't know where the mine is! We can't tell him if we don't know!"

Lurching to his feet, Jennings threw a disgusted look at Callie. "I'm tired of your stupid games, Miss Nolan," he fairly snarled. "I wanted to do this the easy way." He spread his hands wide as if in supplication. "But, hey, you want to do it the hard way? All right. That's just fine with me."

Once again Jennings drew his gun. Jasmine and Callie gaped in horror as he slowly eased back the hammer. A whimper of fear escaped Callie when he stepped behind her and placed one arm gently around her neck, his forearm lying against the wildly beating pulse in her throat.

With great deliberation Jennings raised the gun and poised the barrel against Callie's temple.

"I'm going to count to five, Mrs. Kane, and if you haven't told me what I want to know by then, I'm going to pull this trigger. One . . ."

Callie's terror-filled eyes searched Jasmine's face. "Don't tell him," she pleaded in a voice barely above a whisper. "Don't let him hurt Logan."

"Two . . ."

Jasmine swallowed a sob of despair. "Callie, listen to me. You don't know Jennings. He'll do it. Honest to God, he'll pull the trigger!"

"Three . . ."

"Please, Jasmine, please. It doesn't matter. Think of Logan, think of Hezekiah."

"Four . . ."

A sheen of sweat broke out on Jasmine's brow. Time! She needed time! The rope Claymore had tied her with was loose around her wrists. Maybe, just maybe she could get her hands free, but she needed time!

"Don't tell, Jasmine, don't tell," Callie begged in a tear-strained voice.

"Fi—"

"I'll tell you! I'll tell you!" Jasmine's anguished

331

words rent the air and Callie burst into tears.

The click of the hammer being eased back into place was as loud as an explosion.

"Good thinking, Mrs. Kane," Leroy Jennings purred. "Now, where is Logan Powers?"

"He . . . he's at the mine with Hezekiah."

"Why, Jasmine, why?" Callie asked between soft little sobs.

Jasmine's eyes begged for understanding. "I had to, Callie. I couldn't sit here and watch him shoot you!"

"But he'll kill Hezekiah and Logan!"

There was no answer for Callie's tormented cry. No way that Jasmine could explain she was simply trying to buy them some time in the hopes of being able to work free of her bonds. Jasmine let her chin sink to her chest.

"Very touching, Miss Nolan," Jennings taunted. "I hate to interrupt your conversation, but Mrs. Kane has one more piece of information to give me. Tell me how to get to the mine."

In a slow, halting voice Jasmine began to recite the directions while Jennings listened with avid interest.

As soon as she was finished, Jennings headed for the door. "Don't go away, ladies," he said with a mocking smile. "I'll be right back. Miss Nolan is going to take a little ride with us. I regret, Jasmine, that you're going to have to stay here." With that, he exited the cabin.

"Oh, Jasmine, how could you?" Callie wailed.

"Shh! Listen to me," Jasmine demanded. "We may not have much time. The ropes around my wrists are loose. I had to do something to buy a little time. Don't you understand? And if Jennings follows those directions, it'll take him twice as long to get to the mine. If I can just get free, I'll ride to town for help."

A flicker of hope flared in Callie's eyes. "Do you think we've got a chance?"

"If the good Lord's willing, I'll be able to get out of these ropes," Jasmine answered, her face contorted with the effort of her struggle against the bonds that held her. "Meanwhile, you have to do something to help."

"Anything!"

"Slow them down. Stall for time . . . whatever it takes. Every minute counts, so do whatever you can. And pray. We need all the help we can get."

The thud of footsteps upon the porch put an end to the hushed conversation. Jasmine froze in place, praying that neither man would think to check her bonds before they left.

Her prayers were answered.

Jennings barely gave Jasmine a second glance as he untied Callie and hauled her to her feet. Pinning her wrists together in front of her, he whipped one short length of rope around them. "There, that ought to keep you under control. Now, don't go getting any wild ideas, Miss Nolan. You're gonna ride with me, just to be on the safe side." He gave a low, evil chuckle. "Won't Logan

333

be surprised when he sees what I've got? I'm sure one glimpse of you is all it'll take to lure the bastard out of that mine."

Jasmine's chin tilted at a defiant angle as Callie threw her one last desperate look. *Take care,* she seemed to be saying. *Remember what to do.*

The cabin's flimsy door slammed shut. Almost immediately, Jasmine heard the thunder of hooves. She was hard at work on the ropes around her wrists before the sound faded away.

It took her longer than she'd hoped to free her hands. Next she attacked the knots in the ropes that Claymore had looped around her waist and secured at the back of the chair. Her arms twisted awkwardly behind her, Jasmine struggled to loosen those.

Finally, the last knot slipped free and the ropes fell to the floor. Jasmine sobbed with relief. The chair toppled over with a resounding thud as she jerked upward and ran for the door.

Please, please, she silently prayed. *Let the extra horse still be here.* If Callie was riding with Jennings, and Claymore had his horse, then surely, *surely* they hadn't taken the one Jasmine had ridden to the cabin.

Jasmine flung the door open and went weak-kneed at the sight of her mount. "Thank God. Oh, thank God," she murmured fervently.

Hiking her skirts thigh-high, she climbed atop the horse's broad back. She gave a flick of the reins against the animal's neck and turned him toward the barely discernible path. At the last moment, she hesitated.

Which way should she go?

It had taken far longer to work herself free than she'd expected. Could she reach town and get help in time to stop Jennings's nefarious plan? Did she dare take a chance?

Her frightened eyes darted one way, then another. Town or the mine?

She knew a shorter way than the one she'd told Jennings. She could probably beat him to the mine. But could they defend themselves without help?

What should she do? Dear God, what should she do?

Before kicking the horse in the flanks and urging him in the other direction, Jasmine gave one last fleeting look down the fork of the road that would take her to town. Too many lives hung in the balance. She dared not waste another minute.

If she could just reach Hezekiah and Logan and warn them, they might have a chance.

CHAPTER TWENTY-FOUR

"Would you slow down, Logan?" Hezekiah grumbled. "I don't think we can get everything done the first day. Hell, a man would think you had the devil nipping at your heels, the way you been pushing yourself today."

Maybe I do, Logan thought grimly. He forced a smile for Hezekiah's sake. "Sorry. Guess I'm just anxious to get things going."

Hezekiah eyed the other man and gave a slow shake of his close-cropped head. Something was eating at Logan. They'd been friends too long for Hezekiah not to notice such things. Hezekiah's few leading questions had garnered him nothing but an occasional bitter smile and a mumbled "everything's fine." But Hezekiah knew better. Logan had been driving himself like a man possessed ever since his arrival, and that grim, pinched look to his mouth meant trouble of some sort.

Well, fine, Hezekiah decided. If Logan wouldn't

tell him what was wrong, then he'd just have to talk to Jasmine as soon as he got back to town. Maybe she'd know what was going on.

As if the very thought of his wife had somehow conjured her up, Jasmine's voice rang out from outside the cave.

"Hezekiah! Logan! Where are you?"

The panic in her voice impelled Hezekiah into immediate action. He dropped the shovel he'd been digging with and ran for the entrance. Logan was a half step behind.

"Jasmine! What is it, girl?" Hezekiah cried when he saw his wife's disheveled state. He doubled his speed and covered the remaining distance to her in seconds. "My Lord! What's wrong? Are you hurt?" Alarm rippled through him as she slid from the horse and collapsed in his arms.

"No, I'm all right," she managed to gasp between great gulps for air. Her arms tightened about Hezekiah's neck and she pressed herself close to him, grateful to find him still alive. "Oh, thank God I found you in time." The words were muffled against Hezekiah's chest.

It took Logan only a second to realize that if Jasmine was all right, somebody else must not be. "Callie!" he blurted, suddenly frantic with fear. "Something's happened to Callie!" Wild with panic, Logan didn't even wait for her answer. "I've got to get to her!" he cried, grabbing up the dangling reins of Jasmine's winded horse.

Jasmine launched herself at Logan just as he

put his foot in the stirrup. "No!" she cried, grabbing double handfuls of his shirt and jerking him back. "You can't leave. They're bringing her here! Don't you understand? They're bringing her here!"

Logan slid his foot from the stirrup and turned to stare at Jasmine with total confusion. "What are you talking about? *Who's* bringing Callie here?"

Releasing her stranglehold on Logan's shirt, Jasmine stepped back into the comforting circle of Hezekiah's arms. "Jennings . . . "

"Oh, damnation!" Hezekiah muttered under his breath.

". . . and Claymore," Jasmine finished.

Logan felt as if a blow had been delivered to his midsection. His mouth dropped open in shock. "Claymore? Claymore and Jennings have Callie?" The thought was incomprehensible. "But how . . . why?"

Hezekiah voiced the questions Logan was unable to force from his mouth. "How did those two ever hook up together? And how in hell did Callie get mixed up in this?"

Tears of frustration gleamed in Jasmine's eyes. "I don't know," she said miserably. "What I do know is that we don't have much time to come up with some sort of plan. Come on," she urged, grabbing her husband's hand and pulling him toward the cave entrance. "We've got to get under cover. I'll tell you what I can while we see what we can use for weapons."

338

"Goddammit! I think we've been goin' around in circles," Leroy Jennings growled. "It's got to be somewhere close to here. We've covered practically this whole section of the mountain. If that black bitch lied to me, I'm gonna slit her gullet when I get back to the cabin!"

Renewed fear exploded in the pit of Callie's stomach. "But she said the trail was hard to see!"

Callie felt torn in two. She couldn't bear to hear Jennings's threats against Jasmine, but she also hoped with every fiber of her being that Jasmine's directions would somehow keep Jennings and Claymore from finding Logan and Hezekiah. Remembering Jasmine's admonition to delay them as much as possible, she tried again to distract her captors.

"I'm tired," Callie pouted in what she hoped was a sultry-sounding voice. "And I'm thirsty. Can't we please stop for just a few minutes, Mr. Claymore?"

Some vestige of good manners still lingered in Claymore's warped brain, impelling him to champion a lady's comfort, if not her safety. "See here, Jennings. Miss Nolan is right. We've been at this for hours. Don't you think we could take a short rest stop?"

"Christ!" Jennings mumbled under his breath. When he finished with this mess, he'd never again let himself be saddled with a partner. "All right, all right! Soon as we top that ridge, we'll take five

339

minutes. And then I don't want to hear another damn word out of either of you. Understand?"

But the promised respite never came. What Jennings saw at the top of the ridge elicited a low, satisfied chuckle. "Well, I'll be damned," he said. "There's the trail."

Jasmine had been right about the path to the cave being almost nonexistent. It began at the back edge of a dense clump of bushes and worked itself up the mountainside in a series of steep, switch-back turns. Jennings could see that the loose, gravelly dirt would make for slow going to the high, hidden gulch where Hezekiah and Logan waited in blissful ignorance.

"You go first, Claymore," Jennings said. "It'll be easier for you to lead since I'm riding double with the lady." It would also be a small safeguard to Jennings's safety. If anyone was going to be a target, it could damn well be Claymore.

"Very well," Claymore agreed, clicking his tongue at his mount and urging the animal up the first zigzag of the path.

"As for you, missy," Jennings growled in Callie's ear. "I'm warning you right now. One sound and you're dead. Do you understand?"

Callie managed a nod of her head as his arm tightened painfully around her waist.

"Good." Jennings slapped the reins against his mount's neck. The horse lurched forward, its hooves scrabbling for purchase on the rock-littered trail.

Slowly but surely they made their way upward, past scattered brush and random outcroppings of tumbled rock. Long minutes later, they scrambled up the last section of the trail and topped the final ridge to find a section of fairly flat land stretched away into a small vee-shaped canyon that cut deep into the folds of the mountainside.

"Do you see it?" Jennings asked tersely as he raked the shaded areas for the sign of an entrance to a cave.

"No," Claymore replied, squinting his eyes against the slant of the sun. "No . . . wait! There!" He pointed toward a slice of darker shadow in the far corner of the gulch. "Is that it?"

Shielding his eyes, Jennings peered intently at the shoulder-high clump of gray rocks and at the gaping gash of darkness behind the barrier. "Crap," he muttered. "I think it is, and I damn sure don't like the layout."

Nature had created a natural stronghold. Once inside the cave, a man could peer through ragged sections of the rock pile's uneven top and see anyone approaching. There seemed to be no way to reach the cave except straight toward the entrance.

A sheer rise of scrub-brush-covered ground rose on one side of the gulch. And on the other, not far from the cave, was the bottommost and largest of a stair-step arrangement of rock-lined catch basins. The smallest of the three natural formations was located near the top of the enfolding ridge of mountain. An endless supply of clear spring water trickled from the highest basin to the middle one and then to the one on the floor of the little canyon. Just past the bottom pool was a sheer drop-off.

Fluted outcroppings of rock surrounded all three basins, but a man would have to cover a wide strip of open space to get from the cave's entrance to the promised shelter. Jennings almost hoped Powers or Kane would try to make that dash. They'd be perfect targets and dead within seconds of their first strides.

As for storming the cave, Jennings knew that was out of the question. He'd never be able to get to Powers and Kane as long as they stayed holed up inside.

No, what he somehow had to do was lure the two men out into the open, preferably one by one.

A diabolic grin etched Jennings's face. He had the bait, didn't he? Right there within his arms. Logan Powers didn't stand a chance.

Casting a critical eye about him, Jennings settled on a suitable ambush place, a dense clump of brush halfway to the cave.

"All right, Claymore," he said. "I want you to get yourself into position behind those bushes. Keep out of sight, and keep quiet until Powers comes out. Soon as you've got a good, clear view, shoot him."

"No!" Callie cried, twisting hard against the

342

man who held her captive.

Jennings reached up and locked his fingers in the long black curls that cascaded over Callie's shoulder and violently jerked her head forward. She yelped in surprise, her hand instinctively flying up to stop the torturous pressure.

"Get going," Jennings snapped at Claymore. As soon as the man started to follow orders, Jennings turned his attention back to Callie. "I told you to keep your mouth shut. Remember?"

Tears sprang into Callie's eyes as Jennings's fingers tightened their hold. "Y-yes."

"Then do as you're told or, believe me, you'll think this was fun compared to what I'll do next." With one final vicious tug Jennings slightly relaxed his hold.

Once Claymore was in place, Jennings slowly urged his horse forward. He took great pleasure in the fact that he would personally break the news of their arrival to Logan Powers.

Jennings halted his horse at a spot he thought was out of firing range; and even if he was wrong, he had Callie as a shield. They'd have to shoot her in order to get to him. Perfect.

"Powers!" he shouted. "This is your old pal, Leroy Jennings. I have a little surprise for you. Throw down your gun and come out!"

Inside the cave, in the sooty blackness beyond the reach of the sun, Hezekiah, Jasmine, and Logan froze in place. The pale light of candles flickering on a nearby ledge danced upon faces

343

etched with apprehension.

"Christ!" Logan muttered, making sure to keep his voice low so it wouldn't carry outside the cave. "What do we do now? I was hoping for more time."

"Hell, I don't know. We don't have enough ammunition for a stand-off," came Hezekiah's whispered reply. "These two boxes of bullets are all we have—that and what's already in our guns. Maybe I should try to get a look outside."

Logan gave a terse nod of agreement.

Hezekiah was back within minutes. "We got problems, Logan," he said, his voice raspy with worry. "Bad problems. Callie's on the horse with Jennings—he has her in front of him. I don't think we can hit him from this far, but even if we could, there's no way to get a shot at the bastard without hitting her."

"Son of a bitch!" Logan's eyes were wild. "There's got to be a way to get to him! There's got to be!"

Jasmine looked up from the revolver she was loading. "What about Claymore? Did you see him?"

"No. Not a sign of him."

"Well, he's out there. Make no bones about it." Jasmine's mouth thinned in anger. "Most likely, Jennings is trying to set up some sort of ambush. Is there anywhere Claymore could hide?"

Logan and Hezekiah exchanged glances.

"The rocks around the pools?" Hezekiah ventured.

"Yeah, that'd be one place, but he wouldn't have a clear shot at the cave from there. I'd put my money on that big clump of bushes about halfway across the clearing."

Hezekiah nodded in agreement. "Well, that shoots down any chance of making it out the entrance. If Claymore's that close, there's no way we could safely get to the cover around the catch basins."

"You're right," Logan said with a sigh. "God, we need something . . . an element of surprise. But what?"

"Powers!" Jennings harsh shout put a quick halt to Logan's tortured speculations. "You'd better come on out. I got your lady friend here . . . mighty delectable little morsel she is, too. If you care anything about her safety, you'll do as you're told. Come on out, Powers! My trigger finger's getting itchy!"

Logan paced the cave, raking shaky fingers through his wildly tousled hair. "I've got to go out there. I can't let him hurt Callie."

"Stall him," Jasmine urged. "Keep him talking. We'll think of something — we have to!"

"Lord, I hope so!"

Logan pulled in one last deep breath before he crept to the entrance. Gun in hand, he bent at the waist and scurried the few feet from the cave's mouth to the shelter of the ragged gray rocks. Pressed tight against the back side of the outcropping, he peeked through a jagged slit in the granite.

"I'm here, Jennings!" he shouted. "What do you want?"

Jennings's mocking laughter echoed through the small canyon. "It's not what I want, Powers. It's what *you* want! I guess you can see your lady friend, can't you?"

"Yes, I can see her." The words hurt. He could see Callie all right. See the fear on her face. See Jennings's arm tight around her, his forearm slashing diagonally across the swell of her bosom, his treacherous fingers snared in the long ebony curls that dangled over her shoulder. With a hold like that on her, there was no way Callie could even hope to break free.

"You care anything about this little lady, Powers?"

"Of course I do!" The words exploded from deep inside Logan, and he suddenly knew just how much he did care about Callie Nolan. Everything Jasmine had said came rushing back to him, tumbling and swirling in his head, mocking his stupidity at thinking he could turn his back on Callie and walk away.

Sweet heaven, yes, he cared about her. He wanted a chance — just one more chance — to spend the rest of his life with Callie. The priceless opportunity to watch her grow round and glowing with his children. The precious possibility of growing old with her. He wanted all of that and more.

If they came out of this alive, he was going to wrap her in his love and never let her go. And whatever time the good Lord saw fit to give them—be it a day or a lifetime—he was going to live it to the fullest.

Logan shook his head, but not his heart, free of the dreams. The most important thing now was to protect Callie, to somehow secure her freedom before Jennings could do her any more harm. And anything Logan had to do, any sacrifice, was worth that effort.

"Let her go, Jennings!" Logan shouted. "You have no quarrel with Callie. She had nothing to do with what's between you and me! Let her go, and I'll come out there! We'll settle this between us, face to face, like men ought to do."

"No, Logan! Don't do it!" Callie screamed, raw terror racing through her. "He'll shoot you! Don't come out here!" She clawed at Jennings's arm, trying to break his grip.

Jennings tapped Callie on the side of her head with the barrel of his gun. "Shut up, bitch!" he warned. "And keep still!"

Callie slumped into stillness, her head throbbing and tears of frustration and pain flowing down her face.

Logan called forth every ounce of determination he had to keep from charging across the space separating him from Callie. The knowledge that he couldn't reach her in time to prevent Jennings from shooting her was the only thing that kept him behind the rocks.

"I'll make you a deal, Jennings!" Logan shouted. "Let her go, and I'll throw away my weapon before I come out. A trade, Jennings. You want me, not Callie. Let her go and I'll come out."

"Yeah?" Jennings sneered. "And what about that big black friend of yours? I suppose he's going to just sit there and watch and do nothin'. Right?"

Desperate, Logan was ready to try anything. "Hell, man, what've you got a grudge against Hezekiah for? He was nothing but a piss-poor private in the Army, just doing his job. *I* was the one who figured out you were behind my father's murder. *I* was the one who cooked up the plan that caught you. Hezekiah just took orders."

Silence fell while Jennings pondered the situation. With a swift shift of his eyes, he checked Claymore's position. He was in place behind the bushes — cowered down as if in mortal fear — and the gun in his hand looked less than steady. Could he be trusted to do the job? Jennings wondered.

Greedy and mean, Claymore thought nothing of *ordering* a man's death, but did he have what it took to do the job himself? Jennings knew if he depended on Claymore and the man couldn't put a bullet in Logan, then his last chance at revenge would be gone.

"What do you say, Jennings? We got a deal? You let Callie and Hezekiah go, and I'll give myself up."

"Shut up a minute!" Jennings yelled. "I'm thinking!" Like a squirrel in a cage, Jennings's head was spinning, turning the problem this way and that, trying to find a way to assure the death of both Logan and Hezekiah without having to depend on Claymore.

What if he pretended to go along with Logan's bargain? Could he manage to get both men unarmed, kill Logan first, and then get Hezekiah? Maybe. Just maybe. It was damn well worth a try.

"All right, Powers, here's the deal. You tell Kane to show himself so I can be sure he doesn't have a weapon, and then you walk on out here in the open. *Then* I'll let Miss Nolan go."

Inspiration, wild and reckless, burst within Logan. Jennings had named two people — Hezekiah and himself. Sweet Jesus, they'd forgotten that Jennings had no knowledge of Jasmine's arrival at the cave. *There* was their desperately needed element of surprise.

Logan had a plan . . . nebulous, dangerous, but workable — maybe.

"I hear you, Jennings!" Logan shouted. "But you gotta promise to let Hezekiah go free, too."

"Yeah. Sure. I promise." If they were fool enough to believe he'd let anyone go free, then that was their problem, not his.

"I can't speak for Hezekiah till I talk to him," Logan said. "Give me a few minutes. I'm going back in the cave and ask him to do what you

349

want."

"You got five minutes!"

Logan was halfway to his destination by the time Jennings's shout faded away.

"Jasmine! Quick! Get Hezekiah's coat and hat on!"

Logan's terse instructions brooked no argument. With an economy of motion, Hezekiah stripped the coat off and handed it to his wife.

"What's up?"

"Remember that natural chimney I showed you, that big split in the rock where the smoke can escape from the cave?"

"Yeah, sure. What about it?"

"I think it's big enough for a man." Logan eyed Hezekiah's huge frame. "Christ, I hope it's big enough for you." With a shrug of resignation, he continued. "We have to take a chance. I'd go if I could, but I'm the wrong color."

Jasmine and Hezekiah exchanged puzzled looks. "What the hell are you talkin' about?" Hezekiah asked.

"Simple. Jennings wants you where he can see you. That's why Jasmine's going to be wearing your coat and hat. He doesn't even know Jasmine's here." Logan managed a wobbly grin. "He wants two people. We'll give him two people. From a distance, all he'll be able to see is dark skin. Jasmine can pull the brim of the hat down low to shade her face even more. She's not as tall as you, but from that distance I don't think he'll

350

know the difference. Besides, I hope to keep most of his attention on me."

"Lordy, lordy," Jasmine murmured, comprehending what Logan had in mind. "It just might work."

"I'll keep Jennings talking while you ease your way up that chink in the rock. It opens by the small pool on top and from there, you can use the boulders around the basins for shelter. Work your way down to where you can get a clean shot at the bastard."

"Hell, it's worth a try," Hezekiah said, clapping his floppy-brimmed hat atop his wife's head. "Do what Logan tells you, honey, but stay out of range. Jennings is one crazy bastard." He wrapped his arms tight around Jasmine and hugged her to him. "I love you."

"I love you, too," Jasmine answered bravely. "Be careful!"

"I will." With one last look, Hezekiah loped toward the rear of the cave and the promise of salvation for them all.

"Powers! Your time is up!"

Jasmine's eyes were huge with apprehension. "What'll we do, Logan? Hezekiah needs more time."

"Hang on. I'll try to stall him."

Logan edged toward the mouth of the cave. "I'm talking as fast as I can, Jennings!" he shouted. "You're going to have to give me another minute. Hezekiah doesn't trust you."

351

"Hell, Powers," Jennings shouted back. "Tell him I give my word on the grave of my sweet old mama. All he's got to do is stand behind those rocks and keep his hands in the air so I know he's not armed. He'll be safe enough. I couldn't hit him from here if I tried."

"I'll tell him! Just hold your horses!"

Logan's hand groped for Jasmine's. "If you've got any pull with the Man Upstairs, we can use all the help we can get."

"Believe me, I haven't quit praying since this mess started," Jasmine replied, a courageous smile playing at the corners of her mouth.

Jennings's next bellow wiped it from her face. "This is your last chance, Powers! Get your ass out here!"

"Are you ready?"

"As ready as I'll ever be," Jasmine answered.

Logan gave her hand a reassuring squeeze, and they began their journey.

"Don't do it, Logan! Stay in there where you're safe!" Callie cried out when she spotted his shadowy form moving behind the rocks.

"It's all right, honey. Jennings gave his word." Logan edged to one side of the tumbled boulders. "Stay over there on that side," he whispered to Jasmine. "I want us as far apart as possible. Keep his attention divided so he won't notice Hezekiah."

"Don't believe him, Logan! Please! Stay there! Don't let him talk you into this!" The anguish in Callie's voice sent cold chills racing through Logan.

"Calm down, Callie. Everything's going to be all right. Trust me, honey. I love you. You know I wouldn't let him hurt you. You're going to be safe. I promise."

By now, tears were again streaming down Callie's face. "I don't care about being safe! Don't you know that? What does it matter if you're gone? Please, Logan, please, listen to me. Stay where you're safe. I'm begging you."

"I can't do it, Callie," Logan called back, his voice husky with emotion, his stomach tied in a million knots. "I can't. Just trust me. Please."

"I hate to interrupt this touching conversation," Jennings said, "but time's running out. Where's Kane? I can't see him."

"He's right here," Logan answered.

"Well, have him step over so I can get a look at him. And I want those hands up high. No funny business, you understand?"

"We understand." Logan darted a quick look at Jasmine. "Move around so he can see you through the low place in the rocks," he whispered. "Keep that hat low and your head down. And put your arms up high so he'll think we're going along with his deal."

Jasmine eased into place and did exactly what Logan told her.

"Well, howdy there, Kane!" Jennings shouted as soon as he saw the dark-hued figure. There was a taunting edge to his voice as he continued to play out the game. "Are you surprised to see me again? Well, you can put your worries to rest. Your good friend Mr. Powers has persuaded me to let you go. All you gotta do is stand there nice and quiet and keep those hands in view. Once Powers and I settle our little . . . uh . . . disagreement, I'll let the lady go and you can take her back to town. That a deal?"

Jasmine bobbed her head.

Jennings chuckled. "Guess the darky's too scared to even talk," he muttered under his breath. "All right, Powers. Time's up. Throw out your gun and make sure you pitch it real hard, okay?"

Sunlight glinted on Logan's gun as it sailed through the air and landed with a muffled thud near the rim of the largest catch basin.

"Now, come on out here. I want you to walk nice and slow. No unnecessary moves. No tricks, or the lady gets it. Understand?"

"I understand," Logan called back. Fear coiled deep in his belly as he stepped away from the protecting rocks. With slow, deliberate paces he began to walk forward. *Hurry, Hezekiah, hurry!*

"No, no," Callie pleaded softly. "Don't do it, Logan. Don't do it." Her gaze never left his face as he continued his pacing; her eyes begged him to stop, to turn and run, to save himself. But she knew from the stubborn rigidity of his jaw that he'd do no such thing.

"That's it. Just keep on coming," Jennings crooned as Logan drew nearer and nearer. His gun

354

was aimed squarely at Logan's chest, but he delayed pulling the trigger. He'd waited too many years for this moment and he intended to savor it to the fullest. His eyes darted back and forth between Logan's slowly advancing form and the dark figure behind the rocks, while his twisted mind worked on additional ways to torment his enemy.

"I gotta hand it to you, Powers, you sure know how to pick the women. I've certainly enjoyed having Miss Nolan ride with me today. It's been a long time since I had me a woman this soft and pretty to cuddle up to. Yes, sir, it's been a pleasure, a *real* pleasure."

The suggestive tone of Jennings's words brought a gasp of indignation from Callie, and when he seductively rubbed his forearm across her breasts, she clamped her teeth on her bottom lip to keep from crying out in protest. She could stand anything Jennings did if only it gave Logan a few more seconds of safety.

Jennings had quite forgotten about Claymore. With growing indignation, Owen watched his former employee trespass on what Claymore considered to be *his* property and his alone. His mind was far too muddled to realize Jennings was only using Callie to further torment Logan. Angered at Jennings's brazen encroachment, Claymore stepped forward — and away from the cover of the bushes.

A killing rage raced through Logan, but only the wild flash of fire in his eyes betrayed how close he was to losing control.

"Maybe, after this is all over, I'll take the time to get *better* acquainted with Miss Nolan," Jennings said softly, thoroughly enjoying himself. Just looking in Logan's blazing eyes and knowing Logan was helpless to do anything about the situation, afforded Jennings a rush of pleasure like none he'd ever known.

The words hit Logan like bullets. Muscles coiled as tight as springs, he jerked to a stop. "You bastard," he muttered through gritted teeth. *Where are you, Hezekiah? Where are you?* Logan's fists clenched and unclenched at his sides. *Dear God, please let Hezekiah be in place soon. I don't think I can stand it if that son of a bitch keeps touching Callie.*

"Yep, it's been long time since I had me a woman this tempting. And when I get through with her, she's gonna know what it's like to be loved by a *real* man." Jennings released his hold on Callie's ebony curls and slid his hand downward in a slow, seductive stroke. At the same time, he raised his gun a fraction of an inch and began to tighten his finger on the trigger.

"Goddamn you!" Logan roared when Jennings's hand closed possessively over Callie's breast. Consumed by a blinding rage, he launched himself straight at Jennings.

Desperate, Callie did the only thing she could think of. She sank her small white teeth in Jennings's arm and clamped down with all her might.

356

Jennings yelped with pain and took his eyes off Logan for just a moment. That was all the opportunity Logan needed. He caught Jennings with a flying leap and the three of them tumbled to the ground.

Jennings's panicked horse reared, his flashing hooves raking the air. With a frightened whinny, he bolted across the clearing.

From his place behind a jumble of boulders, Hezekiah surged upward and took aim at Claymore. The sound of gunfire reverberated through the little gulch and Owen Claymore fell dead. Jasmine screamed and ran toward her husband.

Callie's heart almost stopped beating when she heard the shot and the scream. Fear, all-consuming and gut-wrenching, grabbed her as she wondered if Logan had been shot. She scrambled to her feet just as Jennings and Logan came tumbling toward her, arms and legs flailing.

When her whirling mind recognized that Logan couldn't be fighting like that if he'd been shot, there was a split second of relief followed quickly by a burst of sheer panic. The battle was far from over. She had to find a way to help Logan!

"The gun!" Callie cried, suddenly remembering the weapon Logan had earlier tossed aside. Hiking her skirts, she raced toward its landing place. A half-buried rock caught her toes and she stumbled and fell. On hands and knees she scrabbled the few remaining feet. The moment her hands closed on the weapon, she twisted toward the men locked in mortal combat.

By now, the vicious fight had carried the men across the clearing. Thick dust spewed upward as they kicked and rolled and gouged. The stillness of the evening was punctuated with the repeated dull thud of blows landing on flesh and the grunts and groans of their frantic exertions.

Oblivious to the rocky surface beneath her tender knees, Callie clasped the gun with shaking hands and raised it. Sobs of frustration bubbled forth as she tried to aim at Jennings. There was no way she could get a clear shot at him. One second Jennings's back was in plain view, the next it was Logan who was in her sights.

Fear coursed through her as the two men once again tumbled to the ground, rolling over and over toward the edge of the cliff. Callie screamed and surged to her feet. Dear God! If something didn't stop their wild momentum, they were going over!

Locked in a death grip, Logan and Jennings teetered on the rim of oblivion. Jennings gave a harsh cry of terror as his legs slid over the side. He clawed at Logan, hoping to save himself, determined to take his enemy with him if he couldn't.

The gun slipped from Callie's grasp and her hands flew upwards, shaking fingers pressed against her lips. Nothing could save Logan now. Nothing.

Suddenly Callie caught a blur of movement from the corner of her eye. From out of nowhere, Hezekiah launched himself forward, his huge body

358

sailing through space. He hit the ground with an audible thump and skidded the last few inches. At the last possible second, his fingers locked on Logan's wrist.

Jasmine reached Callie just as Hezekiah made his heroic grab. She wrapped her arms around her friend and held her close as their frightened eyes watched the unfolding drama.

Hezekiah lay splayed against the ground, his dark face contorted with the sheer effort of maintaining his grip on Logan. For what seemed like forever, Logan and Jennings seesawed on the brink of eternity. Then, with a harsh cry of sheer terror that echoed and reechoed through the gulch, Jennings slid over the edge just as Hezekiah gave one last mighty heave and pulled Logan from the jaws of death.

Their feet barely touching the ground, the two women raced forward and threw themselves into the arms of their men.

Safe in Logan's embrace, Callie sobbed with relief. He was gritty and grimy and blood-flecked from his battle, but he was the most wonderful, beautiful thing she'd ever seen. Locking her arms about his waist, she pressed herself against him, glorying in the rapid rise and fall of his broad chest as he pulled great gulps of air into his laboring lungs, cherishing the reassuring beat of his heart beneath her cheek.

Logan clutched Callie as tightly as possible and rained kisses upon her tear-streaked face. Between each small torrent of kisses, in a voice that shook with the depth of his emotion, he tried to tell her how much he loved her.

"You're mine, Callie. Mine forever. I'll never let you go, girl. I love you. I love you. More than anything. More than life itself."

"I know," Callie whispered, her face pressed against the strong curve of her beloved's shoulder. "I know, my darling."

And she did.

EPILOGUE

Six adults sat on the shady veranda and sipped fresh lemonade while three toddlers played an exuberant game of tag beneath the softly swaying branches of a twisted mountain pine. The high-pitched giggles and excited shrieks of the children evoked more than an occasional chuckle from their proud parents.

"Gotcha!" the little black boy shouted with glee as he touched the shoulder of his smallest play-mate.

The tagged youngster, the blond hair of baby-hood just beginning to take on the darker hues inherited from Hawk, reversed his momentum and gave hot pursuit of the third child, a little boy with tousled curls the same tawny color as Logan's.

"Where do you suppose they get all that energy?" Logan asked in awe. "Lord, if I could bottle just a portion of what Robert's got, I'd be a rich man."

"You *are* a rich man, my dear brother-in-law," Sterling Hawkins retorted with a chuckle. "The Irish Lady mine has made you a fortune, and you know it."

"Not to mention respected and influential. With Logan's help, George's Independent Miners Association has almost totally wiped out the problem created by Claymore's schemes," Hezekiah added in a rumbling bass that interrupted by two men's playful jibes. "Say, Hawk, do you ever wish you'd hung on to that mine, instead of going back to the lumber business?"

"Nope," Hawk replied without a moment's hesitation, his dark blue eyes locking with those of his wife. "I'm pleased to know that you and Logan are doing so well. I wouldn't change a single thing in my life. I've got Sabra and little Andy there. What more could I want?" His gaze went to the plump little boy who was giggling with glee now that his tawny-haired friend had finally managed to tag their black playmate.

"Be careful, Josiah!" Jasmine called a gentle caution to her son. "You're bigger than Andy and Robert. Don't get too rough with them."

"Yes'm," the little boy piped.

"Um-mm. Can you believe that child is two months younger than Robert?" Jasmine said with a shake of her head. "I do believe he's going to be as big as his daddy."

Sabra picked up the thread of the momentarily

interrupted conversation. "It's lovely to visit Arizona again, Logan, but I don't think I'd ever want to live any place other than Hawkinsville. Hawk's business is booming, and of course there are all of Hawk's relatives to consider." Sabra smiled in remembrance. "It's nice to be a part of a big family. But I guess you know how that is, don't you, Callie?"

"Oh, yes, I certainly do." Callie gazed lovingly at her husband. "And Logan's going to get his first taste of what big family life is all about next year. We're leaving the Irish Lady in Hezekiah's capable hands and taking a vacation to Boston."

"That's marvelous!" Sabra said.

Hezekiah's grin was gleaming white against the chocolate of his skin. "If you two keep going the way you have been, you won't have to visit Boston or anywhere else to know what a big family's all about."

Logan reached over and laced his fingers through his wife's. "I guess when two people have as much love to share as Callie and me, the good Lord doesn't mind giving them a double dose of happiness now and again."

A soft little mewling began to drift up from the over-sized cradle beside Callie's chair. "Speaking of double doses," Callie started to say. Logan was on his feet instantly, his big form bent over the cradle, before she even finished the sentence.

"There's my sweet babies," he crooned to two tiny black-haired infants. "Did Daddy's girls have a good nap? Oh, getting hungry, are you? Well, don't you worry. Daddy's going to take care of everything."

A beatific smile rimmed Callie's mouth as her big husband scooped the small, squalling bundles into his arms. She cast an amused look at the other two couples and gave a small shrug of her shoulders. "I think Daddy might need a little bit of help from Mama on this matter. If you'll excuse us, we'll be back as soon as Elaine and Mary's appetites are appeased."

LOVE'S BRIGHTEST STARS SHINE
WITH ZEBRA BOOKS!

CATALINA'S CARESS (2202, $3.95)
by Sylvie F. Sommerfield
Catalina Carrington was determined to buy her riverboat back from the handsome gambler who'd beaten her brother at cards. But when dashing Marc Copeland named his price—three days as his mistress—Catalina swore she'd never meet his terms . . . even as she imagined the rapture a night in his arms would bring!

BELOVED EMBRACE (2135, $3.95)
by Cassie Edwards
Leana Rutherford was terrified when the ship carrying her family from New York to Texas was attacked by savage pirates. But when she gazed upon the bold sea-bandit Brandon Seton, Leana longed to share the ecstasy she was sure sure his passionate caress would ignite!

ELUSIVE SWAN (2061, $3.95)
by Sylvie F. Sommerfield
Just one glance from the handsome stranger in the dockside tavern in boisterous St. Augustine made Arianne tremble with excitement. But the innocent young woman was already running from one man . . . and no matter how fiercely the flames of desire burned within her, Arianne dared not submit to another!

MOONLIT MAGIC (1941, $3.95)
by Sylvie F. Sommerfield
When she found the slick railroad negotiator Trace Cord trespassing on her property and bathing in her river, innocent Jenny Graham could barely contain her rage. But when she saw how the setting sun gilded Trace's magnificent physique, Jenny's seething fury was transformed into burning desire!

Available wherever paperbacks are sold, or order direct from the Publisher. Send cover price plus 50¢ per copy for mailing and handling to Zebra Books, Dept. 2718, 475 Park Avenue South, New York, N.Y. 10016. Residents of New York, New Jersey and Pennsylvania must include sales tax. DO NOT SEND CASH.